OPER
SOLDIE
DOOR

Justine Davis

HARLEQUIN® ROMANTIC SUSPENSE

ISBN-13: 978-0-373-28202-9

Operation Soldier Next Door

This edition published by arrangement with Harlequin Books S.A.

For questions and comments about the quality of this book, please contact us at CustomerService@Harlequin.com.

Printed in U.S.A.

You might be surprised at the desires I have.

Tate quashed the traitorous thought. “Actually,” he said, “that’s always my first assumption.”

Lacy blinked. Drew back. “What?”

He shrugged.

“You always assume a woman’s not interested? You’re smart, great-looking and sexy as hell. And you volunteered to serve, to protect. Any woman with a brain would be interested.”

He actually felt his jaw drop. He wanted to look away but couldn’t, not when she was looking at him with such genuine puzzlement, after saying...that. And for a moment all he could think of was that she’d seen his scars and still said it.

“You,” he said carefully, “have a brain.”

“Enough of one to see that you’re not interested.”

He sucked in a deep breath. “Then I’m a better liar than I thought.”

Be sure to check out the rest of the books in this miniseries—
Cutter’s Code: A clever and mysterious canine helps a group of secret operatives crack the case

* * *

Dear Reader,

I've always been a huge supporter of our military veterans. More so now than ever, since they are all volunteers. While I once wore a uniform, it was never the kind that would send me out of the relative safety of home, and I admired those who had such nerve. I still do.

I have also always been fascinated with WWII history. I wonder what it was like on the home front both here and in theater, but mostly I wonder about the people who fought it—and the aftermath. How on earth did those people, that greatest generation, go through that and then come home to lead, for the most part, quiet, unassuming lives? How did you spend all that time in a state of such high tension and brotherhood, watching your comrades die, and then come home and adjust to everyday life? How did you feel knowing that most likely you would never experience anything like that again? Would that be a relief? A letdown? Might you miss it?

So take all those rambling thoughts, throw in another cause dear to my heart—dogs who also serve—and you end up with a story that tugs my heart in about three different ways! I hope it reaches you, as well.

Happy reading!

Justine

Justine Davis lives on Puget Sound in Washington State, watching big ships and the occasional submarine go by and sharing the neighborhood with assorted wildlife, including a pair of bald eagles, deer, a bear or two, and a tailless raccoon. In the few hours when she's not planning, plotting or writing her next book, her favorite things are photography, knitting her way through a huge yarn stash and driving her restored 1967 Corvette roadster—top down, of course.

Connect with Justine at her website, justinedavis.com, at Twitter.com/justine_d_davis, or on Facebook at Facebook.com/justinedaredavis.

Books by Justine Davis

Harlequin Romantic Suspense

The Coltons of Texas

Colton Family Rescue

Cutter's Code

Operation Midnight
Operation Reunion
Operation Blind Date
Operation Unleashed
Operation Power Play
Operation Homecoming
Operation Soldier Next Door

Redstone, Incorporated

Just Another Day in Paradise
One of These Nights
In His Sights
Second-Chance Hero
Dark Reunion
Deadly Temptation
Her Best Friend's Husband
The Best Revenge
Redstone Ever After

Visit the Author Profile page at Harlequin.com, or justinedavis.com, for more titles.

Yugo (named after a tour of duty my husband did), nicknamed "Nugget," was my best friend. A Lhasa-poodle cross, a chunky, curly furred bundle of warmth and love. Creamy beige with beautiful brown eyes, he had expressive feet and a pokey little nose. He wasn't much for tricks but he loved cuddles and snuggles and was the perfect reading buddy. His front feet danced when he sat and waited for treats and food. When he was laying down he always stretched one leg out and if he could, up on something. I loved his expressive feet!

Yugo, sadly, suffered with anxiety and panic disorders that left him terrified, crying. We taught him to run for a dark room so he had no triggers from sound and light and he could calm down. His illness limited our lives but he was worth it. Despite his necessary isolation, he was a well loved and happy dog. He had many human friends who cheered him on.

Yugo was a part of our family from Dec 2010 until June 18th, 2015.

We saved him from a puppy mill when he was four months old. We rescued him and in return he gave us a great gift.

He loved us unconditionally. He put all his faith and trust in us.

He made us laugh and filled our home with joy.

He taught us patience, commitment, strength, to love unconditionally, and to never give up.

He gave me, personally, a purpose unlike anything I've ever known. I was his safety, his calm, his person. All he asked was that we love him and keep him safe.

And so, we did!

~Lisa Miller

Chapter 1

Hayley Foxworth lay in the darkness of a quiet night, considering waking her husband after a particularly heated dream. The bedside clock read 4:00 a.m. This time of year, late spring, the sun would soon begin to brighten the sky, and then it would clear the Cascades and spill golden light across the waters of Puget Sound. And he would wake on his own. He never could sleep much past sunrise, anyway, whatever time of year it was.

She didn't mind. Quinn was a complex man, but the core of him never changed; he loved her, and he would always do what he thought was right. Not much more a woman could ask for, she thought as she turned on her side to snuggle up behind him, savoring his heat even on this relatively warm night. He—

A blast shattered the quiet.

Two things happened simultaneously. Her husband bolted upright, instantly awake and alert. And their dog, Cutter, did the same, erupting into a cacophony of barking.

"Damn, that was close," Quinn muttered, already out of bed and pulling on the jeans and boots he'd discarded so hastily last night. By the time Hayley had pulled on enough to be decent he was at the front door, where Cutter was pawing at the knob, demanding to get out.

"He'll be gone like a shot." She knew her clever dog's demeanor too well by now.

"Then we'll just have to keep up," Quinn said.

Hayley spared a moment to be thankful he didn't tell her to stay safe at home while he checked it out, but then Quinn had never questioned her competence or abilities.

And, of course, she'd had some training herself in the last two years.

Cutter seemed to realize his humans couldn't move quite as fast as he could, and when he got too far ahead—Hayley had no idea how he decided when that was, but it was consistent—he paused and looked back, waiting for them to catch up. In the darkness his black head and shoulders were almost indiscernible. Were it not for the lighter, reddish brown of his body and tail, she doubted she'd be able to see him at all.

They were headed west, but at the first cross street the dog cut south, and within a few yards Hayley could smell… something. Smoke. Ash. Dust in the air. She wasn't sure.

"There," Quinn said, just as she saw it. A man, wearing only trim boxers, coughing, staggering a bit, in front of a small house that looked tidy and well-kept. Except for the huge, smoking hole in the north wall.

Cutter reached the man first. He was either too dazed to be concerned, or he was comfortable with a dog of no small size appearing out of nowhere. She guessed the latter when Cutter nudged him and the man moved to stroke the dog's head in a gesture that appeared instinctive. From here, all she could tell was that he was tall, with close-cropped dark hair, and thin, although he looked fit rather than bony. A second figure came into view, a woman, running toward the scene from the house next door, apparently using the flashlight of her cell phone to light the way. She arrived at the same moment they did.

"I've called the fire department," she said, looking at the man rather anxiously. "Are you all right?"

The man's head slowly turned. Hayley saw his face was soot-stained and his right shoulder and left foot were bleeding. Not badly, but definitely. Broken glass? He was looking at his neighbor, his brow furrowed. He gave a slight shake of his head, not in answer but as if to clear it. He didn't speak.

"I'm guessing his ears are still ringing a bit," Quinn said.

The woman glanced at them, then at Cutter. Her expression changed, in obvious recognition of some combination of them and their dog. Hayley smiled briefly in return. She and Quinn ran with the dog through the neighborhood regularly, and this was the woman with the amazing vegetable garden who always waved at them as they went by. The woman nodded and went back to watching her neighbor with concern.

"You should sit down," she told him.

His brow furrowed again. The woman got there quickly. She pointed at her own ears with a questioning look. He shook his head again, wincing. The movement made him sway slightly.

Cutter whined, nudging at the man's hand. He looked down, smiled, and stroked the dog's head again. Cutter dropped to the grass and rolled over, clearly asking for a belly rub. Hayley drew back in surprise since Cutter rarely surrendered his dignity so quickly, not even to them, and certainly not in situations like this. She glanced at Quinn and saw he was just as startled.

But the man bent to comply, marking him as knowledgeable about canine body language. A second later he rather abruptly sat down beside the dog, as if he'd had little choice in the matter.

The woman's mouth quirked up at one corner. "Well, that's one way to get him to sit down."

"Ears. Balance. I think he might need medics to check him out," Quinn said.

"I asked for them, too," she said. "The house has been empty since Mr. McLaughlin died, but I saw a motorcycle arrive last night and lights on, so I figured somebody must be here."

"Good thinking," Hayley said.

"I'm Lacy Steele, by the way," the woman said.

"Quinn and Hayley Foxworth," Hayley said. "We live around the corner."

The woman nodded, clearly thinking anything more by way of introduction could wait, then crouched beside the man, who was giving Cutter the requested rub.

"Let me know if your ears are—"

She stopped mid-sentence as the man looked up quickly. A flicker of relief crossed his face.

"Better?" she asked, smiling.

"Some," he said. "Still ringing, but I can hear you enough to make it out."

"Good," she said. She turned the flashlight on the phone back on and aimed it at his left ear, then moved to his right. "No bleeding there," she announced.

"Thanks, doc," he said, rather wryly.

The woman stared at him for a moment, as if she wasn't sure how to take that. The man said nothing more to her, just leaned over and ruffled the fur between Cutter's ears.

"Thanks, buddy," he said softly. For a moment his hand lingered on the dog's head, gently, as if in thanks. Or benediction.

Cutter's body language changed instantly. He rolled to an upright position, head cocked back. For a long moment he stared at the man. Straight into his eyes. And then he got up, turned to face Hayley and Quinn. Sat.

And gave them The Look.

"Uh-oh," Quinn whispered.

"Indeed," Hayley answered in a tone just as quiet. "Seems there might be something else going on here."

"I wish I knew how he does that."

Hayley glanced at her husband, giving him a loving smile. He'd long ago surrendered to the fact that Cutter did do it, and only now and then idly wondered how.

And there was no question about it here. Their new neighbor had a problem, something beyond his immediate situation. And Cutter's instincts told him it was something Foxworthy, as Liam jokingly put it.

"I get the feeling," Hayley said, "he's going to be a prickly one."

"As long as he's not a—"

"Hush," Hayley said, cutting off the awful pun she knew was coming.

She was surprised at how energized she felt. It had been a quiet few weeks, with nothing much happening since they'd returned from California, where her prodigal brother, Walker, was busily setting up Foxworth Southwest with help from her best friend, Amy.

While she'd relished the extra time spent with Quinn, she had been getting a little antsy. And she knew if she was, Quinn was triply so. He'd kept busy, planning, training, teaching, not to mention clawing at the old case of the mole who had once betrayed them, but she knew he was more than ready for an immediate challenge.

"Looks like we've got one," she said softly.

Because Cutter was never wrong.

Chapter 2

The chaos had ebbed, the firefighters had assured them the danger had passed and Lacy Steele's heart had slowed to a near-normal pace after the adrenaline-induced rush of her rude awakening.

The explosion appeared to have originated in a lean-to shed on the north side of the house. The shed and whatever was in it, they said, had likely directed the force inward as much as outward. The shed was destroyed—the only things left were some shattered boards hanging at all angles. The blast had left a gaping opening at least eight feet wide in the house itself, including the roof. She knew the master bedroom was right there, and thought her neighbor was lucky to have escaped as lightly as he apparently had.

"I'd say welcome to the neighborhood, but I'm not sure it's appropriate right now. You must be Tate McLaughlin. I'm Lacy Steele," she said, holding out a hand to the new neighbor she hadn't yet formally met. That he was wearing only boxers made the gesture a bit silly, she supposed, but she made it, anyway. It helped her to not gape at him; even in the dark, it was clear he was a tall, nicely put-together man with the kind of lean build she liked. What she could see of his somewhat angular face matched, and she wondered what he would look like in full light.

"I'll bet," he muttered, not even glancing at her, focused

completely on the firefighters going over the house looking for any lingering embers or problems.

"Yeah, yeah, I know, I'm an oxymoron." She was used to jokes about her name, and they hadn't bothered her in a long time.

"Not the word I was thinking."

She didn't ask what was. And she forgave him ignoring her proffered hand, figuring he had enough on his mind that she shouldn't consider it rude. In fact, it was probably silly of her to do such an ordinary thing under the circumstances.

"There didn't seem to be much of a fire, really," she said.

"More boom than burn," agreed the man who'd introduced himself as Quinn Foxworth, his wife as Hayley and their rather remarkable dog as Cutter.

To her new neighbor's credit, he didn't respond to Quinn's comment any more than he had to hers. So it wasn't personal. And she guessed if it had been her house that had had a gaping hole blown in it, she wouldn't be much more talkative herself.

Quinn walked over to talk to the fire official who had arrived some minutes after the initial response, leaving her with the man she'd heard so much about. His name, she knew, had come from his grandmother. It had been her maiden name. But in everything else, he was pure McLaughlin, his grandfather had said, usually with a laugh.

"I really liked your grandfather," she said to him. "We used to eat dinner together some nights. He'd do the meat, and I'd provide the veggies." She waved a hand toward her garden, where she spent most of her time when she wasn't at her computer station for her self-created job as an online reading tutor for kids. "I loved hearing his stories about his time in the war."

He looked at her at last. And although there was nothing in his expression to make her uncomfortable, she was suddenly aware she'd come running over here wearing only the summer shorts and T-shirt she slept in.

Of course, she'd been aware from the beginning that he was out here in much less. Aware in a way that was just the tiniest bit unsettling. It wasn't just that he had the lean, rangy build she preferred and a nice backside, it was the sleek-looking skin. So much skin…

"He didn't talk about that much," he finally said.

"I'm sure he sanitized them for my benefit, and he avoided talking about himself, but it was still fascinating."

She looked back at the house, where the firefighters were clearing up, apparently satisfied now that there would be no flare-up.

"I miss him," she said softly. She'd truly enjoyed her time with the feisty old man. She'd never known her own grandfathers, but she liked to think they would have been like Martin McLaughlin.

"You mean that," he said, sounding not quite amazed, but at least surprised.

"Yes," she answered simply.

After a long moment he lowered his gaze and said quietly, "Thank you."

Something crashed and his head snapped toward the house. He winced at his own movement. The medics had bandaged his foot—a minor cut from a sliver rather than a shard of broken glass. His shoulder had a wound on the edge of needing stitches, which he had refused. The medics had suggested they take him to the hospital to be checked for any sort of head injury. He'd refused that, too, saying he'd had a concussion or two in his life and knew the signs.

She hoped he was right, and he'd just moved too quickly.

When his expression cleared she spoke again, hoping to distract him from the fact that the crash had been another chunk of his roof caving in. "He was so very proud of you, and your service."

His gaze seemed to soften for a moment, but his voice didn't when he finally said, "He was the only one."

She blinked. "That's not true. I didn't even know you except by name, and I was proud."

He drew back slightly at that. As if he didn't like the idea that he'd been a topic of discussion.

"Well, Tate, I'm glad this wasn't any worse."

"I'm sure. Could have been big enough to take out a chunk of your place, too."

Lacy sighed inwardly. Acerbic was one thing, and given what had happened he had the right, but it was the middle of the night, she'd stayed up too late reading and she was tired of working so hard to simply have a civil conversation when she was only trying to help.

"In which case you'd probably be dead, and I'd have missed the sheer pleasure of meeting you."

His mouth quirked. It wasn't a smile, not even close, but it was an improvement over the understandably grim expression he'd been wearing.

"Sorry," he said. "I'm a little..."

That was an improvement, too, she thought. "Of course."

He nodded. Then he turned and started walking toward Quinn and the uniformed man. Only now, when the sunrise had brightened the sky, did she see the thick, long scar that wrapped around from his spine to his side, just above his waist. A second, thinner scar ran up the back of his left shoulder, his neck and twisted into the hair at the back of his head. Short hair, still almost military short, but long enough that she could see the new hair growth near the scar was coming in a silvery white rather than dark like the rest.

That scar had the reddish tinge that said it was newer rather than old. The thought of the kind of injury that would have left that, that had actually made his hair change color, made her shiver despite the early sun's warmth. She guessed that was the injury that had sent him home from overseas. Guessed his recovery had been long and hard.

And then to come home to this, on his first night in his grandfather's house… She'd be on her knees, probably wailing, she thought with a grimace. And he was merely a little cranky.

Martin McLaughlin had said his grandson was smart, tough and brave. She supposed the scars were proof enough of that, if she'd needed any after the medals Martin had shown her.

I think the boy sends them to me because I know what war is.

I think he sends them to you because he loves you and wants you to be proud of him.

She'd forgotten that conversation until now. And again she felt the tug of sadness since she genuinely had liked Martin and truly would miss him.

He'd also said the grandson who shared his birthday had a generous soul, a good heart that had been hurt too often and was a gentleman to the core. She remembered smiling at the word rarely used these days. Those qualities she wasn't so sure of, but it was hardly fair to judge him under these circumstances.

Martin had definitely been right about one thing. His grandson was a hero. And for that he deserved all the patience she could muster.

She walked over to where the man who had rolled up in the car labeled Battalion Chief was standing with the

Foxworths and Tate. She got there just as another man in turnouts walked up. The chief frowned when he saw the dog at the man's heels. She supposed they were worried about the dog getting in the way, or perhaps messing up whatever investigation they had to do. But the firefighter quickly forestalled his boss.

"Yeah, I know, Chief. But in fact, he probably just saved us a lot of time."

The frown deepened. "How?"

"We found that propane tank here, right? Well, he just led me right to what's left of a second five-gallon propane tank a few yards from the house. In really bad shape. Looks like that might have been our explosion."

The man drew back. And Lacy saw that Quinn Foxworth was frowning, as well—although clearly not surprised that his dog had apparently provided a major clue to the cause of this middle-of-the-night chaos.

"Those things don't blow up easily," he said.

The chief nodded. "Not without a leak and some pretty extreme heat."

"The arson guys and the lab'll have to figure it out." The man grimaced. "Maybe in a month, if we're lucky. They're pretty backed up."

"I've got some friends with access to the fed's lab, if that'll help," Quinn said, and Lacy guessed his tone was purposefully neutral.

Lacy saw the chief's gaze shift to Quinn. "Heard about you Foxworth folks. Word is you know what you're doing and you don't get in the way."

"A reputation we've worked hard to build," Quinn answered.

"Brett Dunbar's a friend of mine," the man said.

Quinn smiled. Widely. "And of ours. A good friend. As is his girlfriend."

Both men nodded, connections established. Lacy was pondering the interesting way things worked when something occurred to her.

"I saw someone out here, just after midnight," she said. "I was up reading, and when I turned out the light I looked outside and saw someone in the yard." She glanced at Tate. "I thought it must have been you, still getting settled in."

He shook his head, and finally spoke.

"It wasn't me. I was tired, crashed early. And my grandfather," he added, "would never keep a leaking propane tank, even a small one."

The chief considered that for a moment. "When was the last time you saw him?"

Tate grimaced. "A while before my last deployment. So a couple of years ago."

Lacy bet he wished he'd had a chance to say goodbye. She felt awful for him, but glad for Martin that the illness that had taken him had been quick. He would have wanted it that way.

"How did he seem?"

"Fine. Like always."

"How old was he?"

Lacy realized where the man was going, and hastened to head him off. "Martin McLaughlin was sharp as a tack until the very end. We should all be so clearheaded and active now, let alone at ninety-three."

The chief shifted his attention to her. "You knew him?"

"Yes. I was there, and talked with him barely an hour before he passed, and he was still mentally together."

Tate went very still. "You were…with him?"

She glanced at him. "Yes. Your father hadn't arrived at the hospital yet and I didn't want Martin to be alone."

He stared at her silently. In the morning light she realized his eyes were a greenish hazel, like his grandfather's.

The moment stretched, the voices of the others as they discussed the situation fading out somehow. Only when she sucked in a deep gulp of air did she realize she had actually stopped breathing.

"—to board up that hole when we're finished, if you've got something we can use," the chief was saying.

Tate shook his head, as if he were still fuzzy.

Or as if he'd been as caught by that long moment as she had been.

"I'll handle it," he said. It sounded automatic, as if it were a standard response. As if whatever it was, he was used to handling it.

"I've got some panels from my greenhouse you could use temporarily," she said. "I think a couple of them would cover that gap. That and a tarp for the roof would keep the wildlife out, at least."

His mouth twisted ruefully. "I'll take the local raccoon over scorpions."

She made a face. "I think I'd take anything with fur over scorpions."

He gave her a fleeting smile. Definitely improving, she thought. "Speaking of fur," he said, looking at Quinn, who in turn was studying him assessingly, "that's quite a dog. Yours, I assume?"

"My wife's first," he said, "but now, yes."

"Interesting that he headed *for* an explosion."

Lacy hadn't thought of that, but he had a point. Her mother's ball of fluff would still be cowering under the bed.

"To be expected, once you get to know him," Quinn said.

"And finding the cause of explosions?" She might just have met him, but she could tell Tate McLaughlin had an idea in his head.

"That, in particular, is a new one to me," Quinn answered, "but again, knowing him, not surprising."

"He looks too young to be retired. But he acts trained."

So that was it. He was wondering if the dog had been a working dog, military or police, she guessed.

"Don't know. He just showed up on Hayley's doorstep one day and stayed. So while I wish I could take the credit," Quinn said with a grin, "he came that way. I've only fine-tuned what was already there. He's a wonder, that dog."

Lacy couldn't argue with that. But it wasn't the finding of the cause of the explosion she was thinking of.

She was thinking of those moments when the dog had somehow managed to make Tate McLaughlin do what he needed to do—sit down. When the man had responded to the dog in a way he didn't to the sudden influx of concerned neighbors.

If the animal hadn't been trained as a therapy dog, he surely had the instincts.

And it appeared her new neighbor just might need that kind of help.

Chapter 3

As he stood in the bedroom doorway, surveying the damage after the fire department had finally cleared out, Tate rubbed a hand over the back of his head. His fingertips instinctively traced the scar that thinned out and stopped an inch or so into his hairline. It wasn't even tender anymore, and the occasional headache and stiffness in his back were the only lingering aftereffects of that bloody day.

He'd not only been lucky that Sunny had been with him that day, he'd been lucky that Lori Collins, the best damned medic he'd ever served with, had been on duty at the aid station when he'd been brought in. Otherwise he might well be dead instead of back home, relatively intact. If he kept to his physical therapy regimen, he'd be in a lot better shape than many.

His mind skittered away from the memory of two funerals, funerals he'd missed because even though he was stateside, he was still in the hospital. He still felt guilty about that, although he'd done what he could when he was released. He had visited each family of his fallen brothers, shared stories of their talks about home and family, and assured them all of the love their lost ones had for them. It was all he could think of to do, but when he left he felt sadly inadequate. He was still alive, and they would never see their sons, brothers and husbands again.

Survivor's guilt, they'd told him. He supposed it fit. He'd survived, and sometimes he felt damned guilty about it. Guilty enough that while he was in the hospital he'd seriously thought about trying to re-up when his active duty period ended. But then Gramps—

"RPG?"

Quinn Foxworth's voice came from close enough behind that it startled him. He turned, looked at the man. Saw he was looking not at the smoldering ruin but at his scars. Normally this would have bothered him, but what he saw in that steady gaze told him this man understood.

"IED," he answered.

"Sucks."

Tate nodded. "You've been in the sandbox."

"Not lately. Thank God." He looked at the hole in the wall of the house. "No wonder this got your attention."

"Rattled my cage, that's for sure," he admitted. Somehow it was easier, with someone who knew.

"You're lucky it wasn't worse. And that you weren't injured worse."

Tate knew it was true. "I wasn't in there. I sat down on the couch in the living room last night, and that's the last I remember until it happened."

"Still bothers me, that tank," Quinn said. "It's not just unusual, it's darned hard to get one of those to blow."

Tate looked back toward where the dog had led the firefighter to the source of the blast. "Welcome home," he said, his mouth twisting.

He wasn't feeling bitter, but knew he could without much effort. More than one of his buddies who'd come back before him warned him about that, that the everyday problems of life back home could seem either petty or insurmountable, making you ignore them and thus they got worse, or turn bitter because you felt like you'd paid enough already and deserved some smooth sailing.

Tate hoped he was tough enough not to go that route. And he had Gramps's example to follow, the man who had come home from a long, ugly war with a trunk full of medals, citations and commendations, but had put them in the past and built a full, normal life back home.

"You need a place to regroup?" Quinn asked.

"No," Tate said instantly, and more gruffly than he should have. But he knew that while he'd been shaken by the explosion in the darkness, it wasn't that bad. He had too many brothers in arms diagnosed with PTSD to compare to, and was more than grateful he wasn't one of them. Since this last injury, he'd felt only a bit numb to life in general. They told him that would pass. He wasn't so sure.

"I'll bunk in the shop for now, until I can get the repairs done," he said, regretting the sharpness in his first response.

Quinn seemed to understand.

"Keep it in mind. We're just around the corner a bit. Got a spare room." The man grinned. "And a dog."

Tate ignored the wistful longing that crept in at the thought of loyal canine companions. "And some dog he is."

"You don't know the half of it."

Quinn gave him a solid but not jarring clap on the shoulder as he turned to go.

"Thanks, anyway," Tate said belatedly, realizing some response was appropriate to the generous offer. His social skills needed some repairs, just like the house.

"Always open," Quinn said, then left to round up his wife and dog.

Tate went back to surveying the interior damage, calculating what it was going to take to fix it. He wanted it back the way Gramps had built it, the way it had always been. He'd do whatever it took. He knew enough to repair the guts of the wall and the siding outside, but the roof and the drywall patching would take pros. He should probably have a structural check on it, too, the way the roof was damaged.

Then he could handle the paint, and maybe repair the scorched flooring, depending on whether it could be sanded down and refinished, or had to be replaced. He could—

"You're lucky you hadn't unpacked yet."

He nearly jumped. As it was, he whirled too quickly and the cut on his foot, he guessed from the broken bedroom window glass, protested. He supposed he was staring at her, but he was a little stunned that twice now people had come up on him without him being aware. Quinn he could understand. He moved like the fighter he'd been—and still was, Tate guessed—but the girl next door?

"Sorry, didn't mean to startle you."

"I didn't realize you'd come in."

She took a half step back. As if she were offended. Or hurt. He wasn't sure. He'd gotten out of the habit of reading civilian reactions, especially women's. But he realized he must have sounded curt when she held up her hands, palms toward him.

"My apologies. I'm afraid I got used to coming in on my own to check on Martin. I didn't think."

He didn't know what to say. His thoughts were careening around, bouncing off each other. He hadn't meant to sound so sharp. Should he say he was sorry himself? Or never mind? And how could he be irritated at her uninvited intrusion when she'd explained it was a habit from checking on his grandfather? Not when he was glad she had. What was it about women that made them do things like that?

The same thing that made Lori the best medic. And Sunny the most determined to protect. Whatever it was women had…

And his new neighbor was most definitely a woman. The T-shirt and shorts she wore did nothing to hide that fact. A sudden image, an imaginative one very unlike him, shot through his head. Of her curled up asleep, that long, dark hair in a tangle around her head, eyes closed, those soft lips slightly parted… It was more a peaceful image than a sexual one, he told himself. Not that another glance at the soft swell of her breasts, the curve of her hips, couldn't change that in a hurry. For a girl-next-door type, Lacy Steele—she of the oxymoronic name—was having an odd effect on him.

Abruptly he was aware he was still standing around in nothing but the boxers he'd been sleeping in. And if he didn't derail this train of thought in a hurry, it was going to become obvious.

"Guess I should put on some of the clothes I'm lucky to still have," he said, looking toward the two duffel bags still unopened on the floor of the living room. Again, it sounded more gruff than he'd intended, but he hadn't been in a position like this in too long. A long hospital stay tended to make you surrender whatever dignity you thought you still had anyway, so he hadn't even realized how he must appear, standing around all this time in just underwear. With his scars visible to everyone, including her. Not a pleasant sight,

"At least it wasn't raining."

Her tone was just a shade too cheerful, leavened perhaps with a touch of sarcasm. He was not doing well in this first contact with his new neighbor. Even the image her words invoked of the rain this region was known for pulled him two ways; it would have lessened the threat of fire after the explosion, but also would have left what little he had on soaking wet and him as good as buck naked.

That it would have done the same to her was something he didn't dare think about.

She turned to go. He felt a sudden urge to stop her somehow, but felt hopelessly out of practice at this.

He wasn't even sure what "this" was.

Was even less sure what had brought on the urge to tell her not to go.

She turned back, and for an instant he wondered if he was so rattled he'd spoken without realizing it.

"Come get those panels later, if you want them."

"I… Thank you." That seemed safe enough.

"I'm really sorry your first night here ended up like this. It's normally a very peaceful neighborhood."

"That's what I wanted."

Again that look flickered in her eyes. Was she thinking he meant she was disturbing that peace?

Did he mean that?

Before he could formulate an answer she was gone, leaving him alone with the rather startling revelation that he felt alive again in a way he hadn't since he'd come home. Interested, rather than just going through the motions. Is that what it took, a middle of the night explosion? Had he truly become one of those people who only found purpose amid chaos and destruction? One of those guys who comes back from war unable to live in peace? He suppressed a shudder at the thought.

But the alternative was just as unsettling. That the new energy and interest he was feeling was the result of his attractive new neighbor.

Don't make any big decisions for a while. And for God's sake don't fall for the first normal girl who catches your eye. You're on a pendulum, and at first it's going to swing back hard the other way. Give it a little time.

Greg Parker's words, spoken in their last counseling session, had resonated with him. He knew the man had been there himself and trusted him the way he'd trusted his squad mates, with his life, albeit in a different way. And he'd been right; the euphoria of being back in the States had eventually given way to a moody depression that had lasted awhile, especially when Gramps died while he'd been trapped in a hospital, unable to get to him.

After that his focus had been to battle back to health, and then to readjust to a life where a crack of sound behind him was more likely to be a car backfiring than a shot. Finally he'd leveled back off, and only then had he made the decision to do what had been in the back of his mind all along. To go to the place he'd loved above all else as a kid, the house Gramps had left him. There he would decide what to do with the rest of his life.

...don't fall for the first normal girl who catches your eye... Give it a little time.

It had been more than a little time, but no one had caught his eye in that way. There had been only that enveloping numbness.

At least, until tonight.

It was just the circumstances, he told himself. Who could fail to notice a woman like his neighbor when she was standing in your yard wearing next to nothing, with a look of concern in her big, blue-gray eyes? He was just numb, not dead. In fact, maybe this was just a sign he was coming back to life.

Problem was, he wasn't sure he liked the idea. For a long time he just stood there, amid the smell of scorched wood, until there was a swath of dawn's first light coming through a breach that shouldn't be there.

Chapter 4

Her new neighbor was going to be a pain, Lacy thought decidedly.

And within three seconds she was chastising herself for leaping to that judgment. You could hardly decide about somebody under circumstances like this, after all. Or you shouldn't, although she knew people did.

He deserved better, anyway. Anyone who carried scars like his, earned volunteering to protect people he didn't even know, deserved better. The best, she told herself. Besides, he was Martin's grandson, and that alone should earn him some slack.

She poured herself a cup of coffee and carried it over to the workstation she'd set up in what had been intended to be a dining alcove but was now her office. It was the only space that seemed suitable, and she liked being able to look out over the garden, and then to the thick trees beyond.

Her cottage was small, designed for one person with a great room that held the kitchen, living area, a small powder room and the alcove she was in now. On the other side of the house was a large bedroom with a master bath. Scattered throughout were various nooks and crannies for storage that she'd found charming at first, but frustrating when it came to actually finding anything.

Her favorite spot was the large deck, which overlooked

the garden and a small grassy yard that was getting smaller as she took over more growing space. Her landlady, a prosperous dentist from Seattle, had given her carte blanche to expand after the first time she'd visited and seen what Lacy had begun. Sending her home with a basket of fresh tomatoes, squash and peppers, and a bouquet of beautiful dahlias hadn't hurt any.

Lacy sipped at her coffee as her computer booted up, wondering if the full pot she'd made was even going to be enough after last night. She'd like nothing more than to go back to bed for a nap, but even if she didn't have work to do, she knew her mind wouldn't cooperate by shutting off. It was too full of thoughts, and too stubborn to stop wondering about Martin McLaughlin's grandson and how he was doing.

At a sudden thought she abandoned the steaming coffee and went back outside. She'd meant it when she'd offered the Plexiglas panels to him, but she wasn't at all sure he'd come over and get them, even if they would save him having to go buy sheets of plywood and cart them home. She didn't know if he even had a car, since he'd arrived on a motorcycle.

She doubted Martin's classic old El Camino, that sleek cross between car and truck that he'd just called "the buggy," was running at the moment, although she was sure it was in perfect condition. The old man had puttered with it constantly. The engine rumbled happily, and the cherry-red paint always gleamed. She'd watched him often enough, handed tools to him, a bittersweet process because it reminded her of all the times she'd helped her father the same way as a kid.

She felt a pang as she remembered the last time she'd seen the car, the day she'd helped him put it into storage in the garage next to the workshop, carefully on blocks and covered. She'd had no idea then that it would be the last time. Would he keep it, this rather cranky grandson of his? Or sell it off for the no doubt nice bit of cash it could bring from a collector? She hoped not, hoped that his willingness to move in here was more than just that he needed a place to live.

She walked to the west side of her house, where the extra panels were leaned against the wall. She picked one up, thankful it was fairly light despite its size. She could carry it alone, although it was a bit awkward because of the width.

There was no fence between the two properties, and both she and Martin had liked it that way. She crossed over, walked to the big maple tree and set the panel down, leaning it against the trunk where he couldn't help but see it when he came outside. Then she went back for the second, which she thought would be enough. Only then did she pause and look at the house that was nearly as familiar to her as her own.

She couldn't see the damage from here, and for a moment an ache overtook her. Everything looked the same, as if Martin would look out at any moment, smile, wave and invite her over for a chat and some of his own coffee. Now that stuff would keep her awake, she thought. For a week.

"He's here," she whispered, as if to the old man. She had caught herself speaking to him now and then when she looked over here, or came over to check on the place. It was a silly, wistful thing, but it eased the ache a bit. "He's here and he's safe, Martin. A bit cranky, but no more so than he has a right to be, all things considered. I'll keep an eye on him for you."

From a distance, she added to herself as she turned to go back home. He'd made it pretty clear he'd rather be left alone. It went against her instincts not to help a neighbor who was having some trouble, but if that's the way he wanted it, she'd give him time to settle in before she made any more overtures.

And you neglected to mention he was so hot, Martin, she thought with an inward laugh at herself as she headed back to her house. She'd only seen pictures of him much younger, as a baby, a child and a gangly adolescent before they'd shifted to a man in uniform and often loaded down with gear. She knew herself well enough to know her first reaction to military personnel was always positive, but she'd always thought him genuinely nice-looking.

She just had never thought of him as camo-wrapped sexy. For that matter, she'd never quite realized how sexy just a pair of plain, simple boxers could be on a tight, fit male body when you were looking at the real thing, not an artfully posed photo.

And Tate McLaughlin was definitely the real thing.

Tate screwed the last corner of the second panel down tightly, tested the seal, decided it would do nicely for the moment. There was no rain predicted for the next several days, so the heavy tarp on the roof should hold. He'd gotten the charred edges of the hole cut away, so that should help with the burned smell. He stepped back and looked at his makeshift repair. The large acrylic panels were the perfect size, as she'd guessed, and the predrilled holes had made attaching them a matter of a few long wood screws. It would also make working on repairs easier, only having to remove the panels.

It was nice of her to offer the temporary fix.

Nicer of her to leave them out for him to find rather than making him come get it. He appreciated that. After years of having to react and respond to rapidly changing circumstances instantly, he wanted the chance to ease into things more gradually.

And thinking about easing into things in conjunction with his new neighbor was not the smartest move he'd made this afternoon, he thought wryly. Neither had been the moment this morning in the thankfully undamaged bathroom, when during his shower he'd caught himself thinking about her ratio of leg to body. She wasn't strikingly tall, maybe five foot six or so, but she surely had a lot of leg.

Lovely, shapely leg.

His thoughts had taken a decidedly raw turn then, and one she certainly wouldn't appreciate when all she'd done was try to be helpful and neighborly, that's all.

Really nice, neighborly young woman, sweet, thoughtful and helpful.

The memory jabbed at him, the words from the email Gramps had sent him after she'd first moved in next door.

Leave it to Gramps to omit the salient detail that she was a looker. And, of course, he'd had advice to offer at the end of that email.

You admire the pretty ones, but you marry the real ones. If you're smart.

Not likely. Not him. Sometimes he thought about his grandparents and their sixty-year-long marriage, in love up until the day his grandmother had died five years ago. This had been their dream, this simple home surrounded by trees and life, and Gramps had never even thought about leaving. He still loved her, and Tate knew he had until his last breath. It was sometimes the only thing that gave him comfort about his death, knowing that the old man wouldn't have minded going because he missed her so much. He even understood; his grandmother had been a heck of a woman—smart, tough, and yes, pretty—up until the disease that took her had robbed her of everything but that indomitable will.

And if you're as lucky as I was, you get both in the same package.

Even now he smiled at the pure love in those words. They made him think of their wedding portrait, the black-and-white image stiff, formal, but yet still unable to erase the twinkle in her eyes or the amazement in his. Gram had been a looker, too, no question.

Which brought him careening back to an image of a woman with big eyes that seemed to go from blue to gray, a mane of long, dark hair and legs that went on forever. Legs that had been bare to his view. Legs that made a man think about sliding between them, of feeling them wrapped around his—

"Get your mind out of the gutter, McLaughlin," he ordered himself sharply.

The moment he derailed that dangerous thought he became aware of a tickle at the back of his neck. Once, it would have meant he was being watched, and given where he'd been at the time, that was never a good thing. But he wasn't there anymore, and he was relieved to see that the time it took to remember that was getting shorter and shorter.

He wanted it to be zero. He wanted his reaction to such things to be curiosity, not the instant urge to go into protect mode, or worse, attack mode. He was getting there, but he wanted to be there. Gramps had always said he was impatient. Tate supposed he'd been right. Because he was very impatient for his mind and gut to match the peace around him.

It's normally a very peaceful neighborhood.

That's what I wanted.

Yes, above all else, that's what he wanted.

He turned around and found himself face-to-face with a dog. This was the dog from last night who belonged to the Foxworths.

The animal was sitting politely a few feet away, watching him. Very politely. As if at attention. And yet right at the edge of his comfort zone, as if he knew where the boundary was, somehow.

"Cutter," he said. The dog's tail wagged, but he didn't move. Just watched, alertly, intensely. That steady gaze was unsettling, as was the intelligence behind those amber-flecked dark eyes.

He'd seen that kind of intensity before, in another set of canine eyes. Eyes that had belonged to the dog who was one reason he was alive today.

His stomach knotted. Cutter made him realize how much he missed that dog. Sunny had saved a lot of lives that day, alerting him and the squad in time to get nearly clear of the IED that had been set beside the road, awaiting their passage. Spahn had been killed instantly. He and Cav and Owen had only been injured, and the rest of the guys had escaped unscathed, thanks to Sunny's warning.

This dog looked nothing like the yellow-furred Sunny, yet he still reminded Tate of her in that fierce intensity and intelligence. He had the feeling that when intent on something, Cutter would be as unswayable as Sunny had been while working, with nothing in her mind but the task of sniffing out danger in the form of explosives.

And he didn't like the memories that the dog's presence was stirring up. Didn't like thinking of Sunny still over there, doing her job. Saving others as she'd saved him, intent on her work. Loyal, steadfast and unwavering until it was time to play. He'd give anything to have her race up to him again, crunchy water bottle in her mouth, banging it against him in an invitation to play.

It hurt too much.

"Go home, dog," he said gruffly.

The dog didn't move.

"Get," he said, louder, fiercer.

For a moment longer the dog just sat, staring at him. And then, finally, he got to his feet and, with a last look, trotted off.

Relieved, Tate turned to go pick up his tools.

And saw his neighbor standing next to the tree where she'd left the panel. Watching.

He had no idea how long she'd been there. Maybe she was the reason for the tickle at the back of his neck, not the dog. She was frowning, clearly not happy about something. She shifted her gaze to the departing Cutter and back to him. Then she gave a shake of her head, turned on her heel and headed back toward her house.

She couldn't have said more clearly that she didn't like the way he'd reacted to the dog. He wasn't proud of it himself, but it had come from someplace deep inside. He didn't want the dog around. He brought on too many memories Tate couldn't do anything about.

And it was just as well Lacy Steele was peeved at him. Maybe she'd stay away.

Chapter 5

It really wasn't fair, Lacy thought as she paused in the garden to check the status of her recently transplanted tomatoes.

Grumpy people should look it, wear permanent scowls or have eyebrows forever lowered over irritated expressions.

They should not be tall, built and sexy, with gorgeous hazel eyes that seemed to change color as you looked.

So quit looking, she ordered herself.

Besides, no amount of sexy attractiveness made up for coldness toward an innocent animal. A helpful innocent animal, in fact. Hadn't the dog discovered the source of the explosion, led the investigator right to it?

She herself found the dog charming, with his alert look and apparently instinctive knowledge of what was needed. He'd gotten her prickly neighbor to sit down when he needed to, when he'd been clearly determined to stay on his unsteady feet, hadn't he? The dog was clever and—

Here.

She thought he'd gone, but Cutter had merely decamped to her yard and was now approaching her, slowly. She straightened from her inspection of a branch filled with tiny yellow blossoms that would hopefully become tasty, sweet, homegrown tomatoes, and some that had already begun growing tiny green rounds the size of a pea. She smiled at him.

"Well, hello, my fine lad. Looking for a better welcome? You'll certainly find that here."

At her first words, or maybe her tone, the dog's tail began to wag and he trotted up to her. She was scratching his ears, smiling at the way he leaned into it. When she glanced back next door, she almost hoped her new neighbor was there, noticing the welcome the dog was getting here. A proper welcome for a sweet dog. The kind of welcome Martin would have given him. Funny, she still thought of the house as Martin's, even though—

He was there, all right. Movement caught her gaze, and she looked in time to see him bend to pick up the tools he'd been using to affix the panel she'd provided over the damage. But he suddenly stopped, grabbing at his left shoulder in an oddly jerky motion. As he rubbed at the back of it, she remembered the scar. And the new damage done in the blast. Remorse flooded her. He had reason to be cranky. She chastised herself for judging—again—and vowed not to do it anymore, no matter how grouchy Tate McLaughlin got.

A sudden bark from Cutter drew her attention back. It was a short, happy sound, and the dog whirled and left at a run. Lacy wasn't surprised when she looked up to see the Foxworths approaching. She followed, albeit much more slowly, smiling as they got nearer.

"Morning," she called out.

"Hi," Hayley Foxworth said. "Sorry about the trespasser. He just took off on us. I think he wanted to be sure everything was okay around here."

Lacy nodded. "He checked out next door first, but my neighbor's in a mood." Remembering her vow she added, "I think he's hurting a bit."

"New or old?" Quinn asked.

"Both, I think," Lacy said, assuming he was asking if there were any aftereffects from last night. She indicated the back of her own left shoulder. "He was kind of rubbing at the scar there."

"Poor guy," Hayley said.

"Don't say that to him," Quinn recommended. "I doubt he'd appreciate it."

"I'm not sure he appreciates anything at the moment," Lacy said frankly. "Not that he doesn't have cause," she hastened to add.

"It was a heck of a welcome to the neighborhood," Hayley said. "We should go apologize for Cutter's intrusion."

"Apparently so." Quinn's tone was dry, and when his wife gave him a curious look he nodded toward their dog, who was already started that way. Cutter paused and looked back over his shoulder, and Lacy would have sworn his expression said, "Hurry up!"

Hayley smiled. "You know he's got a plan."

"He always does," Quinn agreed, but with a roll of his eyes.

"And Tate has a problem."

"Yes. That was definitely Cutter's 'fix it' look last night."

Lacy watched the exchange in quiet fascination, and when they started to follow the dog, she went along. Torn between what to ask first, she blurted out both of her questions. "This is a dog we're talking about, right? And do you mean more of a problem than what happened last night?"

Hayley grinned at her. "Sort of, and yes."

Lacy blinked. "In that order?"

Hayley laughed. "Yes."

So, Cutter was "sort of" a dog who somehow knew that Tate had more of a problem than a freak explosion that had taken out a big chunk of his wall, barely feet from where he would have been sleeping had he not been too tired to make it to the bed? She wondered what on earth could be more of a problem than coming that close to dying, so soon after surviving another close call. It had to be big, to top that.

Then she realized she was taking them seriously about the animal knowing about said problem. She knew dogs could be incredibly sensitive and perceptive about their humans, but Tate was a complete stranger. Yet Quinn and Hayley, two perfectly normal people she suspected were very smart, had accepted easily that their dog not only knew about this problem, but had A Plan.

She watched as Cutter came to a halt, not near the hole in the wall and the temporary fix, but near the back door that opened out onto the flagstone patio Martin had been so rightfully proud of, having done it himself. The dog sat and stared at that back door as if willing it to open, sort of in the way she'd seen border collies will sheep to do their bidding.

Quinn and Hayley waited silently. Or, at least, not communicating with words; she saw them look at each other and guessed they were one of those couples who didn't always need to talk to know what each other was thinking. Or apparently what their dog was thinking.

It wasn't that she didn't know dogs were amazing. She loved them, had often thought about adopting one since she'd moved here, but she'd been too busy getting her home-based tutoring service up and couldn't give an animal the attention it deserved.

And she could accept that Cutter was particularly perceptive; she'd seen it herself. But however sensitive, perceptive and amazing dogs were, it was a jump from that to reading minds, hearts and the unseen. Wasn't it?

"What kind of problem do you think he has?" It was all she could think of to say.

"Quinn has his doubts about the explosion," Hayley said.

Lacy frowned. "What do you mean?"

"Just what I said last night," Quinn answered. "It takes a great deal to get one of those tanks to explode. Just a leaky or open valve wouldn't do it. It takes something like that plus extreme heat."

"You mean it must have caught fire?"

"Even then the escaping vapor would likely just burn, not explode. But if that second tank was close, or stacked on top of the leaking one..."

"Then it would explode?"

"Could."

Lacy looked toward Martin's house. Her brows lowered in puzzlement. "But how could it just catch fire?"

"Exactly," Quinn said, his voice grim.

She was pondering the ramifications of that when Hayley said quietly, "Here he comes. Probably wondering what we're all doing out here."

The door Cutter had been so intent on swung open. Tate stepped out and let it shut on its own behind him. He stopped a yard or so away. Outside personal space, Lacy thought. Expressing that he didn't consider them friends enough to get closer? Wary, or just unsociable? Or perhaps just plain rude?

"Make a habit of trespassing?" were his first words.

Lacy's brows rose. Okay, rude won that one, she thought.

Hayley, with more benevolence than she herself would have shown at that—although perhaps living farther away she had less reason to be concerned about this man's attitude—answered with a smile.

"Only to apologize for this one trespassing." She gestured at the dog, who was watching him steadily.

"Ought to keep him under control," Tate said to Hayley, still sounding stiff and cold.

"Many people should keep many things under control," Quinn said. His voice was steady, inflectionless and nearly as cold as Tate's, but somehow Lacy heard warning and threat and heat in it. She had the feeling that Tate would be unwise to ever talk to Hayley Foxworth like that again.

He seemed to realize it. She saw his gaze flick to Quinn, then back to Hayley. After a second, he nodded. "Yes. They should. Especially me. I'm sorry."

It came out clipped, and rather flat, but it was an apology and Hayley moved quickly to accept.

"It's all right. You've had a rough twenty-four hours, just when you should have had peace."

At her gentle words he seemed utterly at a loss. For an instant he closed his eyes and looked chagrined enough that even Quinn appeared satisfied.

"And we'll leave you to that peace," he said, and slipped an arm around Hayley as they turned to go. Cutter seemed less than willing, but eventually, at a sharp whistle from Quinn, the dog followed, looking back at Tate the whole time.

"They're nice people," Lacy said. "Good people."

"Mmm."

Nice non-answer. Prodded by his gruffness, she added, "So am I."

He looked at her then. She couldn't read anything in his shuttered expression.

"Have it your own way, then," she said, exasperated. Then, unable to stop herself in the face of his coldness toward people—and a dog—she found so likable, she added, "But Martin would be ashamed of your manners.

"Nice way to keep your vow," she muttered to herself as she turned on her heel and went back to her house.

It was just as well the rest of her day would be taken up with work.

Chapter 6

Okay, so she had a point, Tate thought as he rubbed a hand over his stubbled jaw the next morning, debating whether to bother shaving. There was a difference between being aloof and being downright rude, and he'd crossed the line.

Martin would be ashamed of your manners.

That had stung like few things could. The thought of his grandfather being ashamed of him for any reason had the power to truly unsettle him. Much more than his parents, who had never agreed with most of his life choices, anyway. Of course, his father agreed with his mother if she said grass was purple. He was quite capable of standing up to anyone else—especially his son—but Michelle McLaughlin's word was law.

If they'd had their way, he'd have gone to that Ivy League school, taken that knack he had for numbers and built a career around it. Wall Street, maybe. Never mind that the thought of being shut up in an office for hours a day made him twitchy, or worse. He shook his head at himself.

Shave, he thought. Then get started. It was already late, after a restless night trying to catch up on sleep. His makeshift bed on the big air mattress in the shop had been okay—he'd slept in much, much worse—but he didn't want it to be long-term. He'd had to dig a blanket out of Gram's linen closet, since everything that had been on the bed had been destroyed.

And the smell. The too-familiar smell, the lingering odor of destruction, that crept into the nostrils and stayed, haunting his dreams.

Maybe fresh paint would help that, though. At least it would smell like something had been done. But he was a long list of repairs away from painting.

He finished shaving, ran a hand over his still-damp hair, which was all it needed. He was going to keep that, he decided. Worrying about what his hair looked like was way down on his list of civilian habits to reacquire.

He pulled the list he'd made out of his pocket and read it again, looking for anything he'd forgotten. And trying to figure out how he was going to get it here when his only wheels were a motorcycle. He thought of Gramps's pride and joy, that classic red Chevy El Camino, but it was sealed up on blocks in the back of the shop, and it would take more time to get it ready to drive than he wanted to spend before getting started on repairs. Although the makeshift fix with the Plexiglas had worked better than he'd expected, and it was nearly summer, dry and warming up already, so maybe he wasn't in quite the rush he'd first thought he was.

Thanks to one Lacy Steele.

What a name. But he'd liked the way she'd kidded about it. She'd probably heard so many jokes she just blew them off.

In the end it went well enough. He found that the local lumber store he'd feared would be too small to have what he needed actually had a decent selection, thanks to a storage yard a short distance away. And there he found a guy who seemed to have a good knowledge of what he'd need and some tips on how to proceed, and the name of a good drywall guy for the texture coat, which Tate wrote down, thankfully. Best of all, they had a small pickup he could borrow to get the stuff home, then come back and get his bike.

No, he thought as he made the trip back, the best thing was that everyone he'd encountered on this supply trip had known, and obviously liked, his grandfather. The steady condolences were a little rough when he was still grieving rather fiercely—being in Gramps's house, amid his things, was turning out to be both blessing and curse—but it was good to know he hadn't been forgotten.

There was a lot to be said for this small-town stuff, he thought.

And Mom would cringe at the very idea. Reason enough to stick it out.

He was honest enough to admit tweaking her prejudices might be the tiniest bit of his motivation for not just accepting this inheritance, but actually coming here with the intention of staying. His ultra-cosmopolitan mother had shuddered at the very idea of living in a town of less than five thousand.

By late afternoon he had the last scraps of the destroyed shed cleared away, tackling that first to give the area more time to dry out from the fire department's efforts to keep the damage to a minimum. He might need to give the guts of the damaged wall time to dry completely, as well, so he limited himself to cutting away the ruined drywall with his newly acquired drywall saw and clearing out the section of damaged roof and ceiling.

He assessed the situation and his condition. There was still plenty of light, but he could feel the slight hum in his head that told him he was tired. And that was when mistakes happened. So he decided further work should wait until tomorrow, when he would hopefully have had a decent night's sleep. This wasn't his area of expertise—he wasn't sure what, if anything, was anymore—and he wanted to go slowly and carefully. So he would—

The doorbell, with Gramps's selection of the chimes of Big Ben in tribute to his time in England before and after the war, interrupted his thoughts. Since Tate knew no one else here, it wasn't a surprise to find Lacy on his front porch. His first thought was that she was even prettier than he remembered, although he thought he preferred the sleep-tousled look for rather primal, male reasons.

His second thought was that whatever she had in that pot she was carrying smelled so good it woke his stomach up with a vengeance.

"I rang this time," she pointed out.

He nodded. Made an effort. "I thought maybe you were that dog again." He realized suddenly how that sounded. "I only meant—"

She waved it off with a laugh. "He does seem clever enough to figure out how to ring a doorbell, doesn't he?"

He was relieved she hadn't taken offense; he'd already ticked her off quite enough.

"I was making beef stew for dinner, so I made extra." She held out the pot, which she was holding with a towel between it and her hands, so apparently it was hot.

"Extra?"

"For you," she said patiently, lifting the pot slightly. "I figured you'd be too busy to fix anything. You could have borrowed my car, you know."

He blinked. "What?"

"My car. To go get your stuff."

"Oh."

If he had ever done worse at casual conversation, he couldn't remember when. And she clearly noticed, because after a moment of silence she gave him an amazed look and a slight shake of her head.

"I would have invited you over for dinner, but since you don't seem inclined to socialize, I brought it here."

A sudden image shot through his mind of sitting across a table from her, like a normal person, chatting easily rather than stumbling along like this, uncertain of why he found it so difficult.

"It would help," she said, rather pointedly again, "if you took this. It's getting heavy."

Hastily he reached out.

"Take the towel, too, it's hot," she warned.

"You didn't have to do that," he said as he took the indeed heavy pot, wondering if he sounded as awkward as he felt. And as if on cue, his stomach growled loudly.

Her smile was genuine this time. "Obviously somebody needs to feed that beast."

Somehow he found the grace to smile back at her. "Guess so."

"When was the last time you ate?"

His brow furrowed as he thought.

"The fact that you have to try to remember means it's been too long. No wonder you're grumpy. Eat something."

His mouth twisted wryly. "Grumpy was a dwarf," he said.

She arched one eyebrow at him. "Old Disney references?"

"Gramps," he explained.

"Ah. A traditionalist."

"Still on videotape, if I remember right."

She laughed at that. He liked the sound of it.

"Thank you," he said, lifting the pot. His stomach growled again.

"Eat before it gets cold. If you have leftovers, it's good over noodles."

He nodded. Realized much too late that he'd made her stand outside holding a heavy pot for far too long. Feeling that required…something, he said hastily, "I'd ask you in, but it still reeks in there."

"Like a place that's had a big hole blown in it?"

He nodded again. Drew in a deep breath as he set the pot on the glass table beside the door, which thankfully hadn't shattered from the concussion of the blast. And wondered why this seemed so hard. "About the grumpy… It was a long trip, and then the explosion. I—I'm sorry."

She gave him a look he couldn't quite interpret. "Actually, I think it's the dog you should apologize to. I can at least understand."

He sighed then. "I know."

"You don't like dogs?"

"I love dogs. I just… He reminded me of another one."

"Does he? I've never seen one with coloring like that."

"I don't mean looks. More intensity."

"He is that, isn't he." It wasn't a question, so he didn't answer. "Who's the other dog?"

"Sunny. Well, Sunniva, which is Latin for something. But we always called her Sunny, because…well, she's that, inside and out. She's an MWD—Military Working Dog—who was with us overseas. She's the reason I'm still alive, along with most of my squad."

He was a little surprised he'd said so much. Normally he would have said, "Just a dog I knew," or some such. But nothing seemed to be normal just now, him least of all.

"Dogs are amazing, aren't they? They give so much and ask so little." Her voice was soft, her tone utterly genuine and more than a little awed. Exactly how he felt when he thought of Sunny and what she had done. "She wasn't hurt, was she?"

He liked the urgency in her question, the concern for an animal she didn't know and never would.

"No. She got clear."

"Where is she?"

"She's still there."

He didn't add that because of that, anything could happen; he could see that Lacy got it.

"You miss her," she said, still in that soft tone.

"Yes," he admitted.

"It must be a bond like no other."

Yes, she got it all right. "Yes," he repeated, unable to think of anything to add. Then abruptly he remembered what he hadn't said. "And thank you. For the food. When I cook, it usually requires a meat identifier."

She smiled. "You're welcome. But…a what?"

"You know. Potatoes mean beef. Applesauce says pork chops. Cranberry says it's turkey. Otherwise you can never tell."

She laughed, seemingly delighted by the old, corny military joke. But at that point he was out of things to say and was grateful when his cell phone rang, ending this silence that he thought should feel awkward, but oddly didn't.

To his surprise, it was the county arson investigator.

"Foxworth has even more pull than I realized," the woman said when he asked. "We got the report back from the federal lab just now. I didn't expect it for days yet."

Somehow he wasn't surprised. Quinn Foxworth had that air about him, not just of confidence and authority, but genuine power, the power to get things done.

"And?" he asked.

"You want the whole thing or the bottom line?"

"Bottom line, please. I probably wouldn't understand the rest."

"No leak. The valve on the bottom tank was open."

Tate opened his mouth to protest, then stopped. He had no proof, but he knew. Gramps would never, ever do that. He was meticulous, always had been, and age hadn't changed him. Besides, Tate would have smelled it. He'd had the window open, and it was right beside the shed. And there was no mistaking the purposefully distinctive odor of propane.

"So what does that mean?" he asked.

"It's early yet, but if I had to guess…"

"Please guess. I won't hold you to it."

"The tank that blew is pretty scorched on the bottom."

Tate got there quickly. "So you think the lower tank valve got opened somehow, the leak got ignited somehow and the extreme heat from that fire blew the tank stacked on top of it?"

"That's the theory, yes. There's some additional recovered material we have yet to identify, but right now…"

That was a lot of somehows, Tate thought. But he said only, "So…a freak accident?"

"Sorry, I can't say. That determination hasn't been made yet. I'm only calling now because Brett Dunbar asked me to let you know something ASAP."

It took him a moment to place the name. And after the call had ended he shook his head at the oddity of having a man he'd never met intercede for him at the request of a neighbor he'd met less than a day and half ago.

Yes, there was a lot to be said for this small-town stuff. And people—and dogs—named Foxworth.

Maybe even girls next door.

Chapter 7

It was the dog again.

Tate scowled. Counting the first night, this was the fifth time in the last two days the dog had shown up. It was as if the dog made rounds, and he'd added Tate to the list. And each time he was followed by his people, one or the other or sometimes both. They seemed remarkably unperturbed at having to retrieve their pet so often.

But this time he'd made it into the house, through the patio sliding door that Tate had left open while he carried out debris he'd found thrown into other areas of the house. Even more irritating, he was in the kitchen. Sitting in that same alert way Tate had seen before.

At first he thought the dog was expecting a dog biscuit or some kind of treat. But then he realized the dog wasn't just sitting, he was staring. As Sunny had, when something was wrong with the familiar landscape around her. Intent, undistractable, until something was done about the offending intrusion. Once it had been a visiting general, who landed high on the "don't like this" scale. Once it had been a new video game with lots of loud car noises that somebody had brought into the mess tent. The last time he'd seen it had been a celebrity visitor she had pointedly turned her back on.

Tate shook off the memories, telling himself to focus

on how he was going to get this dog out of here. It didn't seem wise to grab a sizable dog he barely knew and try to drag him out. Something had him fascinated, and—

The pot.

He realized suddenly that the dog was staring at Lacy Steele's cooking pot. Or whatever it was. That kind of big, tall pot had a name; his grandmother'd had one, but he couldn't remember what she'd called it. He'd finished the stew last night—and it had been as good as it had smelled—and had thoroughly washed the pot when he'd finished. And there on the counter it had been ever since, because he couldn't quite work himself up to taking it back to her.

"It's empty, dog," he said sourly.

Cutter glanced at him then, and Tate had the strangest feeling that had he been human, it would have been the equivalent of "Well, duh." Maybe it was because obviously the dog's nose would have told him that.

But he went back to staring at the pot, anyway. Only now he started glancing at Tate every few seconds, expectantly.

"What is it you want?" he asked after the third time through the cycle. "You know it's empty. And you can't possibly know it doesn't belong here."

Or maybe he did know, Tate thought suddenly. And almost on the thought, the person to ask knocked on his front door.

"Morning, Tate. I'm assuming my errant dog is here again?" Hayley Foxworth asked cheerfully as he opened the door. She was in running clothes, with her hair tucked up into a Seahawks cap. Her green eyes were bright, as if reflecting her mood. Or maybe the green on the cap.

"Leash?" he suggested wryly, then regretted it; he wanted to ask her something, not make her mad. At least her husband wasn't with her to give him that warning look again if he didn't like the way Tate spoke to his wife. And the man was impressive enough that Tate knew a fight would be a real one. Quinn Foxworth wasn't someone to trifle with. He was the kind of man you wanted on your side, and the kind you dreaded to come up against.

"Wouldn't do any good," Hayley said, her cheerful tone unchanged. "He's on a mission, and he'll find a way."

"A mission?" Tate repeated, diverted for the moment. "What mission?"

"You," the woman answered simply.

Tate blinked. "Me?"

"Whatever your problem is."

"My problem," he said, speaking carefully, "is a dog who keeps showing up and interrupting what I'm trying to get done."

"Maybe you should put him to work."

"What?"

She smiled, and it matched her tone. Quinn Foxworth, Tate thought, was a lucky guy.

"He knows a hammer from a screwdriver from a wrench, and he's happy to fetch and carry."

He blinked. Again. "You're saying if I tell him to bring me a hammer out of a pile of tools—"

"He will. Helpful if you need to nail something you can't let go of." As if she hadn't just boggled him she went on in that same jovial tone. "So where is the lad?"

"In the kitchen. Staring at a pot. An empty pot," he added, to explain how odd it was.

"Hmm" was all she said.

"He must hear you out here," Tate said, truly puzzled now. "Why hasn't he come out?"

"Told you. Dog on a mission."

"So you said. But I don't have a problem. At least, not one he can fix."

She laughed. "You might be surprised. But I'll go get him, if it's all right?"

Smothering a sigh, he nodded. When she hesitated and he realized she didn't know, he pointed toward the kitchen and remembered what he'd wanted to ask in the first place.

"Has he been here before?" he asked as he followed her into the room where the dog's tail wagged happily, but he didn't move from his selected spot. "Before the explosion, I mean."

"Not that I know of."

"So he didn't…know my grandfather?"

"I don't think so," Hayley said, an understanding look dawning on her face. "Nope, it's all you."

Tate wasn't sure how to feel about that. Or the knowledge that his theory that the dog kept showing up here because he was looking for Gramps had just been shot down.

"So, that's the pot?" she asked, looking at it where it sat innocently on the counter.

"Yes."

"Doesn't fit with the rest," she said with a glance at the overhead rack his grandmother had so loved, but that he was seriously considering taking out now that he'd banged his head on the low-flying skillet once too often.

"No." She just looked at him, waiting. *You and your dog*, he thought, his mouth quirking. Finally he gave in. "It belongs next door."

"Ah. Your charming neighbor."

When she wasn't sniping at him for his bad manners, Tate thought. *Rightfully so*, his conscience nudged.

"He probably wants you to take it back to her, then."

For a third time Tate blinked, this time long and slow, and with a shake of his head.

"Dog," he said—unnecessarily, he thought.

"Yes," Hayley agreed. "And I would have thought you, of all people, would realize some dogs are different than your run-of-the-mill house pet."

She had him there. And, judging by her expression, she knew it.

He was saved from trying to answer by yet another knock on the door. He stifled a grimace.

"Grand Central Station here this morning, huh?" Hayley said with a grin.

"Seems like," he muttered, and wasn't really surprised when he opened the door and found his charming neighbor on the porch.

"Sorry to bother you," she began.

"That ship already sailed this morning," he said, gesturing at the dog, who had suddenly abandoned his obsession and had come trotting happily out to greet the clearly very welcome Lacy Steele. As if the dog lived here, and not him, Tate thought wryly.

"Well, hello there, furry one," Lacy said, reaching to pet the dog then scratch behind his ears. Cutter sighed happily and leaned in as Lacy looked up and smiled at Tate. He was still taken aback at the jolt that had given him when she looked past him and said, "And you, too," telling him Hayley had followed her dog out of the kitchen.

"Good morning," Hayley said. "I'm here to retrieve my dog. Again. Before Tate's patience runs out."

"Might be a bit late on that," Lacy said, without looking at him.

"I got that feeling," Hayley agreed.

"He'll get over it. Nobody could stay mad at this sweetie."

"Unless they're really mad at something else."

"Standing right here," Tate pointed out, feeling a bit aggrieved.

"So you are," Lacy said. She sounded as cheerful as Hayley had. None of them—including the dog—had any qualms about intruding or interrupting, obviously. "And speaking of retrieving, I need to retrieve my stockpot, if you're done with it."

"Stockpot," he repeated, the memory coming back now.

"The pot the stew was in?" she explained.

"I know, I just couldn't remember what it was called. I don't cook much."

"Well, I do, and I need it for spaghetti sauce tonight. My tomatoes aren't ready yet so I had to buy some, but I've got some other veggies I need to use up."

"That garden looks like you'd have enough to feed my entire squad."

"Invite 'em over," she said.

She was kidding, of course, but as he looked at her serene expression he had the oddest feeling that if he did just that, she would welcome them. And deal with the influx graciously and feed them well.

"I'll leave you two to it, then." Hayley glanced at her dog, who had inexplicably given up his fascination with the stockpot and was at the front door, clearly ready to leave, and added, "Since it appears his work here is done for the moment."

Tate's brow furrowed. What was that supposed to mean? But before he could ask, both woman and dog were out the door and headed home at a steady run.

"Seems you're making friends in the neighborhood whether you like it or not," Lacy said when they'd gone out of sight.

That stung, although not as much as her manners comment. "Why wouldn't I like it?"

"Just saying you don't go out of your way to be welcoming."

"Doesn't seem like I have to, with everybody showing up, anyway." What was it about this woman that had him snapping like this? Maybe he wasn't an easy charmer like Cav, but he'd never turned into a grouch at the sight of a beautiful woman. And Lacy Steele was certainly that, as his body kept reminding him. He sucked in a breath, willing himself to speak evenly. "Look, I only meant I thought it would be…slower here. Small-town slow. And I thought I'd left stuff like middle-of-the-night explosions behind for good."

"I'm sorry," she said immediately. "Of course, you're right. And you have every right."

Her instant contriteness, so obviously sincere, made him feel even worse. As if he'd somehow traded on his service to get out of a situation his own rusty social skills had gotten him into.

"I'll get the pot," he said, turning to go to the kitchen before he could make things any worse. When he brought it back, feeling he had to say something, he handed it over with what he thought should be safe enough—a sincere, "The stew was great. Really. Thank you."

The smile she gave him then made him forget the awkwardness, and all the irritation he'd been feeling over his disrupted morning. It did nothing, however, to remove that uncomfortable awareness that had him so edgy.

"You're more than welcome. And if you like, I'll save some spaghetti sauce for you. I always make a ton so I can freeze some for later."

"I…"

"Just say 'yes, thank you.' It's easier."

He lowered his gaze and let out a rueful chuckle before echoing her suggestion. "Yes, thank you."

Her smile widened. "All right then." She looked around, her nose wrinkling. "That smoke smell is still pretty strong." He nodded as she pointed out the obvious odor of burned materials. "It would give me a headache."

It had, in fact, given him a headache the one time he'd tried to sleep in the house. Not to mention nightmares. "That's why I've been sleeping out in the shop."

She nodded in understanding. "Fresh paint'll fix that when you get there." She grinned at him, as if he were the friendliest guy in town. "Whole different kind of headache."

He smiled back. He couldn't seem to help it. It even lasted a second or two. It seemed enough for her, because she turned to go, stockpot in hand. Then she turned back.

"Anything more on your explosion?"

She'd been here when the lab had called, he remembered. As if he could forget. "No. I think they still suspect Gramps left the valve open."

"Bull."

She said it so bluntly he drew back slightly. She kept going, rather fiercely.

"One, Martin was sharp as a tack and would never forget something like that. Two, he was always aware and careful about propane in the first place, double-checking everything when he was done with the grill. Three, I've been around the back often, checking on the place, and I never once smelled even a trace of it. And the back corner of my garden is close enough, and I'm there often enough, I would have smelled it, anyway. It wasn't leaking all this time."

Halfway through her surprisingly impassioned declaration he was nodding. By the time she finished, he was nodding and smiling again as she echoed his own thoughts and reinforced his position.

"Thank you," he said, meaning it from somewhere deep

inside him, where his unfailing love for his grandfather resided.

"And I thought of something else last night," she went on, clearly not done yet. "I never saw two tanks. In fact, a few times I took the one tank he had to get it refilled, to save him the trouble since we used his grill so often."

Now, that he hadn't known, Tate thought, feeling both gratified that she was echoing his confidence in Gramps, and sad that he hadn't known. He should have spent more time with him. But he'd spent as much as he had. When he got enough leave to come home, it had been here he'd come, not the fancy, over-decorated house in So Cal where his parents lived.

"You don't believe it, do you? That he was careless or forgot?"

She seemed as concerned as if he'd been her own grandfather. And Tate felt an odd kernel of a different kind of warmth finally blossom inside him.

"No," he said softly. "I don't."

She smiled, seeming to be relieved. "Good. Because he wasn't. And didn't." But then a frown creased her brow. She shifted the big, heavy pot in her arms. "But that leaves us with a big question."

Us.

Funny how she assumed that kind of involvement.

Not at all funny how that simple, ordinary, two-letter word made his stomach knot up.

"A couple," he said, trying to ignore the odd sensation. "Like where'd the second tank come from? And what really did bring on the explosion?"

"I was thinking more like—was it an accident at all?" she said, her tone grim.

Chapter 8

Lacy stirred the sauce, her nose telling her she had the blend close to right. She wondered if it needed a bit more basil, so she lifted out a tiny bit in the spoon. She blew on it to cool the hot sauce, then took a careful taste.

"Nope," she said aloud, happy she'd hit the balance right off the bat. Everything had come together as planned, flavor and timing, and the afternoon-long project was done.

And this time she would put the portion for her neighbor in a storage container, one he could just throw away when he was done, since the pot had apparently caused too much trouble.

"Stop it," she muttered to herself. He had his reasons for being less than sociable. He'd come here for peace and quiet and had gotten little of either so far. She would drop this off and then leave him alone. This would fulfill her ingrained instinct to help a neighbor—strengthened immeasurably by the fact that he was a wounded veteran—going through a rough patch.

Once the sauce was cooled, she portioned it out into containers, including one for next door, leaving some in the pot for her own dinner tonight. She limited her intake of her favorite pasta dish because it spiked the number on her scale if she went overboard. And although it would taste even better after it sat and the flavors mingled, the making of it had whetted her appetite and she couldn't resist.

She'd just leave the sauce on his doorstep with a note, except she wasn't sure how long it would take him to find it. So she would take it over, hand it off and leave quickly without bothering him too much.

She hoped.

And then she would spend what was left of this lovely, warm, late spring day in her garden, catching up on tasks she'd put off when the quiet had been so severely ruptured Monday morning. And tonight she would finish up her study plan for the book she had chosen for her newest student. After chatting online with the boy for nearly an hour last week, she'd picked a newly released story about a boy whose fascination with a world-building video game led him into a fantastical place where his game expertise had turned him into a hero. She had a good list of questions she hoped would result in her student reading more carefully, which would spark thoughts of his own.

When she stepped outside, the still-warm container in hand, she heard the whine of a power tool coming from the back of Martin's house. His grandson was clearly determined to get the damage repaired quickly.

And just as determined, it seemed, to do most of it himself.

As she picked her way across the yard, she wondered if that was because he wanted to or couldn't afford to do it otherwise. But he was surely going to have to have roofers and such come in, so perhaps that was where money was going. Martin had said he was leaving his grandson everything, including what money he had saved, but he couldn't have foreseen anything like this. Either way, Tate clearly had no hesitation about diving in. It was clear he was used to tackling things himself, which she would have expected since he was—

Her breath jammed up in her throat as she rounded the corner of the house. He was there, all right, leaning into the damaged wall with some sort of long, narrow power saw, lit up by the afternoon sun shafting through the trees. And wearing only a pair of low-slung jeans, lace-up boots and a serious-looking black watch.

He hadn't heard her over the sound of the saw so she had a chance to just look as she tried to regain her equilibrium. It made no sense, really; she'd certainly seen this much and more of him the night of the explosion when he'd been propelled outside in just boxers. But somehow it was different, seeing him like this, working, a slight sheen of sweat on his skin from the work and the warmth, the muscles of his arms and back and ridged abdomen all involved in the effort.

A sizable wood chip flew out from the cut he was making, and only then did she notice he also had on sunglasses, a wise bit of protection given that piece bounced off the side of his face. He barely flinched, she noticed. She probably would have dropped the saw on her foot and done untold damage, she thought wryly.

Stop gawking at him, she ordered silently. She drew in a deep breath to steady herself, then started to walk forward again.

The sound of the saw stopped. His head snapped around at her first step. She noted the instant the tension faded as he saw her, recognized her. He put down the saw, reached down and picked something up from the ground. A T-shirt, she realized as he shook it free of chips and sawdust and pulled it over his head. A sight she regretted, even as her gaze lingered on his flat belly as he did so.

Stop it! she repeated to herself, embarrassed to think

she had been staring at him so blatantly he felt the need to cover up. She hurried over, set the container down on the board set across two sawhorses, making a temporary workbench.

"Spaghetti sauce," she reminded him. He looked at the large container, then back at her. "This way you can focus on repairs, not cooking."

He hesitated, then said only, "Thank you."

"How's it coming?" Well, that was inane, she thought instantly, seeing all the detritus around after he'd taken down what was left of the lean-to shed.

"Slow. He built well."

"Yes." She tried again. "But if he hadn't, the whole thing might have collapsed."

He glanced at the huge hole. "Maybe," he said. "It was quite a blast."

"Better you than Martin." His head snapped back, and realizing how that sounded she hastened to explain, "I only meant he would probably have been in the bedroom, and might not have been able to get out. He wasn't moving quite as well the last few months."

"Better me than him, in any case," Tate said. And she could both see and hear that he meant it. He would take a lot worse than some cuts and a singeing if it would have protected his grandfather. Yes, Tate McLaughlin might be gruff and a bit surly, but there was much to admire about him.

An echo of the heat that had hit her when she'd come around that corner shot through her again at her own thought. She needed to change the subject, and fast. Or just turn tail and run. The latter appealed, but she'd never been much of a runner.

"I still don't believe Martin left a valve open. He was never, ever careless. Especially with dangerous things."

"I know."

"Besides, even if it was true that he did, and even if he did suddenly get a second tank I never saw, what are the odds that it would happen to leak enough but not so much it emptied itself, and that there would just happen to be a spark, or whatever, the very night you arrive?"

"I hadn't thought of it quite like that," he said, his brow furrowing slightly.

"But it's a good point, isn't it? It just sits there leaking, with nothing happening until you get here?"

He stared at her for a moment. "What exactly are you suggesting? That I set it off?"

Her brows rose in shocked surprise. That hadn't even occurred to her. Oddly, he looked relieved at her reaction, as if he'd really thought that was what she'd been hinting at.

"No, not at all," she said with a fervent shake of her head. "I just meant it seems impossible to be just a coincidence."

"They happen. That's why there's a word for it."

"I'm not some conspiracy theorist, if that's what you mean. I'm just saying it doesn't figure, doesn't make sense, no matter what way you twist it. Martin wasn't careless, but even if he was, the timing is suspect. No way it could have been leaking all this time unnoticed, and yet still have enough left to explode like that. It's been three months, after all."

He winced at that, and she felt instantly contrite. The man had just lost his beloved grandfather. Three months was no time at all when it was someone you loved that much.

"I'm sorry. I should go." *And stay away, since I apparently can't stop making things worse.*

She hurried back to her house and went in through the

back door without even glancing at her garden. She shut the door behind her and leaned against it.

Even spaghetti wasn't going to cheer her up tonight.

Of course it was an accident, Tate thought as he rolled over onto his other side of his makeshift bed on the floor of the shop. He'd hit it early, trying to catch up a little more on sleep, but the moment he'd closed his eyes the rabbit warren of his brain had opened up full force and he couldn't find the off switch.

Sometimes I wish brains had an off switch, Tate.

But Gramps, if it's off, how would you switch it back on?

He smiled into the darkness. He always smiled when that childhood memory came to him. Mostly of how Gramps had roared with laughter, as if Tate'd said the most clever thing ever spoken.

I'll not worry about you, boy. Your brain works just fine.

It was working overtime now. But it had to be an accident. What else could it have been? He was no longer in the world where any explosion was assumed to be enemy action until proven otherwise.

Unless…

What if she really had meant she thought he'd somehow set it off himself and just hadn't wanted to admit it?

He closed his eyes, remembering her startled reaction. It had seemed genuine. So genuine he'd been relieved to see it. Not that that had done anything to ease the tension he felt every time she was around.

She made good spaghetti sauce, though. Really good. And if it hadn't been for that huge tub in the fridge, he probably would have ended up eating odds and ends of unbalanced stuff instead of a full, satisfying meal.

You owe her, he told himself. And frowned. He wasn't

sure if it was because he didn't like owing anyone, or because he didn't like owing her. Because owing her meant more contact, at some point.

She lives next door, you're not really going to be able to avoid her all *the time.*

His common sense told him that, but the inward discomfort he felt at the thought made him wish he could. Which in turn made him frown again, at himself, because she'd been nothing but nice and helpful.

Really nice neighborly young woman, sweet, thoughtful and helpful.

Yeah, Gramps. The beautiful part was just frosting, right?

You admire the pretty ones, but you marry the real ones. If you're smart.

Smart? Well, Gramps, there's book smart and then there's life smart.

And if you're as lucky as I was, you get both in the same package.

Tate shook his head. *Not many are that lucky, Gramps. And I think you and Gram may have used up all the McLaughlin luck in that arena.*

Chapter 9

When she caught herself contemplating buying more chicken at the market to make a larger batch of her four-cheese bake so there would be extra, Lacy grimaced and stopped herself. And wondered if the fact that most of her cooking lately had been aimed at easily reheatable things was for the same reason.

Her troublesome neighbor.

Not that he was troublesome in the usual way of some neighbors. No, were it not for the sound of tools when he was working on the repairs to the house, or the sight of a light on in the workshop at night, she wouldn't even know he was there.

She wondered about that, the workshop. Rather, how much time he spent in there. Yes, the house wasn't repaired yet, but surely in his time in the service he'd been in worse? And he could easily sleep in the living room, away from most of it. So why was he still sleeping out in the workshop? True, the nights weren't that cold anymore, in fact, they were having a rather warm June, and besides, she knew there was a woodstove in the back of the shop, although she hadn't seen any smoke rising from the metal flue above the roof. Not that she checked all that often, but—

Quit kidding yourself. You're always looking over there. And now you're standing here in the produce section with a no doubt idiotic expression on your face while you contemplate how much of your life has been sucked up by your new neighbor.

Forcing herself to move on, she quickly finished her shopping so she could stop at the post office and still make it home in time for her next session. She had two completion certificates pending and she wanted to get them in the mail today so her proud students could show them to parents who didn't quite believe the good news. She was focused on that when she heard someone call her name.

"Lacy?"

She turned and saw Hayley Foxworth, headed toward the store she'd just left.

"No dog?" Lacy asked lightly.

"Too warm already, and besides, Quinn took him to the office. One of our guys is at our headquarters in St. Louis, and Cutter's been worrying about him."

Lacy smiled. She already knew the dog was beyond clever, but that seemed a bit much. "Worrying?"

Hayley laughed as they stepped out of the way of another customer going into the store. "Rafe left his car here, and he works a lot in the warehouse, where the backup generator and the helicopter are. Every time we get there, Cutter's off to inspect both, to see if there's any sign he's been back."

Lacy laughed in turn at that. "Okay, that's pretty clear."

"After that, he'll finally settle down. Usually with a mopey sigh. He really does worry about Rafe."

Lacy wondered what there was to worry about with this particular Foxworth guy. But she was even more curious about something else Hayley had said. "Headquarters? Helicopter? You guys must be big."

"We're growing." Hayley's smile turned satisfied in a

very personal way as she went on, "We have a southwest office open now. My brother's running it."

"So, it's literally the family business?"

"When family's the best person," she said. "Quinn's loyal, but if he didn't think Walker could do it, he wouldn't have offered it."

"So, what exactly does the Foxworth Foundation do?"

Hayley met her gaze levelly. "We fight for those in the right who can no longer fight for themselves."

Lacy blinked. "I... That's quite a mission statement."

"Yes. And we mean it. Even if the person we're helping doesn't realize it."

"So, you fight for the little guy?"

"Not always. Sometimes the little guy is wrong. We helped a fairly big company last year that was being sued over something that never really happened. Their attorneys wanted to give up the fight and settle. We helped their founder prove it was all lies."

Lacy was really curious now. "How did he find out about you? I mean, you're right here and I've never heard of you. No offense."

Hayley laughed. "None taken. We don't advertise. We run strictly on word of mouth and referrals. Often from people we've helped in the past, who come across someone in a similar situation. And who want to help someone else the way they were helped."

"Sounds...noble."

"In a way, it is."

"And expensive."

Hayley shook her head. "If we take on the case, we take on the cost. Quinn and his sister set up the Foundation with insurance money from their parents' deaths, and that funds it to this day."

Lacy's mouth tightened with emotion. "What a wonderful tribute."

Hayley smiled, widely now. "Yes. Yes, it is. I knew I liked you."

"Mutual," Lacy said, echoing the smile.

"So, how's your neighbor doing?"

"You mean Mr. Leave-Me-Alone?" She grimaced at her own words. "I shouldn't have said that. He has his reasons to want to be alone."

"He's dealing with a lot."

"Yes. He truly loved his grandfather. And then being wounded. Leaving the service. And now this explosion."

"Enough to send anyone into curl-up-and-heal mode."

"Exactly," Lacy said, feeling guiltier by the moment. "And I'm a—"

"Caring neighbor," Hayley said, cutting off her self-rebuke.

"Thank you, but I really need to knock that off. Oh," she added, "your friend Detective Dunbar really did come through. Tate already got a call about the explosion."

"I know. Quinn talked to him."

"They seem to think it was an accident."

"So far, yes." Lacy thought Hayley's gaze narrowed slightly. Her next words confirmed it. "You don't?"

Lacy gave a half shrug and a slight shake of her head. "I only know Martin was never, ever careless. And as far as I know, based on regular contact, he never had a second tank. Not to mention the timing of it all."

"Hmm."

"I know. I sound like a conspiracy theorist."

"And some theories are proven true. And that would explain Cutter."

Lacy drew back slightly. The memory of the night of the explosion shot through her mind. "His 'fix it' look...?"

Hayley grinned. "You are quick. Yes. He thinks Tate has a problem. And if this wasn't an accident, I'd say he's right. As usual."

"You have a…remarkable dog."

"Yes." Hayley studied her for a moment. "That look has brought us a lot of cases. Even when it didn't seem like there was one."

"You mean your husband takes the dog's word for it?" Lacy joked. To her surprise, Hayley nodded seriously.

"He—and all of us—have learned he's never wrong."

"Never?"

"Not yet, anyway. And," Hayley added, "he never gives up."

"Meaning?"

"I think Foxworth is going to end up helping Mr. McLaughlin, whether he likes it or not."

Lacy nearly laughed at the idea—she couldn't help it—but only asked, "Helping him with what? The sheriff will figure out the explosion, won't he?"

"Probably. Doesn't mean we can't help."

"But this is such a small thing, really, for an operation with multiple offices, and…and a helicopter."

"Quinn's favorite case was returning a stolen locket to a girl who had lost the only thing she had from her dead mother. It wasn't small to her, so it wasn't small to Quinn."

Lacy stared for a long, silent moment at the woman with the vivid green eyes before saying softly, "You're a lucky woman."

"That I am. Especially since I believe I've found a new friend."

As they parted Lacy was smiling, warmed inside at the simple words. Hayley Foxworth, she thought, would be a good friend to have.

Chapter 10

Thanks to the encounter with Hayley, Lacy had managed to completely divert herself from thoughts of her neighbor. That is, until the moment when she managed to drop a grocery bag—thankfully, the one without the glass jar of artichoke hearts—halfway between her driveway and the back door.

He appeared within a moment, clearly he'd been outside. Without a word he began to gather up the loose items, including the orange that had rolled off into the grass. He was wearing cargo pants this time, a garment she'd never thought particularly attractive. But the way he looked in them as he bent to pick up the loaf of fortunately unmashed bread could make her reconsider. Of course, the snug T-shirt that clung to his flat abdomen might have something to do with it.

"Thank you," she said with a rueful smile. "That's what I get for being so 'One trip or die.'"

He gave her a startled glance, and she thought she saw, just for a moment, his mouth quirk as if he were fighting a smile.

"Don't tell me—you, too?" she asked.

"I'm more of a gambler." At her look he added, "All in one big bag and gamble nothing gets crushed and it doesn't rip."

She laughed. "I should try that."

"Don't think it would work. You buy a lot more than I do." He straightened, the refilled bag in his hands. "But then, you've been cooking for your neighbor. Who, contrary to appearances, really has appreciated it."

As apologies went, it was one of the better ones she'd gotten. "He's welcome."

"He's thankful."

She grinned, unable to stop it. "Is it easier for him to accept in third person?"

He had the grace to let out a low chuckle. "Apparently."

"Does he like lasagna?"

"Loves it."

"Good. It's on the menu tonight."

His gaze shot back to her face. His eyes really were a fascinating combination of colors, she thought. They looked almost green this morning, the flecks of golden brown barely discernable.

"And if you—he—comes and eats at the source, he'll have fewer dishes to clean up and not have to worry about returning them."

She couldn't believe she'd really done that, but it was out now and she couldn't pull it back. When he just stared at her and then lowered his gaze, she sighed inwardly. "Or, option two, he can just stay in his comfort zone and I'll bring some over later."

"There's a third option," he said after a moment.

"What's that?"

"You could realize you've done more than enough already and leave him to fend for himself. I'd recommend that one."

She considered that, studying his face as she did so. He seemed sincere enough, but there was a weariness around his eyes that made her ask, "Is that because he's feeling obligated, or because he genuinely wants to be left alone?"

"Does it matter?"

"Yes. Because he shouldn't feel obligated. I only did what neighbors should do. But if he sincerely wants to be alone, I get that."

"Do you?"

"Yes." She waved toward her house. "It's why I work at home. Large groups of people wear on me, except in small doses."

He was studying her in turn now, and for some reason she was glad to see the spark of curiosity. "What is it you do?"

"I'm a reading tutor, for kids."

His brows lowered. "Haven't seen any kids around."

"Online," she said. "I have students from Seattle to Sydney."

He blinked. "That must be...challenging. Different cultures."

She was oddly pleased he'd gotten to the crux of it quickly. "It can be. But worth it. I'm often a last resort, so success is very sweet."

She was surprised with every passing second that he didn't make some excuse and escape. But he appeared truly interested, and asked, "How do you define success?"

"Turning a reluctant reader into an eager one, and a downright stubborn refusal into acceptance, if not enthusiasm."

"How?"

Yes, the interest seemed genuine. So she explained. "I have a pretty detailed and varied questionnaire I have my students answer. They—and their parents—sometimes don't get it, but the key to that student's success is most often hidden somewhere in the answers. I'm always searching for stories that could spark interest in those reluctant readers, plus I have a network of children's librarians I've built up over the years, and they're invaluable when I have a tough case."

He nodded, slowly. "Good work."

"You're a reader?"

He looked away then. "I... It got really hard for a while."

His injury, she thought. The thought that his brain might have been so impacted made her wince inwardly, and she clung to the hope it was something more benign. "It's hard to focus when you're hurting."

His gaze shot back to her face. She kept her expression matter-of-fact, guessing he wouldn't want any sympathy. She saw by the relief that flickered for a split second in his eyes that she was right.

"Yes."

"Is it better now?"

"Mostly. Just haven't had much time to get back into it."

She glanced toward the back of Martin's—well, his now—house. "Can't imagine why."

Again one corner of his mouth quirked with an almost smile. He might just be coming around, this grumpy neighbor of hers. She decided not to push her luck.

"Dinner's at six," she said, taking the bag he was still holding. "Either show up, or I'll bring leftovers later."

"I—"

"Gotta get this inside," she said. "Thanks for the help."

She left him standing there, staring after her as she left.

And wondered why she felt as if she'd battled a dragon and survived.

Tate tried to concentrate on getting the drywall screws tight yet not break through the paper surface, as the guy at the lumber store had advised him. He wanted this damned wall up and ready for the plaster guy next week, but he had to wait to finish the last section until the roofer got here. He just had to hope that wouldn't take more than a day or two.

The drywall man who would do the texture coat had made room for him on a busy schedule, and he didn't want to repay him by not being ready for him when he got here. Then he'd end up having to do it himself, and while he was good enough at the basics—he'd been taught by the man who'd built this house, after all—trying to match a new wall texture to an already existing one was a skill he didn't have.

He finally ended up doing the last few turns of each screw by hand, to better control the process and pressure. It slowed him down, but it worked. And then his power screwdriver's battery died anyway, so he finished all three of the final screws on this panel by hand. It took more time and effort than he would have liked, and made him think again of Gramps, who had only grudgingly accepted the use of power tools to do what he'd always done by hand.

He'd been a tough old bird. And yet losing Gram had taken the heart out of him. Tate stood for a long, quiet time staring at the simple tool that had belonged to the man he'd admired above all others in his life, running his fingers over the worn handle.

Taking the temporary demise of its powered cousin—and the growling of his empty stomach—as a sign he should break for something to eat before tackling taping the joints, he moved the Plexiglas panel back over the remaining gap, picked up the power screwdriver and walked toward the shop. Then he glanced at his watch and realized it was well past lunch time. Hours past. In fact, it was inching perilously close to that 6:00 p.m. decision time. If he ate now, that would make the decision easier, since he wouldn't be at all hungry at six. But that seemed like a cop-out to him, and he didn't like that idea. As someone had once said, and Greg Parker had been wont to quote in their sessions, not to decide was to decide.

So decide, he ordered himself.

He steadfastly did not look toward his neighbor's garden, even though he had a clear view as he approached the workshop. But he couldn't dodge the words that invaded his mind even as he tried to keep her and everything about her out.

Dinner's at six.

He hadn't had a dinner invitation from a beautiful woman in a long time. Hadn't wanted one, hadn't sought out one, hadn't let anyone close enough to even make the offer.

He still hadn't, but somehow Lacy Steele had managed it.

Of course, she'd given him an out, too. Just don't show up, and he'd still get a share of what would probably be another delicious meal. But then she'd be on his turf, with no way to get her to leave without bordering on rude. At her place, at least he could leave whenever he wanted. In fact, he could probably do it so rudely, the proverbial eat and run, that she wouldn't offer again. And that was what he wanted.

Wasn't it?

You can just stay in your comfort zone…

She hadn't said it like a dig, but rather like she completely understood the concept and the desire. Had even, honestly, admitted she had her own.

In uniform, he had once spent his life living outside anybody's comfort zone. And yet now here he was, drawing his own in tighter and tighter. Even knowing that if he kept it up, someday even he himself could end up outside that zone. And if he reached that point, it was a steep downhill tumble from there, and he'd seen too many of his buddies go that route.

He'd plug the screwdriver in first, so it would be recharged enough to finish out the day. Even if he went next door, it was staying light late enough now that he could get at least an hour or two of work in after. Assuming he ate and ran, of course. He wondered if he could do it without hearing Gran's voice chiding him in his head. She'd been a stickler for showing proper respect to someone who bothered to feed you.

So, he'd eat, clear the table, put dishes in the dishwasher—assuming there was one—and run. That should do it, he thought as he found the charger for the tool and carried it over to the workbench below a free power outlet. It had better, because he wasn't about to sit around and do the after-dinner chat thing with Lacy Steele.

He froze in the act of reaching out with the plug. Had he decided to go? Really? Was he really going to subject himself to this?

Swearing under his breath because he apparently had decided just that, but telling himself it was because he couldn't reach the outlet and had to change hands, he shoved the plug in rather fiercely.

He didn't even have time to yell at the slamming shock that went up his arm.

Chapter 11

Lacy was just turning on the oven to preheat when a bark made her jump, because it sounded like it was just outside her kitchen door.

Then she realized it really was just outside her kitchen door.

She ran over and opened the top half of the Dutch door she'd installed so she could look at her garden no matter the weather. When she saw Cutter there, she started to smile. Obviously Quinn was back from the office, wherever that was. But then the dog's actions cut off her thought. The moment he had her attention he ran across the deck to the steps. There he stopped, looking back at her. She frowned slightly. Cutter barked urgently, went down two steps and looked back again. And barked again. There was no missing the inference. He definitely wanted her to follow him.

Feeling like a stereotype from a hundred movies, she opened the door. "Coming, Lassie," she muttered.

The moment she stepped outside Cutter took off at a startlingly fast run.

Toward the workshop next door.

He slowed only once, looking back a third time, as if to be sure she was coming. Something about his demeanor had her heart picking up the pace as well as her feet.

The door to the workshop was standing open and Cutter darted through. When she caught up, she heard him whining in the moment before she stepped through herself.

Tate was down.

He was huddled on the floor in front of one of Martin's long workbenches. Bent over as if protecting some wound. Cutter was crouched beside him, but looking at her. The words "Fix it!" shot through her mind the moment she met the dog's fierce gaze. In a split second she was on her knees beside them both.

"Are you all right?"

"Don't touch..." She jerked back the hand that had instinctively gone to his shoulder in reassurance as he tilted his head toward the wall. "The plug."

She wondered briefly if that was supposed to be one sentence or two, decided quickly it didn't matter. He was cradling his left hand, flexing the fingers as if he wasn't sure they would move. She glanced in the direction he'd indicated with that twitchy nod. It took only a moment to piece it together; the singe marks on the outlet were pretty clear. She looked back at the hand he was favoring, saw the smear of matching black.

"I'll call 911," she said, starting to rise.

"No!"

"You should get checked out. Sometimes with an electric shock problems don't show up right away."

"I know. Gramps gave me the lecture a thousand times."

"Did you listen?" she asked dryly.

"Always," he said solemnly. "I'm all right. Will be," he amended, and she had to admit he already sounded better. Steadier. And he wasn't hunched over the way he had been.

"You're sure? This could be worse than it seems. Internal stuff."

"I know. But this was low voltage. And quick. I was able to pull back."

On those words he looked down at the hand he'd been protecting.

"Well, that's going to hurt for a while," she said, managing not to wince at the sight of a burn. A thankfully small burn.

"It's not too bad. I think I was just sho—"

He stopped with a grimace. Lacy frowned, then found herself unexpectedly grinning. "Shocked? Maybe you are all right, if you managed to stop what would have been an awful pun."

She thought she heard the slightest of chuckles as he shook his head. She got to her feet and went quickly to the far wall, where she knew Martin, ever careful, had kept a basic first-aid kit. She pulled the plastic box down from the shelf and carried it back, opening it as she went.

All the necessary items were there, and she began to pull them out as soon as she was beside Tate, who had gotten back on his feet. Cutter stationed himself directly in front of him, against his legs, as if to steady him. Tate brushed the fingers of his uninjured hand over the dogs head.

"He is a clever beastie, isn't he?" Lacy said conversationally as she got out a gauze pad that looked the right size.

"Very." Then he gave her a sideways look. "He didn't really need to drag you over here."

"There was no dragging involved."

"I would have been fine."

She set down the burn ointment she'd been checking the date on. Turned to face him. Very carefully she said, "It will be easier for me to take care of this than you to try to do it one-handed. Your alternative is for me to make that 911 call. Choose."

Cutter made a low, rumbling sound that wasn't a growl

but was clearly an expression of displeasure. Probably wondering why they were disputing the matter instead of just handling it. She couldn't blame him, she was feeling a bit that way herself.

"The 911 call, of course, will likely end in you carted off to the ER for an EEG, EKG and probably some other E's I don't know about. But again, your choice."

"You'd do it, wouldn't you?"

"No question. You want rid of me that badly?"

"I don't—" He stopped, ran his good hand through his hair. "I'm sorry." His mouth quirked. "I keep having to apologize to you."

"Easy fix to that," she said blithely, turning back to business. "Stop doing things you have to apologize for. And come to dinner."

Cutter, apparently satisfied that the sniping had stopped, backed away a short distance. He looked from Tate to her, and then, suddenly, his ears swiveled toward the open doorway of the workshop. With a final bark that seemed aimed at them both, he turned and trotted out the door.

"Did he just tell us to behave?" she asked as she watched the dog go, wondering if he'd heard Hayley or Quinn coming to retrieve him. Again.

"Sounded like it," Tate agreed. "Although I'm guessing it was aimed more at me."

"Smart dog."

He winced, but it was with a wry smile. He stayed quiet throughout her cleaning and bandaging the burn that was less severe than it had first appeared, although she had the feeling that even if it had been agony he probably would have been just as silent.

"Thank you," he said when she'd finished. Rather stiffly.

"Thank Martin," she said, putting the first-aid kit back to rights. "He was always prepared." She snapped the lid shut again. "Which brings us to—what the heck happened?"

"I plugged that in," he said, gesturing to the now-scorched charger. "There must be a short somewhere." He walked over to a panel and opened the hinged cover. "It tripped the breaker."

Lacy frowned. "Martin inspected the wiring regularly. He would have seen if something was developing."

"Maybe he did," Tate said, leaning in to look closer at the row of circuit breakers. Even from where she was Lacy could see that two of them had flipped, showing the red that indicated they were off. "Maybe he just hadn't gotten it fixed yet."

"He had a healthy respect for electricity. He wouldn't have waited on something like that."

He said nothing, drawing her gaze. He was looking at her with a rather odd expression. And she flushed as she realized this was his grandfather she was talking about, telling him, of all people, what the old man was like.

"I'm sorry," she said. "That was…presumptuous of me. He was your grandfather. I was just a neighbor."

"A good one," he said quietly. "I like that you're so quick to defend him."

"He was a wonderful man."

"Yes."

He didn't go on, but then, there wasn't much else to say. She didn't want to ruin the mood, but felt she had to at least broach the subject. "This is all very…suspicious, isn't it?"

"It was an accident. Things happen. Maybe a critter got in, chewed on some wires or something. I'll look tomorrow." Again the sideways look, but this time it was a much brighter thing. "With the breaker off."

She smiled, glad to hear the almost teasing note that had come into his voice. But she couldn't help asking, "But it's a bit much, isn't it? Two...accidents, one right after the other? When Martin lived here for thirty years without anything like this happening?"

"Bad luck," Tate said with a half shrug. "I seem to be having a run."

She studied him for a moment. "I would think that given who you are and where you've been, you'd be quicker to think something was going on."

Something flashed in his eyes then, some combination of weariness and foreboding that stabbed at her.

"Enemy action?" he said. "I left that behind in the sandbox."

She thought she would carry that look and his words with her forever. Because, underneath it all, she sensed that some part of him was afraid she was right.

Chapter 12

"You know that situation we talked about this morning?"

Lacy had gotten through explaining where she'd gotten their number—Cutter's collar tag—and apologizing, both of which were brushed off quickly as unnecessary by Hayley Foxworth.

"Something happen?"

She explained quickly about this afternoon's drama. "So that's where Cutter disappeared to the moment Quinn came home. To check on his new worry."

"Who is insisting it was another accident, but..."

"You don't think it was?"

"I think he needs it to be. And I can't blame him for that, after what he's been through."

"It all does sound awfully suspicious, if what you've said about his grandfather's caution and care is true."

"It is. Martin was meticulous, up to the day he took ill. Two accidents with his equipment, so close together?"

"Does Tate know you're calling us?"

And there was the fly in her plan. "No. And I doubt he'd like it if he did."

"Well," Hayley said, her tone light, "he won't be the first recalcitrant client we've dealt with."

Lacy drew in a quick breath. "You mean, you'll look into it?"

"Isn't that why you called?"

"Yes, but…"

"It's why we exist, Lacy. Besides, Cutter says something's up. And he's—"

"'Never wrong,'" Lacy quoted with a smile. "Come to dinner tonight," she said impulsively. "He's coming over, and it's a full pan of lasagna, so more than enough."

"Thinking we can gang up on him?"

"I'd rather call it convincing him," Lacy said, although she thought he might see it more Hayley's way. "Oh, and Cutter's welcome, too. He's such a good dog."

"What time?"

"He's supposed to be here at six." Her mind was racing with new plans. "Come a little after."

Hayley chuckled. "Figure he won't walk out if he's already there?"

"He's not intrinsically rude. But if he sees you arrive first, he might just beg off."

"I'd offer to bring a salad, but I've seen your garden. I'll bring garlic bread. Make it seem more social."

"Just thanking you for Cutter's watchfulness."

"He'll see through your tactics, you know," Hayley warned.

"I'm counting on that veneer of civilization—and Quinn glaring at him—to keep him from saying so. To you, anyway."

When Tate arrived on the dot of six, Lacy thought she might get away with it. She was inexplicably touched by the fact that he was freshly showered and shaved, and wore neat khakis and a yellow polo shirt that, while not the epitome of style, seemed to turn his eyes golden. He'd even brought a bottle of wine.

"Gramps had a small collection," he said as he handed it to her. "But you probably know that. You mentioned dinner and wine with him. I thought we could... I mean, you liked him, he liked you, so maybe...if we each had a glass...we could..."

He was floundering, and she could sense his growing embarrassment. "A toast to Martin?" she suggested. "What a wonderful idea."

Clearly relieved, he nodded. She got two glasses, he poured and at her suggestion they stepped outside to look over at the house Martin had so loved. Tate seemed to hesitate, so she said softly, "To Martin McLaughlin, the wonderful man who became the grandfather I never had."

Her words seemed to loosen his. He stared out over the carefully tended grounds, and she saw him swallow before he spoke. "As you always said when your friends passed, Gramps, and told me you wanted said over you...may you be a hundred years in heaven before the devil knows you're dead. Godspeed, sir."

The pure respect and love in his voice made Lacy's throat tighten and her eyes sting as she lifted her glass to his. The clink was pure and satisfying, and the first sip of the deep red liquid warming, as Martin had been to her heart.

Tate turned to her. "Thank you," he said. "For... everything."

She only knew a tear had begun to track down her cheek when he lifted a hand to wipe it away. His touch was incredibly gentle, and the delicate touch from this gruff, tough man moved her in ways she didn't have time to analyze just now. Their gazes locked, and held for a long, silent moment. So long that it became awkward, even as it hovered on the edge of becoming something else. He drew back first, turning just slightly away as he took another sip of wine.

Only when she took in a gulp of air did Lacy realize

she'd momentarily stopped breathing. She stood there silently, hoping he wouldn't close off again, not after this.

She also hoped the imminent arrival of the Foxworths—she wondered how Hayley would explain the last-minute invitation to her formidable husband, but given his apparent utter faith in their dog, perhaps it wouldn't be a problem at all—didn't send him running and ruin the sentiment.

When they went back inside, he looked around with apparent interest. "I like your place," he said.

"It suits me. Despite the fact that the only storage is odd places scattered all over, and I can never remember what's where."

"Alphabetize it."

She blinked. "What?"

He shrugged. "Alphabetize the stuff by whatever you usually call it, then start at due north and work your way around the compass."

She looked out into her house, feeling as if she'd never seen it before. She thought of the items in the various narrow closets and cubbyholes. Realized it might just work.

"Wow. That would work." She grinned at him. "Now that's some McLaughlin-style problem solving."

The smile flashed again, longer this time. That pleased her. "Better than remodeling," he said.

"Yes. My landlady drew the line at that, but otherwise pretty much gave me free rein," she said. "And I like it."

"It's nice. Not…fussy."

She thought of Martin, who had left the interior of his house exactly as it had been. Tate's grandmother's taste had been for florals and dark, intricately carved wood, while Hayley's own ran more to clean lines and a minimalist approach.

"You've got some redecorating to do, then," she said with a grin.

He looked startled, but smiled again. He had a great smile, and she hoped it would appear more often.

She hoped she didn't erase it altogether tonight. She looked at the cupboard that held the plates she'd avoided setting out ahead of time, which would betray the number of guests. And she changed her mind. After this quiet, almost intimate moment of sharing, laden with grief yet warmed with love, it didn't seem fair to just spring it on him.

"I ran into Hayley Foxworth this morning at the market," she said. "I really like her. So I hope you don't mind, but I asked them to join us."

He froze in the act of setting his glass down on the counter.

"I thought it might be easier than one on one," she hastened to add, keeping him in her peripheral vision, trying to gauge his reaction. "Oh, and they're bringing Cutter, too."

He winced slightly, and belatedly she remembered what he'd told her about the clever dog reminding him of the canine friend who had saved his squad from near-certain death. Perhaps she shouldn't have asked them to bring him, but she couldn't help thinking of that moment in the workshop when he'd stroked the dog's head.

"More people to carry the conversation," she said. "Fewer awkward pauses. More getting-to-know-you stuff to keep things going."

His mouth quirked. "I'm that bad?"

She raised a brow at him. "I was thinking about me."

The quirk became a smile. A small one, but he let it out and it made her smile in turn. And suddenly things felt more relaxed, and she knew the difficult moment was over. At least, that kind of difficult moment. She wasn't so sure she was going to be able to quash her own silly reactions to him. Yes, he went beyond attractive, he was downright sexy, but he was also a guy going through a tremendous adjustment. It just seemed to be harder than it should be to remember that, at least when he was standing here, bare inches away.

"I'm sorry about the dog, though. If it's going to really bother you."

"I need to get over it, I guess. And it's not like he looks anything like Sunny, it's just..."

"They're both intense?"

"Very."

When the intense dog and his people arrived, several minutes passed in the usual niceties. At dinner, the food was good, the wine as well, and the conversation even easier than she'd hoped. Hayley and Quinn were charming, and after a brief mention of the electric incident, the talk stayed on inconsequential things, although Lacy found the story of how they'd met quite amazing, and the tale of Hayley's brother Walker's quiet, determined heroics even more so. She'd seen the incredible stories in the news. Even Tate was clearly fascinated. He'd still been in the hospital at the time it all hit the news, but he'd heard bits and pieces.

When he did speak, which wasn't often, it was about his grandfather, and the respect and love in his tone made her smile. Everyone should have someone like that in their life, and she was so lucky to have had Martin in hers.

It was after dinner that Cutter, who had been politely quiet and snoozing on her kitchen rug throughout the meal, stirred things up. When he went to Quinn and sat, staring up at him, Lacy thought he just needed to go outside. As if sure that now he had their attention, he walked back into the kitchen, stopped at the door to the deck, turned and sat. Staring in the same way.

"I'll let him out," she offered. "If you're sure he won't run off."

"He never gets more than fifty feet from us, unless he's working," Hayley said.

"Working?" Tate asked.

"He's made his own job," Quinn said. "We just follow along."

Tate smiled at that. "He looks like a furry Mal. I knew some, over there."

Quinn shifted his gaze from the dog to Tate. "Yes. The vet thinks he's a Tervuren, the long-haired version of the Malinois. Mostly, anyway."

"They can do DNA tests on them, can't they?" Lacy asked.

"He offered," Hayley said, "but we haven't decided if we want to yet. Things are so perfect with Cutter now, I'm afraid knowing what he is might change things. I mean, if we found out he's half Lab, we might try to get him to swim more, when so far he'd just as soon avoid it."

Lacy laughed as she walked toward the door. But when she opened it, the dog never moved. He just kept staring, clearly at Quinn. Then he took two steps outside, turned back and continued staring.

"Uh-oh," Hayley said.

"So it seems," Quinn agreed.

"What?" Lacy asked, watching the fascinating interplay.

"That job Quinn mentioned?" Hayley was serious now. "Cutter's on it."

"All right, boy, I'm with you," Quinn said softly and stepped outside.

Cutter took off, as if the words had been the firing pin to his bullet, and headed straight for Martin's—Tate's, Lacy corrected herself—workshop.

Tate didn't say anything, but Lacy sensed him stiffen.

"Maybe that critter you mentioned came back," she suggested.

That suggestion seemed to appeal, and he followed easily enough. She had a moment to wonder at humans, willingly letting an animal lead them.

Smart of us, she thought with an inward grin. Maybe she did need to get a dog, now that she was fairly established, her client list was nearly full and still growing, and the differing time zones around the world allowed her daylight to work in the garden. And she was home most of the time. Surely a dog wouldn't mind that? One a bit less intense than Cutter, anyway.

They reached the workshop, and Cutter again sat—purposefully she realized now—at the closed door.

"I haven't inspected everything yet," Tate said as he undid the latch that held the door shut. "I know it's still light out, but I was going to wait until morning. Go at it fresh." His mouth quirked as the door swung open. "Still not quite used to living where you don't have to lock things up."

As they stepped inside, Lacy wondered what sort of invader Cutter was on the track of. A mouse, or a rat, even? Tree rats were common here, so it wouldn't be—

Her thoughts were interrupted by the sight of Cutter darting under the workbench, dropping into a motionless crouch as he stared at something. Maybe the critter, whatever it was, had managed to electrocute itself? What had been a minor shock to a strong man like Tate would likely fry something as small as a mouse. She hung back, not really wanting to see a singed, furry carcass.

You're such a wuss, she told herself, but there it was.

Tate knelt beside the dog. He was tall enough that he had to bend double to see what the dog was staring at.

"Hmm," he murmured. "Could somebody hand me that flashlight?"

Quinn moved quickly, handing Tate a heavy, red metal flashlight from the shelf above the workbench where Martin always kept it. He had been, Lacy remembered, as scrupulous about keeping the batteries fresh as he had been about everything else. Nothing worse, he'd always said, than having to stop the momentum of a project to get new batteries.

And she found herself smiling because Tate was taking this seriously, not even questioning the possibility that Cutter had indeed found…something.

Tate took the flashlight, crouched down and clicked it on. It was only a couple of seconds before she heard him mutter something under his breath.

"Better clear out, dog," he said.

Quinn quietly ordered Cutter out from under the bench. The dog obeyed, but sat barely a foot away, his gaze still fastened on whatever had his attention. Tate straightened and went to the breaker panel, shutting off the main switch at the top. Then he went back and dropped down to his knees. He inched forward under the bench, a tight fit. The flashlight came on again.

"Screwdriver?" Tate asked. This time he added, with emphasis, "Not the electric one. Should be one next to the grinder."

Lacy spotted it and grabbed the yellow-handled tool. When she handed it to him their fingers brushed, just above where she'd bandaged his burn. For an instant she thought she'd somehow hit the same electric current that had shocked him, because her fingers seemed to tingle. For the same instant he seemed to freeze.

She backed away. He switched the tool to his right hand

and began to unscrew something under the bench. Then lifted the flashlight again. Leaned in closer to the wall.

This time what he muttered was clearly audible. "Son of a—"

It stopped there. She didn't know if it was because she and Hayley were present, or if, like Martin, he just didn't swear much. She watched as he backed out from under the bench and stood up. Her breath caught in her throat as he went to the outlet that had shocked him and removed the plastic cover.

Quinn gave him a questioning look. Tate's jaw was tight as he answered, "Down there the ground is disconnected from the rest of the system. Up here, the neutral is wrapped around the ground wire."

Quinn's normally unreadable expression shifted, became somehow harsher. "What does this line supply?"

"The whole workshop," Tate said grimly.

Quinn scanned the array of tools. "So anything you touched…"

"Exactly. And some of the older stuff Gramps has are in metal casings, not plastic."

"What are you saying?" Lacy asked. Her knowledge of electrical danger was pretty much limited to not mixing it with water and calling an electrician at any sign of a problem.

"That combination could back feed the entire system," Quinn said. "Touching anything—especially the older metal tools that don't have insulation—could have been lethal."

Lacy felt a chill that made her shiver. She might have believed that one or the other of these incidents had been an unlikely accident, if she had to. But both?

No way.

Chapter 13

Tate stared at the power outlet. The streak of black flared out in an oddly symmetrical shape from the receptacle. He focused on a faint scratch on the plastic cover. Old or new? He hadn't noticed it before, but he wasn't sure he would have. Everything here was familiar to him; he hadn't felt the need to explore.

"Lucky I was plugging in a new power screwdriver with an insulated case and protected plug," he said.

"Indeed," Quinn agreed.

"How can you be so calm?" Lacy sounded incredulous.

"Probably because he's faced a lot worse," Hayley said, speaking for the first time.

"But this is *home.* He shouldn't be in danger here."

Tate felt a kernel of warmth deep inside, odd given the circumstances. But he liked the way she'd said that.

"You're right," Hayley agreed, looking at Tate as she went on. "I assume, from what Lacy has told me about your grandfather, that he wouldn't have made a mistake like this?"

"Never," Tate said with fierce emphasis. "Ever. He was a meticulous engineer with decades of experience. He wouldn't make even one of those mistakes, let alone two. Not to mention—why would he be rewiring in the first place?"

"Besides," Lacy said firmly, "he was using that—" she gestured at the old but immaculate circular saw that sat beside the grinder "—just days before he took ill. He was cutting a board for me, for one of my raised beds. And I'm sure it was plugged in right there."

No one said anything for a moment. Hayley bent to Cutter and gave him a long scratch behind his right ear. The dog leaned into it, clearly loving this touch from her. Quinn took a look at both the outlet and the lower plate with the flashlight.

"They look clean," he said when he straightened.

It took Tate a moment to realize he meant clean of fingerprints. "Gloves?"

"Or cleanup after." Quinn said it so matter-of-factly Tate wondered exactly what he'd done in the service. He would have guessed Special Ops—the man had the cool of a snake eater—but maybe it had been MPs.

"That dog of yours," Tate finally said after watching for a moment, "is really something."

"He is," Hayley agreed. "I noticed you followed him without question."

"Old habit," Tate said, the memory of a canine smile, a lolling tongue and a heavy, thumping, ever-wagging tail giving him a familiar twinge.

"Are we agreed that something other than bad luck is going on here?" Quinn asked.

Tate shifted his gaze to the man his every instinct told him he could trust. He drew in a deep breath. He didn't want to say it, as if putting it into words would make it real. But his gut already knew it *was* real.

"You have every reason not to want to believe it," Lacy said quietly, spookily echoing his thoughts. "But Tate—"

He held up a hand, stopping her words. "I know." He let out the breath. "You were right."

"I don't care about being right. I care that after everything you've been through you come home, where you should be completely safe, and things like this happen."

He met her gaze then. Her eyes were alight with something bright and fierce. She was angry. Very angry. On his behalf. The realization made him feel…

He wasn't sure how he felt.

"Normally I'd say twice is merely coincidence," Quinn said, "but…"

"Twice with clear intent makes a difference," Tate said, sounding as grim as he was beginning to feel. "But if it is…why?"

"That's the real question, isn't it?" Quinn said.

"With no answer likely soon," Tate said, his mouth tight. "I know they'll think this was just an old man screwing up, just like the explosion."

Cutter moved then, coming to Tate and sitting beside him. When Tate didn't move, he leaned in until it seemed almost cruel not to scratch the offered spot behind his right ear, as Hayley had been doing. And the moment he did, the pressure eased a little. He wasn't surprised, not really. Sunny had had the same effect, and the tension had spiked much higher then.

"Can't really blame them," Quinn was saying. "Call them, of course, get it on record, take some pictures for documentation, but…they're pretty stretched, and there's not much evidence."

"Just my say-so that Gramps wouldn't make mistakes like this."

"And mine that he was sharp as a tack to the end," Lacy added.

Quinn nodded. "They'll pursue it, Brett will see to that, but probably not in the way you'd like."

"We, on the other hand..." Hayley put in, almost cheerfully.

"We?" Tate asked.

"The Foxworth Foundation," Quinn answered.

"This kind of thing is what we do," Hayley said.

"What are you, some kind of private investigators?"

"When that's what's required," Quinn said.

"Or bodyguards." Hayley was grinning. "Property retrievers. Sting artists." Cutter barked, startling him. "Sorry, boy. Or trackers," Hayley added with a grin at the dog. "Missing person locaters. Or, on occasion, a small, very mobile army."

Tate knew he was gaping, couldn't help it. "I can't afford anything like that."

"Yes, you can," she told him, her voice solemn now, the grin replaced by an earnest expression. "Because the only criteria for our help is that you be in the right and need it."

"And who decides that?" he asked, his tone a cross between sour and wary.

"Spoken like someone who's had to deal with too many stiff-necked, over-educated bureaucrats or brass who think they should be the ones to decide that." Quinn was grinning now. And Tate couldn't help grinning back.

"Exactly," he said.

"That's the joy of being private," Hayley said. "We get to decide. And in our book, you've already earned our help ten times over."

Tate thought. It seemed impossible. They seemed impossible. Hell, everything that had happened since he'd gotten here seemed impossible.

He was rubbing at the back of his neck. The tension that had been building since he'd had to admit something malicious was going on had tightened him up, bringing on that ache in muscles that weren't fully recovered.

"Is that what this is? Pity for a wounded veteran?"

"Pity? Hardly," Quinn said gruffly. "We just get it. I'd say half of our staff across the country are vets."

"Including you."

"Yes," Quinn answered, although it hadn't really been a question. "And we're self-supporting, thanks to my genius of a sister who handles the money. All you need to do is accept. And promise to help us help someone else somewhere down the line, if you can."

Tate hesitated. It sounded too good to be true, and as Gramps had always said, that was when to doubt.

"Let them help," Lacy urged. "Martin deserves that much, doesn't he? Not to have his memory besmirched."

Spoken like a reading teacher, Tate thought, although her words and the sincerity behind them moved him.

"But you wouldn't have anything more to go on than the officials do," he said to Quinn.

Hayley answered him. "No. But we're willing to start with the assumption it was not your grandfather's fault."

She couldn't have said anything better designed to get to him than that. He let out a long breath. They waited. Not pushing, just letting him think it through. Only the dog pushed, leaning into him, nudging at his hand, as if petting him was tantamount to agreement.

"All right," he finally said, because the bottom line was Lacy was right. Again. Gramps deserved this.

"Good," Hayley said. Her dog let out a small sound that held a very human-sounding satisfaction.

"First things first," Quinn said briskly. "And this is only precautionary at this point. Do you have a weapon?"

He frowned. "I think Gramps's old 1911 Colt is around. Don't know what kind of shape it's in after seventy-odd years, though."

"It's in perfect shape," Lacy said quietly. Tate's gaze

shot to her face. Her expression was incredibly gentle. "He would take it out once a year and clean and oil it. I think that's the only time he allowed himself to dwell on those days."

"The yearly salute," Tate said, his voice harsh as he put it together. "I knew he took time each year to remember the friends and brothers in arms lost, said it was a ritual he went through, but I didn't realize that was how he did it. He never told me."

"I only know because I walked in on him last year, so he explained."

She said it as if she were afraid he'd be hurt that Gramps had told her, and not him. But knowing how little his grandfather had liked to talk about those times, he wasn't bothered. That didn't mean he didn't appreciate her tact. But his damned throat was so tight he couldn't say the words. So he appreciated Quinn's brisk tone as he went on.

"I'd recommend you get it out. Let us know if you need ammo."

He nodded.

"Now. Anyone approach you about buying the place?" Quinn asked, so quickly that Tate knew he'd been thinking way ahead.

Tate blinked. "No. You think that's it?"

Quinn shrugged. "Just thinking possibilities out loud."

"Martin never mentioned anyone wanting the property," Lacy offered. "And he paid off the mortgage right after I moved here." She looked at Tate. "With your help."

She knew about that? Apparently Gramps really had told her everything. "Mutual birthday present," he said.

"I know. And a great one."

Again he felt oddly gratified. When had her opinion come to matter so much? "There was self-interest in it," he said, wanting to be honest about it.

"So you knew he was going to leave the place to you?" Hayley asked.

He nodded. "He asked me, years ago, if I thought I could be happy here. Since this is the only place that ever really felt like a home to me, I said yes."

"Anyone who wasn't happy about it? Someone else who might have expected to inherit?" Quinn again, with more possibilities.

Tate's brow furrowed. "He outlived pretty much everyone. There's no other family except my parents, and my mother hates it here. Too wet and too few glittering parties."

Lacy made a noise he couldn't quite define, but he thought it might have been, in a less gracious woman, a snort. At his glance she blushed.

"I shouldn't judge someone I don't even know. Sorry."

"Don't be. You're right," he said. "I have no illusions about my mother. If you aren't socially advantageous to her, she's not interested."

It was a cold assessment, he knew, but he'd paid the price for his mother's ideas about how life should be often enough to not care much anymore.

"She wouldn't fit here, then. Most people here just care about other people."

"I'm beginning to see that."

And he was. He was amazed, that in only a week here there were already three people—and a dog—who cared enough to get involved in…whatever this was.

Chapter 14

"So, now what?" Tate asked when they were back inside, gathered in Lacy's small but comfortable living room.

They'd left the workshop power off and unplugged everything for good measure. They'd reported it, with the expected polite but doubtful reaction. Quinn called his friend the detective, but had to leave a voice mail. Then Tate and Quinn had done a search of the area, or what they called a recon. Neither of them found any sign of intrusion they could isolate.

"There's a trail back there, through the woods," Tate had said. "But it's always been there."

"No convenient pile of cigarette butts to mark the spot, like in the movies?" Lacy had asked, earning a smile from them both.

"No," Quinn said. "But Cutter alerted us to a spot just off that trail. Nothing obvious like broken branches, but the dirt looked a little too smooth, like it had been brushed over."

"And," Tate had added, "there was a perfect view of the back of Gramps's house."

The idea that someone had been hiding in the trees, spying, was disturbing, but the idea of that someone targeting a man who'd finally gotten home after nearly dying in the service of his country infuriated her.

So now Lacy poured the last of the wine into her own glass, having topped off all the others, then went to sit in the chair beside the hearth, her favorite spot in cooler weather when she usually had a nice fire going. Tate was in the chair opposite her, while Quinn and Hayley sat—closely, she noticed—on the couch. Cutter politely stayed on the floor at their feet.

Yes, I should definitely consider a dog, she thought as she took a sip.

"Intel, then plan of attack," Quinn said, and ticked off questions so fast Lacy stared at him. "Target. Is this aimed at the property or you personally? If the former, why? And if the latter, also why? Or is it both, which opens up a whole new set of whys?"

"That electric jolt felt pretty personal," Tate said wryly.

"Agreed," Quinn said. "But perhaps it wasn't personal to you specifically."

"You mean me because I own the place now, not me because I'm a pain in the ass?"

"Are you?" Hayley asked with every evidence of innocent curiosity.

"Ask my neighbor," Tate suggested wryly.

Hayley looked at Lacy. "He has his moments," she said, straight-faced. "But given the lousy welcome home he's gotten, I'm willing to believe it's not permanent."

When she shifted her gaze to Tate, he looked away.

But he was smiling.

"So is there any reason you can think of that somebody would want this property so badly?" Hayley asked.

Tate shook his head. "I mean, Gramps loved it, and I love it, but there's nothing intrinsically special about it. That I know of," he amended with a look at Lacy.

She shook her head. "Nothing I know of."

"No developers wanting to put up condos, or native artifacts found or oil bubbling up in the backyard?" Quinn asked.

Lacy shook her head again. "I can call my landlady. See if anyone's been after her to sell for any reason. But I talk to her fairly regularly, and I think she would have mentioned something like that."

"We'll have Tyler—our resident tech-head—poke around into that, too, see if there's any interest that hasn't registered publicly yet," Quinn said.

"Anyone hanging around in the last few months?" Hayley directed that to Lacy, as well, obviously because she'd been here all that time, while Tate had only arrived a week ago. Even as she thought the words, it gave her a little shock to realize that a week ago she hadn't even known Tate McLaughlin—he'd been only a grandson she'd heard about from a loving grandfather, details she'd only remembered because he was so important to a man she cared about.

And now, it was a constant battle to keep him out of her thoughts. He was no longer some vague, indistinct figure with no real form in her mind; he was vivid and alive and consuming entirely too much of her energy. And when you put him and Quinn Foxworth in the same room, the air seemed to get a little thin.

"No," Lacy answered the question hoping the delay would be interpreted as her trying to recall something rather than being lost in contemplating the powerful presence that was her new neighbor. "I'm home much of the time, and I kept an eye on the place, so I think I would have noticed."

"Thank you for that, too," Tate said. And if Quinn or Hayley wondered about that "too," they didn't show it.

"Any chance someone hid something they don't want found?" Quinn asked. "A property where the owner has died might be tempting to certain sorts, looking for a place to stash something."

Something tickled at Lacy's memory, but she thought it was something not really related so she brushed it aside for a moment, watching Tate for a reaction to the reference to his grandfather's death. But this discussion was brisk, businesslike, and if it bothered him, he didn't let it show.

"Not something I would have been looking for, but I haven't noticed anything out of place or changed since I was here last. That was a couple of years ago, though."

"Is there more acreage than what's cleared for the yard?"

He shook his head. "Just the lot. He would have liked more, but didn't want the upkeep."

Quinn nodded. "So, no overgrown areas where something could be hidden. Or buried."

It hit her then. "The governor! That was you guys, that's where I know the name Foxworth from."

Hayley smiled. "That was Brett Dunbar, with a little help from our Rafe, actually. We weren't even in town." She gave her husband a lingering look, and Lacy saw a smile curve his mouth, a smile that in a less imposing man she might have called smug.

Tate had looked over at her exclamation, but turned back to the Foxworths quickly. "Wait, that was you? Gramps wrote me about that, back in the spring. He was not sorry to see that particular governor taken down."

"He wasn't alone in that," Quinn said. "But back to the matter at hand. If it's not the property—although we're taking nothing off the table at this stage—then the next obvious target is you."

Tate grimaced. "I don't even know anybody here. Except Lacy, and she's not the type." He gave her a glance. "Even if she does agree I'm a pain in the—"

"I never agreed," she said. "I just said you had moments. We all have moments."

"Can't argue that," Hayley said with a laugh.

"So, no childhood enemies lurking about?" Quinn asked.

Tate shook his head. "I didn't get to grow up here. I only got to visit during the summers."

Lacy didn't miss the way he'd phrased it. What his choice would have been, had he been allowed. Martin had always been oddly silent on the subject of his son, and she was beginning to realize now it was probably because he didn't care for his choice of a wife. From what Tate had said, she saw why. Thankfully, he seemed to have taken after his grandfather more than his father. Those summers spent here must have been something really special. She could imagine a young Tate, full of childish energy, racing about or watching his grandfather in the shop with teenage intensity.

The vision made her both smile and feel sad. She wished she could have known him then. Both of the McLaughlin men, for that matter.

"What about where you did grow up?" Lacy asked.

"Where I grew up you never got close enough to anyone to make enemies," he said with a grimace. "Play dates and nannies at the park. And later most kids weren't welcome at her house. Too messy."

Lacy absorbed that for a moment, wondered if this was at the root of Martin's dislike of his daughter-in-law. "I'm glad you had Martin, then."

His gaze shot to her face, and after a moment he smiled. It was a good smile, the best she'd seen from him yet. "So am I."

"You must have wanted to go play in the dirt now and then, just for spite."

He blinked, then chuckled. Not yet a solid laugh, but she'd take it. "Not just wanted to. Did."

"I'll bet you got her attention then."

"Mostly for tracking it in the house. That was good for a month's restriction to my room."

"Sounds like a better place to be," she said, enjoying this more than the simple exchange probably warranted. But for the moment she avoided the implications of that. And wondered what kind of person he would have become had he not had Martin McLaughlin's sterling example.

Cutter lifted his head, looking from her to Tate with interest. And Lacy suddenly realized she and Tate had been talking as if the others weren't even there. Quinn was watching them without expression, but she thought she caught an oddly speculative look in Hayley's eyes before Quinn spoke, bringing them back to the matter at hand.

"So, no one from those great teenage years? Most of us cross somebody in those days."

Tate shook his head. "Only one I got sideways with got himself and his buddies killed in a drunk driving crash the night before our high school graduation."

"Ouch," Hayley said.

"And in college, I was too busy trying to survive."

He's putting himself through. I'm proud of him.

Martin's words echoed in her head, along with the memory of something about his refusing to go to the prestigious college his mother had selected for him, and so being cut off from any financial support. She'd wanted to ask how his son could go along with that, but it had sounded like criticism of Martin so she never had. She had always had the feeling he blamed himself for how William had turned out.

"Then let's move on," Quinn said. "You were in combat, so obviously there are enemies. But that's in a general sense, tracking you back here is very specific."

Tate shook his head. "I didn't stand out any more than most. There were a couple of guys who made a name among the local militants, who probably got their names on their first-to-kill list, but I honestly don't think I was one of them. They wanted us all dead, but not me specifically."

He was so calm about it all, as if he was discussing some sports contest, Lacy thought. But then, so was Quinn. Perhaps it was simply the nature of those who had served to take in such stride things that would terrify ordinary citizens like her. That they were all volunteers never ceased to fill her with both amazement and gratitude.

Quinn nodded at his answer. "Again, taking nothing off the table at this point, and assuming this isn't random or a stranger after something we don't know about, we're down to the ugly possibilities."

Tate frowned. "Meaning?"

"If it's not someone who's an obvious enemy…" Hayley said quietly.

Lacy saw the moment when he got it. And the change in his expression was what she'd needed to get there, too.

"If it's not a stranger or an enemy," she whispered, "then all that's left are…friends."

Chapter 15

"Thanks for the help," Lacy said as she set the controls to start the dishwasher.

Tate said nothing. And he was still pacing, as he had been since the Foxworth trio had left. Clearly his foot wasn't bothering him any longer. She realized after a moment he hadn't even heard her. He was dealing with so much she couldn't even start to take offense. She was surprised he hadn't taken off to go home the moment the Foxworths were gone.

When he finally stopped in front of the kitchen door, she walked over to him. With sunset not until after 9:00 p.m. this time of year, there was still enough light to see out to the garden, so she'd opened the top half of the door.

"Thank you," she repeated.

He looked at her then, brow furrowed. "For what?"

"Helping clean up."

"Least I can do." One corner of his mouth quirked upward. "Besides, Gram would skin me alive if I forgot that lesson."

"I wish I could have known her."

"You would have liked her. You kind of remind me of her. She—" He looked suddenly like a man who feared he'd done something very wrong. "I don't mean you look old, I just..."

"From what Martin told me about her, and the pictures I've seen, I could never take offense at being compared to her in any way."

Tate looked at her for a long, silent moment before asking, "Are you always so gracious?"

Of all the things he could have said, that one somehow complimented her the most. "I was raised by someone who believed if you have to *tell* everyone you're a lady, you're not. Maybe it rubbed off, after all."

"It did."

"She'll be glad to hear that. She despairs of me, always digging in the dirt."

"I didn't realize the two were mutually exclusive."

Lacy laughed. She liked this Tate, really liked him. Wondered if this was the real man, or if he still had guest manners on.

"You need a screen on this," he said, gesturing at the opening.

"I know. I love the fresh air, but don't like looking through mesh."

"Better love mosquitos, then."

"They sure love me." She grimaced. "Screens are just so…"

"Functional."

"Yes. Very." She laughed at herself. "I know, it's silly."

He shrugged. Went back to looking out of the opening. And his brow furrowed again.

"What's bothering you? You've been kind of wound up since they left."

For a moment she thought he'd deny it, but then he said, rather gruffly, "It just goes against the grain, that's all."

"What does?"

"To give a list of my buddies for somebody to investigate."

It had been obvious that he'd been reluctant when Quinn had asked, but when Hayley assured him they were looking to clear them, not accuse them, he'd done it.

"I can see why it would," she said carefully. "But Quinn promised they would never know, and I believe him when he says he's got the resources."

Tate's mouth quirked upward. "Quinn's the kind of guy you'd believe if he told you he could drain Puget Sound by tomorrow."

She laughed. Yes, she definitely liked this Tate. Hoped this was the real man, minus the gruffness.

"You have to admit, their approach makes sense. First the what. Then find the why and it will give you the who, or find the who and it will give you the why."

He nodded. "I don't doubt they're good at what they do."

"They helped bring down a corrupt governor," she said. "So, yes, I'd say so."

"I just don't get why they do it. I mean, it's noble and all, but..."

"There has to be quite a story there," she agreed. "We'll have to ask next time we see them."

He went very still, then his gaze shifted abruptly back to the garden.

"Thank you for dinner."

Her brow furrowed, the gruffness was back.

"You're welcome. Sorry the extra bodies meant no leftovers."

"You don't need to feed me anymore."

"I didn't mind—"

"Good night."

And that quickly he was gone, leaving her staring after him, wondering what had just happened.

We'll have to ask next time we see them.

The words echoed in his head as he shifted again, trying to find a comfortable spot on the large air mattress. He'd considered sleeping on the couch in the house despite the lingering smell. He'd certainly spent many a night in much rougher conditions. But he couldn't quite bring himself to do it.

We'll have to ask next time we see them.

Stop it, he ordered himself. He tried to focus on tomorrow. He'd call the electrician Quinn had referred him to first thing. Wondered about his man Rafe Crawford, who he'd said could have handled it had he not been on assignment elsewhere. Wondered why Cutter worried about him. Wondered who these people were, deep down, and how they had ended up in this rather quixotic quest for justice where there was none.

We'll have to ask next time we see them.

Finally he made himself face it. The source of his restlessness. Just like that, she'd moved them from barely acquainted neighbors to "we." A couple. She fed him a couple of times, had him to dinner with other neighbors, and now they were a "we?"

It wasn't that he hadn't enjoyed the evening. He had. He liked the Foxworths, had done okay with Cutter once he focused on the differences instead of the similarities between him and Sunny, and had thought Lacy one of the most efficient and pleasant hosts he'd ever seen. *Gracious* was truly the word for her.

And then she'd made that jump.

We.

He shook his head. Why did women do that? Hayley and

Quinn were a couple. A cohesive unit, a team. It was obvious in the way they moved together, the way they looked at each other, the way they talked, with and without words.

He and Lacy were…nothing. He'd known her exactly a week. And that she'd seen him practically naked that first night didn't change that. Nor did those odd little jolts he felt every time they inadvertently touched.

His mind darted away from that subject. Latched on to something else. That at least if his scars had bothered her, she hadn't shown it. But then, she wouldn't. *Gracious*, he thought again. An old-fashioned word, maybe, but it applied.

We'll have to ask next time we see them.

It was still ringing in his mind when he finally dropped off to sleep. And his dreams were of that "we" his conscious mind swore didn't exist. Lacy looking at him, smiling at him, touching him…

In the morning, after a restless and far too heated night, two things happened in rapid succession that had him reeling in two different directions.

First, he found a note folded up and tucked into the shop door. At first he was more concerned that he hadn't heard a thing. There was too damned much going on around here that he was missing. And this time he didn't have the excuse of being dog tired after a cross-country trip.

And then he unfolded the note. It was handwritten, the writing bold rather than flowing or flowery, and done with a pen with a thick point.

T—I meant the plural we, as in either of us, doofus. L.

He barely had time to wonder which embarrassed him more, that she'd figured out what had set him running or that he'd completely misinterpreted what she'd said, when his cell phone rang.

The number was familiar, because he'd only gotten it last night. Quinn Foxworth.

He answered, wondering what new questions had arisen overnight.

"McLaughlin," he answered automatically.

"Foxworth," Quinn replied, and Tate thought he heard a bit of a grin in the man's voice.

"Need something else?"

"Got something. Can't take credit for it, though. Brett Dunbar just called me. I told him we were looking into the situation, so he called the county forensics lab."

"Quite a network you've got."

"It's the foundation of the Foundation, as our Liam says."

That was a name that hadn't come up last night. "How many guys have you got?"

"This office? Six, counting all of us."

"I assume that includes the dog?"

"Absolutely," Quinn said. "He pulls more than his weight."

"So I saw. How many offices?"

"Five, now. Southeast, Northeast, HQ in St. Louis and now Southwest. And here, of course. We're a bit bigger than most, though. Wife and dog. Ready now?"

Tate felt himself flush. He didn't think he'd been dodging, but maybe he had been. "Go."

"The lab finished going through all the evidence the arson investigator shipped them. Your grandfather into home fireworks?"

Tate blinked. "Fireworks? Not that I know of. Not since I was a kid, and we'd do them on Independence Day. Why?"

"In the stuff from inside the shed, they found a remnant of bamboo that appeared to have been coated with a sawdust mixture."

"You mean like a punk?"

"Not hard to come by around here, this close to the Fourth."

"But why would he have one of those?" It hit him then. "Wait, are you saying that punk was lit, somehow? That that's what set off the explosion?"

"That's the theory. It would make for a nice, slow burn until enough escaped gas built up."

Tate's mind was racing now. "And give whoever time to get away?"

"Get clear, at least," Quinn agreed.

"Damn."

"Yes."

"I guess that settles the *what*," he muttered.

"Yes." Quinn's voice was flat, undeniably grim.

So now he knew. And it only stirred things up more. The explosion—and by extension the near-electrocution—had not been accidental.

Someone wanted him gone.

Permanently.

Chapter 16

Tate followed Quinn's directions and found the Foxworth office easily enough, although it was a very discreet building tucked away some distance off the road with no signage at all. It was also painted green and blended into the trees surprisingly well for a three-story structure. But he knew it was the right place because he recognized the big SUV that was parked near what appeared to be the entrance as the one the Foxworths had arrived at Lacy's in.

He parked his motorcycle next to it and took off his helmet. He hung it from the handlebar and rubbed a hand over his flattened hair as he looked around. There was a dark gray pickup, older but well-kept, also parked near the main building. Farther down was a rather nondescript, even older and somewhat dinged-up silver sedan, parked near the warehouse-looking building that sat a good distance off to one side and was the same shade of unobtrusive green as the bigger building.

It occurred to him then that he was going to have to get four wheels under him when winter came. He'd need to get Gramps's car back up and running, but he had plenty of time before the weather shifted. Even June had been uncharacteristically mild this year, with more sun than clouds.

His attention snapped back to that building when the front door swung open and a familiar dog came out.

"Hey, Cutter," he said.

The two-tone dog raced toward him, and Tate belatedly realized there was no one with him. Odd, he thought. The dog greeted him happily, almost effusively, in a dancing way that made it impossible for Tate not to smile. Cutter nudged his hand, then carefully placed his head beneath Tate's fingers so that the only natural thing to do was to stroke or scratch. He suspected the dog would be happy with either.

After a moment of blissful, eyes-closed leaning, the animal straightened and trotted back toward the door he'd come out. Tate followed, vaguely noting that the cut on his foot was barely noticeable now as he wondered why no one had come out with the dog. But then he saw the small pressure plate to one side of the door. In the same moment he noticed it, Cutter rose up and batted at it with his front paws. The door obediently started to swing open.

"Clever," he said to the dog, who vanished inside.

"Get him? Good boy."

That was a voice he didn't know, and automatically Tate's steps slowed. He guessed it must be whoever belonged to the truck, and kept going.

The inside of the building wasn't at all what he'd expected. Given the utilitarian appearance of the outside he'd expected an office sort of interior, or maybe an industrial feel. Instead he felt as if he'd walked into the living room of a spacious, well-kept home. The focal point was a large gas fireplace, before it a comfortable seating arrangement with a couch and two chairs around a large area rug. A large, square coffee table, at the moment holding a couple of books and a laptop, completed the setup.

"Hey. I'm Liam Burnett. You must be Tate." A young man with a hint of a drawl in his voice came toward him, holding out a hand. Tate placed the name that Quinn had mentioned as one of theirs. The man had buzz-cut hair that looked as if it would be a sandy blond if it grew out, and a lean yet muscular sort of build Tate usually associated with quick movement and surprising strength.

He also looked about eighteen, and Tate felt suddenly old.

"I could be anybody," Tate pointed out, but he took the proffered hand. The shake was firm but not challenging; he might look young, but this guy clearly didn't think he had anything to prove.

"Nope. Cutter knew it was you the minute your bike hit the gravel road out there. I could tell you were a friend because of the way he reacted."

Friend? He wasn't sure he qualified, but he wasn't going to complain. He was getting the feeling the Foxworths would be very good friends to have. And there wasn't one of them yet, including the dog, that didn't give him the feeling they were solid and would have his back.

"Besides," Liam added, "if you hadn't been you, that ol' hound never would have let you inside."

Tate smiled at the words. "Texas?" he asked, thinking of Marcus, the smart, tall and very tough Texan in his squad who'd had the same accent.

Liam nodded. "Can't shake the drawl."

"Do you want to?"

"Nope. It's part of my charm." Liam was grinning now. "C'mon, sit. Quinn'll be down in a minute. You want the fire on?"

"No," Tate said. "It's warm already."

"Pffft. You people don't know from warm."

"I spent an entire year in San Antonio one summer," Tate said, earning a laugh as they reached the seating area.

"Lackland?" Liam asked as he took one of the chairs.

"That's where most of the military dog handler training is, isn't it?"

Tate nodded as he took end of the couch farthest from the hearth. "Eleven weeks slumming with the flyboys."

Liam laughed. "Quinn told me you were Army. Like him."

"I got the feel. Officer?" he guessed.

"Ranger."

So he'd been right in the first place, Tate thought. And his instinctive respect was well placed. "Not surprised," he said.

"He doesn't talk about it much."

"Why'd he quit?" Tate asked, just as Cutter's head came up and the dog looked toward the stairs.

"He quit," Quinn said as he came down the stairs, "because the powers that be no longer believed what he believed."

Tate rose, met the other man's gaze steadily. "Lot of that going around."

"It'll change. People will wake up. But I didn't want to die for reasons I didn't believe in, in the interim."

With a briskness that told him the subject was closed, Quinn put the tablet he'd been carrying down on the low table before them. He took the other chair. Tate noticed that he didn't bother with any niceties like asking if he'd met Liam, probably because he obviously had. Cut to the chase, he thought. He was comfortable with that, it was familiar and he'd found that the ones who didn't stall around the subject at hand were the easiest to deal with.

Like Lacy and her note?

He had to admit her open approach had surprised him almost as much as how quickly she'd figured out what had happened. He appreciated it even as it had embarrassed him to have taken her meaning so wrong. And he'd spent far too long trying to figure out why. Assuming a woman he'd just met was interested in a relationship with him was not a mistake he usually made. It wasn't a mistake he ever made.

Until now, apparently.

"Before we start," Quinn said, breaking in on his distraction, "anything new to add?"

Only that I'm an idiot, Tate thought.

But that wasn't new, Liz had taught him that long ago. The Dear John he'd gotten from his near-fiancée while he'd been deployed had been brutal, even as those go. He'd probably still be stewing over it if he hadn't ended up in the hospital fighting to put the pieces of his body back together. Funny how your priorities changed when you were looking at a long-term recuperation and wondering if you'd ever be able to move without pain again.

Tate made himself focus and shook his head. "I've been trying, but I can't think of a damned thing that would make me a target."

"All right, then. We've done some basic checking, looking for anyone on the list we've made of people you've crossed paths with, who also happen to be here in the area. So far nothing, but that's only commercial transportation records. We're working on military."

Tate decided not to ask how they managed that; Foxworth obviously had resources.

"I want to go over the ones we haven't been able to eliminate. Not that they couldn't be working with someone else, but it's a place to start."

"Someone else? You make this sound like a conspiracy. That's crazy," Tate said.

"Any crazier than the idea somebody's trying to take you out in the first place?"

Tate sighed. He thought he'd accepted that, but maybe

not. "I've only been back in the States six months, and was in the hospital for four of that. How could I have pissed somebody off that bad that fast?"

"It's natural to resist," Liam said. "Nobody wants to think somebody else wants them hurt or even dead. Not here at home."

But this is home. He shouldn't be in danger here.

Lacy's fierce declaration warmed him, even in memory.

"I think it's the jump," he admitted. "You expect it, you know it, over there. And home's the place you want to be, because it's nothing like there."

"As someone who has never had to because of people like you," Liam said solemnly, "I thank you for your service."

Tate drew back slightly; he hadn't expected that. He noticed Quinn had turned to look at Liam somewhat quizzically. Liam gave him a one-shouldered shrug.

"I feel the same way about you. I just never say it because it sounds like I'm sucking up to the boss."

"Teague and Rafe?" Quinn asked.

"I've told them. Teague got embarrassed. Rafe just ruffled my hair like I was a little kid."

"I think he feels that way sometimes."

"He's not that much older than me."

"Chronologically," Quinn said. Then he turned back to Tate.

"Rafe is the one he—" Tate indicated Cutter, who was plopped on a cushy-looking bed near the hearth "—was so worried about?"

"Yes. Teague Johnson and Rafer Crawford are the rest of our team here," he explained.

"Rafer Crawford?" The name rang a bell. A rather loud one. "He wouldn't be a Marine, would he?"

"Once and always."

"Sniper? Name on that trophy?"

"More than once," Quinn confirmed.

"Had a buddy who was a Marine who was at Camp Perry for a while. Said since the day he first saw that trophy there, he wanted to be Crawford-good some day."

"Wish him luck with that," Liam said with a grin.

"Rafe is one of a kind," Quinn agreed. Then he picked up the tablet he'd brought down and turned on the screen. A couple of taps later he looked at Tate. "Names," he said. "I don't want whether you think they could be behind this, just your overall impressions of them."

"Okay."

"Jose Guerra," he said.

"Gorilla? He's okay. Rough around the edges, but when the chips are down, you want him with you."

Quinn nodded. "Eric Caveletti."

Tate grinned. "Cav's the class clown. A joke for everything. We came up together and stayed tight."

"Bart Owen."

He smiled again. "They called him Bart Simpson, after the cartoon. I didn't know him very well. He transferred in just a couple of weeks before we played dodgeball with that IED. Seemed okay, though. Bit cocky, but like maybe he could back it up."

Quinn nodded again. "Daniel Carter."

For the first time Tate frowned. "Bit of an ass, really. Had the need to broadcast his opinion on everything, to everyone."

"Let me guess," Liam said. "With the assumption that everyone else agreed with him?"

"Of course." Tate grimaced. "I mean, everybody's entitled to their opinion, but when you could get guys second-guessing what they had to do, it could get somebody killed."

"So, a malcontent?"

"Pretty much." Tate shifted restlessly. What he'd said was true, but he wasn't comfortable with disparaging one of the guys who'd been beside him in combat. "But—"

"Just impressions," Quinn reminded him. "Not accusations. Let's move back a ways, to stateside before or between deployments. Then we'll back up to anybody you're still in contact with from school, then—"

Cutter's head came up, ears alert. A second later his tail started to thump on the bed and a second after that he was on his feet. He let out a short series of barks Tate could only describe as happy as he trotted purposefully toward the door.

"Hayley," Quinn said, getting up. His voice held the same tone as the dog's bark, and Tate wondered what that must feel like, that the mere approach of The Woman made you so happy.

Then he blinked, realizing what had just happened. He heard Liam laugh. "Trust him, it's Hayley. That's her bark, the happy one." Tate looked at the young Texan, who grinned. "Quinn's is a low sort of rumble. Me and Teague, we share a bark. Rafe gets his own, and I won't explain that or it'll sound even crazier."

Tate thought of another dog, who had had a singular greeting for several of them in their camp. But especially him. They had become much more than dog and handler.

"No," he said softly, "I get it."

He stood as he heard Hayley's voice from the doorway. A moment later he realized she hadn't come alone.

Lacy.

She looked…different. She was wearing a dress, some floaty summer thing, and it transformed her from the jeans-clad gardener to the woman whose long legs had been on display the night of the explosion. Not intentionally, but that didn't lessen the way the image was etched into his brain.

"Hi, Liam, Tate. Look who I ran into," Hayley said cheerfully as they crossed the room, Cutter leading the way.

"Not literally, I hope?" Liam joked, also on his feet.

Hayley laughed. "No. On the ferry. We were both coming back. I wanted to show her the office."

Tate realized Cutter had been staring at him in the moment when the animal shifted his gaze to Lacy. The look had been oddly assessing. Hayley sat and gestured to Lacy to sit. In the same moment Cutter hopped up on the end of the couch and sat next to Hayley. That left only the spot right next to Tate for Lacy.

If he didn't know better, he would have thought the dog had planned it that way. And then she sat, mere inches away, and he could barely think at all.

"I feel blind," Lacy said. "I've driven right past several times and never realized all this was here."

"Quinn's of the 'if you should be here, you'll know where it is' school," Liam said.

They chatted for a minute or two, but Tate wasn't following it very well. He could smell some light, flowery scent that he knew was coming from Lacy. Nothing overpowering, just soft and sweet. Like her flowers.

Like the woman herself.

"Don't worry, I'm not staying."

Tate snapped out of an apparent reverie. He glanced at the others, expecting to see smiles on their faces. But Hayley and Liam were looking at Quinn, who had just said… something. Only then did he realized Lacy had leaned over and whispered it to just him.

And knowing it was targeted at him made it even worse.

Here he'd been lost in a stupid daydream—about her—and she didn't even want to be in the same room with him.

Stupid wasn't the word for it.

Chapter 17

The neighborhood had slipped back into its usual state. A full week of calm and quiet. After the disturbances of Tate's first week here, she should be glad, Lacy thought. If there had been any more incidents, she didn't know about them.

And Tate liked it that way. His expression when she'd walked into the Foxworth building last Tuesday had made that clear. She'd seen more of Hayley, running into her here and there, than she had of her neighbor. She'd even seen more of Cutter, who continued to show up every couple of days.

She knew Tate was alive because she could hear him working. The sound of power tools was distracting when she had a tutoring session—but more for her than the student, who could barely hear it over the connection—so she just kept going. While in her garden she'd seen an electrician come and go from the shop. Then an official-looking man with a clipboard who appeared to be inspecting the explosion damage, probably the structural engineer the county had sent. Then another delivery from the local lumberyard. And later a roofing company truck had been parked out front.

She had seen Tate himself occasionally, going from the workshop to the house in the morning, which told her he was still sleeping in there. Once coming out of the woods late at night, which she thought was odd until she realized he was probably looking for anybody hanging around. She wondered if he had Martin's wartime handgun with him. Once she'd glimpsed him at the local market, staring at the items he had in the small cart as if they were strange to him. She supposed it was odd, to be shopping for himself. Or maybe he was assessing whether he could carry it all on his motorcycle. She'd thought about offering to carry it home for him, but who knew how he'd interpret that. So she hadn't.

Not that she'd managed not to think about him, even when he wasn't around. No, he crept in every time her guard was down. And a few times when it was up. Tate McLaughlin, sexy, heroic presence that he was, was taking up too much of her time. If you counted the time she spent trying not to think about him along with the time she did think about him, it was entirely too much.

And then this morning when she'd stepped outside she'd noticed the Plexiglas panels she'd loaned him were back with the others. Apparently the repairs were done to the point where he didn't need them anymore. Not bad, timewise. Especially with that little problem of nearly being electrocuted thrown in.

But if there had been no further incidents for days now, she was starting to wonder if maybe it really had just been a couple of unlucky accidents. But she refused to believe Martin had been careless. It just hadn't been in the man.

All in all, it bothered her more that she didn't even have a neighborly relationship with his grandson. She'd had an image in her head of him being like Martin, and becoming great friends with him, as well.

But he was, now at least, very little like his open, friendly grandfather. And while she didn't give up easily, she didn't force herself on people either, and that's what it felt like every time she cooked and thought of taking extra next door or made some other neighborly gesture. And the way her thoughts tended to stray when it came to him, it would be far too easy to let neighborly slide into something else, something much riskier. So she stayed away, Tate made no effort to change that and life went on.

She walked over to where the panels were stacked and found a note taped to one of them. She reached up and peeled it off, unfolding the small paper, which was, she noticed, from the notepad with the local real estate office logo on it that Martin had kept by the fridge to make shopping lists. The writing was bold, sharp.

L—Thanks for the loan. It made things a lot easier. T.

So that was that. He hadn't even wanted to thank her in person. Although, to be fair, he might have brought them back so early he didn't want to disturb her. He always seemed to be up and around before her, which at this time of year, when the sun rose at five in the morning and poured into her east-facing bedroom, was saying something.

If he wanted to be left alone, she would leave him alone. She would give him the space he seemed to need, and time. She'd just go about her life as usual, and later, when he'd had time to acclimate, she would try again. For Martin's sake.

Her resolution lasted until noon.

At a couple of minutes past, two things happened simultaneously. Cutter arrived, and through the open half of the Dutch door she heard a familiar sound.

The buggy. Martin's precious classic car.

She couldn't stop herself. She ran outside, an excited Cutter at her heels, and dashed toward the garage next door. She got there just in time to see the low, red vehicle with the passenger-car cab but the practical truck bed in back slowly emerging through the double, carriage-style doors.

She was smiling. And crying. And she couldn't stop either one as she watched Martin's pride and joy roll out into the sun once more. She spared a bit of emotional energy in self-criticism. No wonder she hadn't seen much of him, if he'd been working both on the house and on getting the car moving again.

Tate was clearly concentrating on getting the vehicle through the doorway unscathed, so she couldn't read anything other than that in his expression. Cutter was sitting at her side, watching intently, as if he somehow realized the importance of this event that to him must seem ordinary.

When the car was outside, Tate opened the door and got out, leaving it running. Cutter trotted over to him.

"Back again, huh?" he said, but he scratched the dog's ear as if he didn't really mind.

When he at last looked at her, his expression was again unreadable. But then it changed, a furrow appearing on his forehead.

"What's wrong?" he asked.

She wiped at her eyes. "Nothing."

"You're crying."

"It's just…wonderful to see Martin's baby out in the light again."

He glanced at the car. Or away from her, she wasn't sure. But when he looked back at her again, something had changed.

"Thank you," he said.

For a moment she wasn't sure what he meant. "I saw the note," she began.

He shook his head. "Not that. I meant for being my

grandfather's friend. Looking out for him when I couldn't, the last couple of years."

"I adored him," she said simply.

"I know."

"He wanted so much to come see you, when you were hurt. I was going to take him. But then…"

"I know." His mouth quirked upward in a wry expression. His next words explained it. "In a way, he did come. I had a dream about him. Really vivid. Just him saying everything would be all right, like he used to when I was a kid. I thought it was the drugs they had me on."

Lacy almost held her breath. For this taciturn man to share this seemed almost a miracle. "Maybe," she said carefully. "Or maybe not."

He looked almost grateful. But he looked away, as if he regretted having done it.

Cutter moved then, nudging at Tate, nosing at his right hip and drawing her attention to that nice, tight backside. As if she needed the dog to do that, she thought wryly.

"Oh, yeah," Tate said. He reached into his back pocket. He took something out, handed it to her. "I found this in the glove box last night. Thought you might want it."

It was a photograph. One she remembered well. It had been taken by the local auto parts delivery person, who had teased Martin for being old school and still having a film camera. It was of Martin and her, sitting on the lowered tailgate of the truck bed, laughing. The tears started again, and she again wiped at them.

"Thank you," she whispered. "Truly. I miss him so much."

"And I'm not much of a replacement."

She waved off his words. "No one could ever replace him." She wiped again, then met his gaze steadily. "But then, that's the way it's supposed to be."

He gave her a rather stiff smile, and she suddenly realized all the emotions she was feeling about Martin were there in him, too, just tightly under wraps. And she wondered if he was afraid they would break out, if that was why he turned his gaze back to the car.

"It's a sweet ride."

"Yes, it is." She was wondering how the dog had known he had something in his pocket when something else suddenly struck her. "You won't sell it, will you?" she asked with some alarm at the prospect.

His head snapped back. "Sell it? Hell, no."

She let out a sigh of relief.

"Sorry," he said, and it took her a moment to realize he meant for swearing. His grandmother had taught him well. As had his grandfather. Or rather, he'd been wise enough to choose them to emulate. "I'd never sell it. The house is both of them, and that's great, but this…this is pure Gramps. When I sit in it, it's like…"

He grimaced as if there were no words for it.

"I imagine it's like him putting his arm around your shoulder." Whimsical, perhaps, but it was how she thought it must feel.

His eyes widened slightly, and his expression changed. Became thoughtful, as if he were turning the words over in his mind. Finally he nodded. "Exactly like that. Besides," he added with the trace of a smile, "I learned to drive, really drive, in this thing."

"He taught you?"

"I took a class to get my license, but it was Gramps who taught me smooth and steady, and how to handle weather. He was teaching me long before I was old enough to actually get behind the wheel."

"He would be delighted to have you driving it."

"I hope so."

"I know so. He was so incredibly proud of you."

He looked away again. His voice was tight, husky. "If there's anything to be proud of in me, it's because of him."

She couldn't stop herself, she reached out and put a hand on his arm. "That I believe."

To her surprise, he didn't pull away. Given the way he was staring at the cheerfully red car, she thought maybe he didn't even realize. But then he raised his other hand and placed it over hers, a silent acknowledgment of the connection, the comfort offered.

And she nearly jerked her hand back herself at the little jolt that went through her. Why did that keep happening? Was it just her?

She told herself it was just the shock of the gesture, the unexpectedness of it. But then he turned his head to look at her, and the surprise she caught in his eyes before he masked it told her he'd felt it, too. Or felt something. Enough to make him remove his hand.

"So," she said hastily, "how are the house repairs coming?"

"Too slow," he said, sounding glad of the shift. "The roof damage makes it trickier. Had to take out a lot more than I expected, but the engineer finally came out and said what's left looks sound."

She looked at the back of the house. She hadn't been over here, so she hadn't seen the current extent of the work.

"Wow. That got bigger."

His mouth quirked. "Yeah. One of the fire department guys told me to tear out twice as much as what seemed necessary for the actual repair or I'd be smelling smoke damage forever."

"Ouch."

"He said that wasn't official, but from personal experience, so I believed him."

"And the electrician got things fixed?"

She saw his jaw tighten. "Yes."

She hesitated, then asked, "Did he have an opinion?"

"He agreed it had been rewired."

"Did you tell the sheriff?"

"I called them. They wrote it down."

The words were clipped, and it didn't take much to read the inference. The official assumption was still owner error, based simply on the fact that Martin had been over ninety years old.

Lacy let out a disgusted sigh. "Oh, I wish he was here, I would just love to see him chew them out for their assumptions."

He smiled then, as if he could picture it, as well. "He'd tear them up, that's for sure." He looked at her for a moment before going on. "Are you sure he didn't have anybody come in and do some work on the shop?"

Her brow furrowed. "I can't be absolutely positive, of course, I'm not here every second. But I think he would have mentioned it." She gave him a curious look. "You sound like you're having doubts."

"Nothing's happened in the last week."

"I was just thinking that, but still..."

He shook his head, saying, "I don't know. It all just sounds crazy."

"I know."

"I'm almost convinced it was just...general weirdness."

She saw him glance at Cutter, who was sniffing around the car.

"Are you thinking of calling Foxworth off?" she guessed.

"Maybe."

Even as he spoke Cutter was trotting back to them. The dog came to a halt in front of Tate and sat. He stared up at him, intently.

Lacy almost laughed. "I swear, he's saying 'Don't you dare.'"

Tate did chuckle. "He must really keep them on their toes."

Lacy heard the sound of a motorcycle, but it was coming from the car, clearly audible over the smooth-running vehicle. Tate went over and pulled the driver's door open, reached in and came out with his cell phone. Clearly the motor noise was his selected ringtone. For some reason that made her smile.

"McLaughlin." She watched as he listened, then he looked at Cutter with a grin. "Yeah, he's here."

Lacy grinned herself. One of the Foxworths obviously, hunting down their vagabond dog.

"No, it's fine. He never gets in the way, really." He listened again. Then he glanced at the car, then the dog. "You don't have to do that. I just got Gramps's car started and I need to take it out, make sure it's running right. I can bring him to you."

Lacy nearly cheered inwardly at the overture. Of course, the Foxworths weren't just neighbors, he was working with them, but still…

He listened again, said, "Okay," then disconnected.

"Your mom wants you home, dog," he said to Cutter. "Hope you like car rides."

On the last word the dog trotted over to the car and hopped obligingly into the front seat.

"Guess that answers that," Lacy said, not even trying to rein in the big smile on her face.

Tate looked at her, seemingly pondering…something. He glanced at the dog in the car. Then back at her.

"Do you want to come along? A ride in the buggy?"

Lacy's breath jammed up in her throat. "Yes," she finally managed. "For so many reasons, yes."

She wasn't at all surprised when he walked around and opened the passenger door for her. Martin would have taught him well.

She slid in, fleetingly grateful Cutter would be between them, remembering that jolt of sensation when their hands had merely touched. And ridiculously found herself wondering if it was more than the prospect of a car ride that had put the expression of satisfaction on the dog's face.

Chapter 18

As he turned the buggy to head down the Foxworths' long driveway, Tate wondered what on earth had made him ask Lacy to come with him. He couldn't even say that the words had come out without thinking, because he had thought about them.

But he'd also thought of that photograph and the way she'd looked, all teary-eyed, when he'd brought the car out. She had been there for his grandfather in a way he hadn't been able to be, half a world away, slogging through sand and heat, and then later stuck in a hospital and barely able to move when Martin had taken ill and died.

For that alone he owed her much more than he could ever repay.

Starting with civility would be good, he told himself.

And tried to ignore the little voice that was telling him he was only uncivil with her because she scared the hell out of him.

The drive was narrow, wound through thick trees, and about halfway down something on the left caught his gaze. A clearing, where it looked like a structure had once stood. Vegetation was spreading over much of it, but it was at a different level than what was around it.

"Wonder what that was?" he mused aloud.

"Ask Hayley," Lacy said. "This has been her family's place for years."

Of course she would know that. Women shared details so easily. Maybe too easily, sometimes, if they shared with the wrong person. Hardly an issue here, true. And it wasn't his place to say anything, anyway.

Hayley was out in the yard, doing something with what looked like a rosebush at the corner of the house. Cutter leaped out and raced over to her. She greeted him with mock sternness and a brief lecture on roaming the neighborhood on his own.

Tate pocketed the keys—Gramps's key ring, with the house, car and workshop keys, plus a small gold one he hadn't figured out yet—and followed Lacy, telling himself he hadn't put himself behind her on purpose, just to watch her walk.

"Deadheading?" Lacy asked as they caught up with the dog.

"Yes," Hayley said, apparently seeing nothing unusual in the fact that Lacy was with them. "Hi, Tate. Nice car."

He nodded. "Thanks. Gramps was meticulous about it."

"It shows. Quinn'll like it. He appreciates such things."

"He's here?" Lacy asked.

"Yes. I was about to knock off and meet him on the deck for some lemonade. Join us."

Tate hesitated. Lacy noticed. He could almost read her thoughts, that he was being antisocial. Like it was a bad thing. His mouth quirked.

"I'm really glad you're here," Hayley added to Lacy. "I'd like to pick your brain about what to plant in my problem zone."

Lacy laughed, and it was a light, airy sound that put the icing on a day already sweetened by getting the car out and running. Suddenly, extending this time seemed like the best idea in the world.

"We all have them," Lacy said. "I'm no expert, but I'll be happy to look."

"I've seen your garden. You're way farther up on the expert scale than I am."

"And I'm on the bottom rung of that scale, so I'll listen and learn," Tate said. He had the strangest feeling that the smile Lacy gave him had more to do with his agreeing to stay than the compliment.

"Come, then. Quinn wants to talk to you anyway, Tate." At his look she added quickly, "No news, really, but he wants to update you."

He nodded, and they walked around the house to the back deck.

"How are the repairs coming?" Hayley asked.

"Well, finally. Had to wait on the inspector and the structural engineer for a few days, but it's getting there."

Quinn was already out on the deck, on the phone, a glass of what appeared to be real lemonade in his hand. Hayley went inside for more glasses as Quinn finished his call and set down the phone.

"Nice view," Lacy said even as Tate thought it; through the trees he could see a bit of the sound and the Cascade Mountains in the distance, jagged and impressive.

"Great location," Quinn agreed with a grin. "About halfway between two of the biggest volcanos in the state."

"Better than right next to either," Hayley said cheerfully as she came back out and handed them glasses of the summer brew. She led them to the corner of the deck where a couple of cushioned chairs and a two-person settee were arranged around a fire pit. Cutter followed, wiggling his way between Tate and Quinn to get to Hayley, who had been about to sit next to Lacy on the settee. It was subtle, but Tate was certain he'd seen the dog nudge at Hayley. He saw her look at the dog, then at the seat.

"I see," she murmured, barely loud enough for him to hear.

Then she smiled, scratched the dog's ear and took one of the chairs instead. Quinn had already taken the other chair, leaving the settee for Tate and Lacy. And suddenly Tate remembered that moment in the Foxworth office when the dog had put himself on the couch, thus forcing Lacy to take a seat beside him. Once they were seated he walked, tail gently wagging, over to Quinn and lay down at his feet.

"Glad you're here," Quinn said; if he'd noticed anything it didn't show. But then, perhaps he was used to his dog's maneuvering.

Or perhaps you're imagining it all, McLaughlin.

"Any more trouble?"

Tate shook his head. "I've been running recons, but no sign."

Quinn nodded. "That call was from Liam," he went on.

Lacy glanced at him. "I can leave you to talk in private. I'll go check Hayley's problem spot, if she'll point me."

Tate's first instinct was to agree—he was…not uneasy but unsettled by how thoroughly she was getting woven into his life—but practicality won out.

"Stay," he said. "You were with Gramps more recently than I was, you might have answers."

"All right. But if you change your mind at any point, I won't be insulted."

She made it easy, Tate thought. Much easier than some. And he reminded himself that he had already misjudged her once. The least he could do was take her at her word now. Although taking a woman at her word had cost him before, he was past the stage—he hoped—of blaming every woman for the actions of one.

"He's been digging—and he can dig pretty deep—and found no record of your grandfather paying for any electrical work on the house. Or buying another propane tank. He could only find one credit card so far, though."

Tate nodded silently. When he didn't speak, Lacy did. "Martin only had one," she said.

And, that quickly, she justified her presence. "I knew he didn't believe in them much, but I didn't know that," he said.

"He paid cash for many things," she said.

"So," Hayley put in, "he could have hired someone to do the electric and paid him in cash, and paid cash for a new tank."

"Could have," Tate agreed, reluctantly.

"But he was meticulous about records," Lacy said. "I used to tease him about needing a storage unit just for all his files."

"She's right," Tate said. "Even if he paid cash, he'd have gotten a receipt."

"Unless the electric was under the table," Quinn suggested.

"Doesn't sound like Gramps," Tate said.

"Unless it was to help somebody out," Lacy said.

She had a point, Tate thought. Again. His grandfather might have done just that, if someone was strapped.

"Makes it harder, but we'll keep on it. Something will turn up."

Tate drew in a deep breath. "I'm not sure you should."

Cutter's head came up as if he'd said something attention worthy. Tate stayed focused on Quinn, who lifted a brow at him. "Past few days lull you?"

He didn't like the way that sounded. As if he were being fooled.

"It's only natural," Hayley said. "If nothing's happened, of course you begin to wonder if you were imagining things, if maybe it really was just a string of bad luck and coincidence."

"We will, of course, abide by your wishes," Quinn said. "But I don't think we should quit just yet."

"Why?"

"Two reasons. One logical, one not."

Tate's mouth quirked. "Can we start with the logic?"

"We've also talked to some people," Quinn said. "About your grandfather. People who'd dealt with him right up until he fell ill."

Tate's brow furrowed. He'd given them permission, but hadn't quite realized how this would make him feel.

"Every one of them agreed with Lacy. He was mentally sharp and aware. Made quite an impression on most of them, and more than once we heard people decades younger say they had wished they were as sharp as he was."

Tate felt a sudden tightness in his chest. It spread to his throat and he had to swallow hard for fear it was going to reach his eyes and he was going to start bawling like a baby.

"And that alone," Lacy said softly, "makes starting this worth it."

He gave her a sideways glance. She was looking at him as if she saw and understood every emotion that was rocketing through him. Every bit of pride, love and loss that was swirling around with enough power to put him on his knees, had he been standing. And this time she put her hand over his.

It wasn't a jolt this time. It was a warm, steady connection, as if a circuit had been completed and a light had come on.

And now you're thinking in electrical metaphors.

He shook his head sharply. Blinked a couple of times. Sucked in a steadying breath.

But he didn't move his hand.

"What's the not logical one?" Lacy asked.

Quinn's mouth quirked. He gave a sharp jerk of his head downward. Toward Cutter.

"He still thinks you have a problem. Did you see the way he reacted when the subject of quitting came up?"

Tate drew back. "Are you really saying he understood that?"

"Actually, he said it, in his way. I'm saying we've never gone wrong assuming he does understand what he seems to."

Tate looked at the dog, who was watching him intently. And for an instant, as he looked into the gold-flecked eyes of the animal, he saw…something. Something that once more put him in mind of another pair of canine eyes that had looked at him with love, understanding and the kind of devotion only a dog can give.

"I would have thought you'd have more trouble with him insisting you have a problem," Hayley said, her voice light and her expression saying clearly she knew just how illogical most would find this conversation.

Tate shook his head. "Sometimes dogs have a sense," he said. "I don't know where it comes from, maybe they just feed off our feelings, but they know."

"Yes," Hayley said. "But I have to say, Cutter is… unique. And he's thoroughly established that he has the proverbial nose for genuine trouble."

"And you'll keep going based on that," Tate said, and it wasn't really a question; he had the measure of these people now, and quitting wasn't in their nature.

"You're the only one who could stop us," Quinn said.

"And who," Lacy asked with a wave at Cutter, "stops him?"

Hayley grinned. "Nobody."

"Kinda thought that," she said with a laugh.

Tate found himself chuckling, as well. The talk turned to the progress on his repairs, and then to other things, until the lengthening shadows made him realize with a little shock that he'd spent a couple of hours here and had actually enjoyed it. Not least because in the beginning Lacy had stepped in smoothly whenever he started feeling awkward or said something a bit too sourly. Eventually he was able to relax, and he thought it the most normal interaction he'd had since he'd come home. It was a good feeling.

Very good.

"So, do we keep going?" Quinn asked, when they at last stood to go.

Tate knew there was really only one answer.

"Yes," he said. Because one truth still stood.

Gramps didn't deserve to be blamed for what had happened.

Chapter 19

"Cutter is a very clever critter," Lacy said.

She saw Tate glance at her as they pulled up to the stop sign at the corner. "He does seem to get his way."

He sounded rather determinedly neutral.

"He'd make a great seating usher," she said.

He gave her another sideways glance. "So you noticed that."

"Hard to miss."

"Yeah."

It was a moment before he looked at her again, more steadily this time since they were halted now and there was no one behind them. She missed the easing presence of the dog more than she would have thought possible.

"Good thing I'm not in the market," he said, his tone light.

Well, that was clear enough. Not that she'd thought any different, not after his reaction to her casual use of the dreaded "we." And not that it mattered, because she wasn't looking, either.

"And I've sworn off, so we're good," she said, keeping her tone purposefully just as light at his.

"You have?" he asked as he moved on from the stop.

"Learned my lesson," she said with a shrug, glad that

she was finally able to say it without a trace of the rueful-ness that had been the last emotion to go.

"The hard way?" There was understanding. Experi-ence, perhaps?

"Three years with a guy who went back to his ex."

He didn't answer right away, and she figured he'd been expecting more explanation. It had taken her a while to get it down to that essential statement, and she wasn't going to backslide now.

"Idiot," he finally said.

"Him or me?"

His head snapped around. "I didn't… I meant…"

"I was teasing," she assured him. "Because the answer is 'both.'"

He turned his gaze back to the road as they neared the turn to their street. "You're not an idiot."

"I was to stay that long."

"He was to leave."

He didn't mean it, of course. Not in the way any woman who was looking would want it meant from this man, any-way.

It was a good thing she'd sworn off.

Feeling like she needed to acknowledge the compliment no matter if it had been meant or not, she said, "Nice of you to say."

"Mmm."

Well, that was noncommittal. And very male. But then, if Tate McLaughlin was anything, it was 100 percent male.

"What took you off the market?"

He hesitated, then said, "A ten-word Dear John letter."

"While you were deployed?"

He nodded.

"That is unforgiveable," she said, rather fiercely.

"She didn't want forgiveness. She just wanted out."

He said it with finality, and she knew that was the end of the conversation. And given that she had no desire to talk about her own romantic failure, she could hardly push for more on his.

They made the turn and moments later were pulling down his driveway toward the garage. He stopped the car outside. At her glance, he said, "I want to work on it a bit more. It's running a little hot."

She nodded.

"My fault," he added as he opened his door and got out, as if he feared she would think his grandfather had done it. "I tinkered and obviously should have left it alone."

She had her hand on the door handle before she realized he was, to her surprise, coming around to open it for her. "Martin wouldn't mind," she said. "Thank you," she added as the door swung open.

He smiled, with just a tinge of self-consciousness that she found appealing. And as she headed back home for an evening session she had pending, she felt the warmth of satisfaction. He had done very well today, relaxing with the Foxworths in a way she'd been afraid he couldn't. Or wouldn't.

She would count it an afternoon well spent.

He took a step back and looked at the wall. Then he stepped right up to it, turned sideways, leaned in to put his head against it—glad the headache he'd awakened with had dissipated—and looked down the length of the repaired section.

No question the drywall guy had done a great job. He could only see the borders of the repair now because he knew they were there and it wasn't quite dry yet. When painted they'd be invisible.

But painted what color? That wall had been papered with a flowery print that, with apologies to Gran, he hadn't been sorry to see go. At least she hadn't done the entire room in it. Gramps had probably put his foot down on that.

If it were up to him the whole place would probably be basic white. Not that he didn't like color or pattern, he just sucked at putting them together.

Belatedly it struck him. It was up to him. The place was his now, and there was no one to quibble with his choices. Especially inside, where no one would see it except him. At the sound of a yip that was rather close, and remembering he'd thought the front door hadn't quite latched, he added aloud ruefully, "And maybe him."

He turned to see Cutter sitting expectantly in the doorway to the bedroom.

"Trespassing?" he suggested.

Cutter gave him a head-tilting stare that for all the world looked like "Really? After all I've done?"

But he turned and trotted back the way he'd come without a glance back, leaving Tate feeling a bit guilty. He'd only been teasing, really. He'd gotten used to the dog, and Cutter was such a distinct personality he no longer reminded him of Sunny in quite the same way.

Still, once he started painting he'd have to be sure the door was closed no matter how full his hands were. Unless, of course, the clever dog could open regular doors, too. At this point he wasn't sure he would put it past him.

He leaned into the wall again and saw one spot that he thought could use a tiny bit of sanding. Then he was going to have to decide about paint. Maybe he'd ask Lacy. He liked the way her place looked, the green that seemed to bring the outside in, and the splashes of brighter colors here and there. That was the kind of thing he was lousy at.

He'd probably end up with some combination that looked like the aftermath of a blender explosion.

Odd how the thought of asking her advice didn't unsettle him, he thought as he headed out to the workshop for sandpaper. Perhaps because they'd made the parameters clear the other day. It made it easier to talk when the expectations—or rather lack of them—were clear and out in the open.

And he'd liked that she'd kept it short. Not given him chapter and verse with a dash of whine, as most women he'd known would have.

Three years with a guy who went back to his ex.

Only one word longer than Liz's Dear John.

But what guy would walk away from a woman like Lacy? She wasn't just attractive, she was smart, funny and easy to be with. She didn't seem to be at all self-involved; in fact, if anything, she was too generous for her own good.

And too damned sexy in a pair of jeans and those shirts she wore. They might be made of plain denim or chambray, but they fit her like a glove, unlike the more usual baggy ones he'd seen—and had a couple of himself.

And if he didn't stop thinking about her like that, all that getting it out in the open was going to be for nothing. Because thinking about her like that made him think of that first night, when that vision of mostly bare, incredibly long legs and breasts free beneath the thin T-shirt had been seared into his mind. And no matter how he struggled to hang on to the counselor's stern instructions about women, that image blew all that cool detachment to hell.

The buggy wasn't the only thing running hot.

He tamped down his runaway thoughts and focused solely on what grade of sandpaper he wanted—something very fine, obviously—and pulled out the big envelope of papers Gramps had neatly placed in the appropriately labeled workbench drawer. Extra fine, he thought, and went through the coarser grades until he found what he wanted. He—

"Are you all right?"

He spun around, staring at the woman in the doorway, the woman he'd been trying so hard not to think about. She was wearing jeans that hugged her hips and a knit shirt that clung to every curve and matched her eyes. He barely noticed the dog beside her.

"What?" He only realized how dumbstruck he sounded after the word came out. Natural, he told himself, after all, he'd just been thinking about her—and trying to stop—and here she was.

"Are you all right?" she repeated as she came in, looking him up and down as if checking for damage.

"I'm fine," he said, puzzled now.

She stopped a bare two feet in front of him. "It's just… he came and got me, like before, and I thought…"

The dog, he realized belatedly. Who was now sitting beside her but looking at him. And looking almost smug, as if he'd done something very clever. He shifted his gaze back to Lacy's face. Her worried expression was clearing.

"You thought something else had happened?"

She nodded.

"Well," he said, lifting his arms to the side and nodding down his unscathed self, "I don't know what's up with the dog, but as you can see, I'm fine."

"Yes," she said. "Yes, I can. See, I mean."

It was, Tate realized, two entirely different things, to be inspected by a Lacy who thought he might be injured and by one who knew he wasn't. This inspection made his gut knot up and sent other nerves into heightened alert. And all the shouting his mind was doing, that they'd safely put this off-limits, wasn't doing a damn bit of good.

Running hot, indeed.

Chapter 20

Lacy looked away from him. Reluctantly, but necessary. If she didn't, she was afraid she might gape at him.

He appeared to have put on a little weight, which made her smile inwardly; he'd needed it and it looked good on him. And given the way he'd been working, it was probably all muscle. Taut, fit muscle. She nearly shivered.

She didn't know what it was about a well-built guy in jeans and a half-buttoned shirt with rolled-up sleeves that did it to her. She didn't dare consider the fact that it might be Tate McLaughlin specifically who got her blood pumping.

Cutter provided a distraction, walking toward the back of the shop and nosing at something. She looked and saw the makeshift bed against the back wall. She recognized the full-size inflatable mattress that Martin had had, for nights when he had been up at all hours watching the sky for meteors or a glimpse of the aurora dancing across the northern sky.

"You're still sleeping out here?" she asked.

He only shrugged, but seemed vaguely unsettled.

"I thought the wall was at least sealed up enough."

"It is."

She lifted a brow at him. And this time managed not to state the obvious, that there were other places to sleep inside. He grimaced, and when he spoke there was an edge in his voice. "I'm waiting until I can only smell fresh paint, not burned—"

He stopped, gave a sharp shake of his head. The aftermath of an explosion probably didn't give him sweet dreams at night. Maybe even nightmares, given what he'd gone through.

She felt an instinctive rush of sympathy, but before she could say anything Cutter was back. He sat beside Tate, but he was watching her. And she would swear the dog, ever so slightly, had shaken his head. It was that moment's pause, as she contemplated that silliness, that gave her time to realize sympathy was probably the last thing he would want.

Instead she said as lightly as she could manage, "I'm too big a fan of indoor plumbing."

When Tate's expression softened and he almost smiled, she knew it had been the right move. Her gaze flicked to Cutter, who was now looking at her happily, tongue lolling. Almost, she thought, in approval. Then she laughed at herself. What was it about this dog that had her projecting human thoughts onto him? He was obviously very smart, but this was a bit much.

"There is that," Tate agreed. She noticed he was scratching that spot behind Cutter's ear that the dog obviously loved. He wasn't focused on it. It seemed like it was practically a reflex; if the dog was there, contact was normal. She liked that.

"So, when will you have that lovely paint smell instead?" she asked, thinking it safe enough.

"Next couple of days, I think." He glanced down at the dog, then back at her, and there was something tentative in his expression. After a moment of silence, which she consciously decided not to fill for him, he went on, "Unless I can't decide what color to paint."

Lacy remembered the color the room had been. "I can certainly understand not wanting pink," she said with a grin.

"Gran," he said.

"I know," she said. "Martin said he didn't have the heart to change it after she died, even though he'd always hated it."

Tate let out a breath. "Maybe I shouldn't, either."

"She wouldn't mind. And I can't see you in a pink bedroom." That sounded wrong, somehow, and she hastened to add, "Or me, for that matter." And that sounded worse. Like she was contemplating herself in his bedroom. "It's my least favorite color," she ended, sounding lame even to herself.

She told herself to shut up and waited, half expecting him to turn her comments into something that would turn her face the color they were discussing. He didn't, only saying, "I thought all girls liked pink."

"*All* girls don't like anything."

A little too late to stop her denial of some female monolith, she caught the glint in his eye. He'd been teasing her.

"Brat," she muttered. Cutter yipped, whether in protest or agreement she couldn't tell. And there she went with the anthropomorphizing again.

"So, what color?" he asked. "Left to myself, I'd go with basic white, but that seems kind of..."

"Better than olive drab," she quipped.

His gaze narrowed. In that same moment Cutter nudged his hand, and when he glanced down the dog rose and came to her, turning to sit at her feet facing him. He cocked his head as he looked at Tate, as if to say, "Can't you take a joke?"

Even as she thought it, Tate's expression cleared and he laughed. Actually laughed. It was wonderful, if a bit rusty sounding. And, she realized for the first time, he had a dimple in his right cheek. The combination made her smile.

"Anything," he said with emphasis, "is better than olive drab."

"Indeed."

"What, then?"

"It should be what you want, not me."

"But I don't know what I want."

Join the club.

She hushed her own thoughts again and tried to remember the room. "I'm trying to recall where the windows are."

"South wall. And I changed—" He stopped suddenly, looked for a moment as if he were considering something difficult, then he shrugged. "Do you want to come in and look? Get a better idea?"

Lacy reined in the leap her heart took. Because he'd invited her into his domain. Now, that was progress, she thought, remembering the times when she'd had free run of the house, when Martin had told her to quit knocking and just come on in. She remembered him saying cheerfully, "At my age, I'm not likely to be up to anything you shouldn't see."

He'll get there, Martin. He'll be okay.

"All right," she said.

And it wasn't until they were actually going through the door that she realized he'd essentially invited her into his bedroom. Now that, she thought, would make her heart leap under other circumstances. Circumstances she was not going to think about.

She was surprised when she stepped into the living room and caught the faint scent of burned wood and plaster.

"You really can still smell it."

"I'm not sleeping out there because I enjoy it," he said dryly.

"Be glad it's not winter." They got to the doorway of the bedroom. She realized the entire doorjamb had been replaced. And when she looked in, she was surprised all over again. Shocked, in fact. "I had no idea it did that much damage. I thought it was just the hole in the wall."

"It blew debris all over, into the other walls."

She could see almost the entire north wall had been replaced, and there were large patches on the other three walls. No wonder she hadn't seen much of him. This had been a lot of work.

And he was damned lucky not to be hurt worse than he had been. She was about to say something like that when Cutter bumped her hand. She automatically looked down and saw the dog make that same odd little shake of his head. This was insane, she thought. But she followed the imagined advice anyway, because it made sense.

"I guess you'll be furniture shopping, too," she said instead, only now realizing that some of the debris he'd stacked outside was what was left of the bed and dresser.

"Don't remind me," he said with a grimace.

"There's a nice shop out near the mall."

"I figured I'd just find something I liked online."

"That's good, too. I just like to see something that big in person. Especially a bed. You'd want to try that out first."

Her words seemed to echo in the abrupt silence. He was looking at her, rather too intently. She'd meant the words in an entirely innocent manner, and she refused to blush just because he was watching her like he was wondering what she would consider "trying out" a bed.

Or maybe she was just imagining that. Wishful thinking? Lord, she was being a fool. She looked around the room, trying to focus on why she was here. But something else snagged her attention.

"You put in a bigger window. Martin always said he wanted to do that."

"I know."

Of course he did. Martin was his grandfather, after all. Paint, idiot girl. Paint is what you're here for.

"That will let in more light. You might be able to get away with a darker color in the whole room if you really want."

He looked around. Shook his head. "Cave," he said. "Already dark enough here most of the year."

She smiled at the analogy.

"Blue is the obvious counterpoint to the pink, but light blue tends toward baby blue. I don't like pastels, but your mileage may vary. Gray would be nice and masculine, especially with black furnishings, but with the sky being gray so often here, it may be a bit much. A different shade of green, maybe? Lighter?"

Like the pale green in your eyes?

For an instant she was afraid she'd voiced the thought. Now that would be embarrassing, betraying that she'd spent far too much time pondering the mystery of his hazel eyes and how they sometimes looked green, sometimes gold.

"Lot of that outside, too," he pointed out.

"True."

"I like gray. Even with a lot of it in the sky." He looked at her for a moment. "What about a kind of gray-blue?"

It took everything she had not to read anything into that choice and the fact that her eyes were a grayish blue. She had eyes on the brain, she thought. And even her thoughts were sounding more ridiculous by the moment.

"That would work. The blue would take you out of the battleship category."

He grinned. It nearly took the breath out of her.

"You also need to decide if you're going to paint the whole room the same color."

"What?"

"If you only paint one wall, and do the rest maybe that white, you can get away with a darker color, I think."

He frowned. "Okay, this is getting complicated."

And they, she realized, were having an utterly normal conversation. Like any two neighbors might.

Except for the fact that she kept thinking about his eyes and that newly discovered dimple. Oh, and his chest, broad beneath that shirt. And his forearms, strong, muscular beneath the rolled-up shirtsleeves.

Stop there, she ordered herself sternly.

A movement drew her gaze at the moment something lightly brushed her ankle. She looked down to see Cutter's tail wagging happily. As if he, too, was liking the fact that they were simply talking. And that Tate wasn't as grumpy as he had been just a couple of weeks ago. Amazing what not having your life threatened for a few days could do. Or maybe just a lot of hard, physical work, although clearly he was no stranger to that.

"What would you do?"

"Like I said, it's not what I like—"

"I like your place. So what would you do?"

She was honest enough to admit she was flattered; she'd worked hard on getting the little cottage just as she liked it.

As she looked around the room, she remembered how it had been arranged. Pictured various combinations.

"That wall," she finally said, pointing at the wall opposite the repaired one with the new, bigger window. "A darker color, maybe a nice slate blue. The rest white. Blue and white is classic. Bed against that wall, facing the new window. Then you could go with the same blue for bedding, or gray, or even black if you want. Or white, but that's a pain to keep clean." She looked at the dog who was wandering the room now, sniffing. "Especially with canine company."

"Which it seems I'll continue to have."

"Do you mind?"

He hesitated, but only for a moment. "No. He's a great dog."

"Not too much of a reminder?"

He lowered his gaze. "Now that I've gotten to know him, I can see he's a very different dog than Sunny."

She could only imagine the kind of bond man and dog developed under those circumstances. And she couldn't at all imagine what it would be like to be so far from home, in such a radically different place, in such danger all the time, volunteering for people you didn't even know.

And then getting that letter.

She wondered rather inanely if it had been an actual letter or an email. Or maybe a text? Could she have been that cold? Lacy had spent some time—too much time—wondering what exactly she'd said.

"What were the ten words?" It was out before she really thought it through. He went very still. "Sorry," she said immediately. "None of my business. I just wanted to know how much to hate her."

"Don't."

Hate her, or ask?

"Hard not to," she said. "But I do apologize. It really isn't my business."

"Don't hate her. I don't. I hate how she did it, but…"

"How did she do it?"

"Text. Sent it, then blocked me."

"So you couldn't even answer? Tell her to go to hell?"

His gaze shot back to her face. She thought he might be fighting a smile, but he didn't say anything.

"You got it over there?" she asked.

"In the field hospital, before I was shipped home."

She nearly gaped at him. To her that was even worse.

"She had her reasons. And she was honest."

"Honest."

"'Sorry, I can't do this. You deserve someone who can.'"

It took her a moment to realize he was quoting the ten words.

And, grudgingly, she saw what he meant about honest.

"Would she change her mind? Now that you're out?"

His mouth twisted slightly. "I think her new husband might object."

Lacy stared at him, shocked. "She's already married to someone else?"

"So I was told."

She didn't understand why he was smiling at her. Didn't he realize that had to mean she'd most likely been cheating on him before, maybe long before, she'd ever told him she wanted out?

"How can you smile at that? She had to have been—"

"It doesn't matter anymore."

The phone in her pocket chimed a warning that her afternoon tutoring session was nearly here.

All the way back to her house she puzzled over that smile.

Chapter 21

Tate found himself still smiling as he went back to work. Which was odd enough for him that he pondered Lacy's last question. He didn't think he could explain why he'd been smiling. At least, not in a way that wouldn't be…not insulting, but maybe provoking.

Because he'd been smiling—and still was—because she had looked so horrified at what he'd known from the moment he heard Liz had married, that she had been seeing someone else for some time. It said a lot about Lacy Steele, that reaction did.

Cutter appeared, nudging his hand for a scratch.

"You know, it's a good thing you don't live in the city, dog. They'd have to curb your visiting."

And he realized with surprise that he would miss that.

The dog turned in what Tate now knew was the direction of home and started off.

"Figure your work here is done?" he called out, feeling a bit silly.

The dark head turned as the animal looked back at him. He was noticing the contrast between that head and the reddish brown of the dog's back and hindquarters when his gaze snapped back to Cutter's face.

Had the damn dog winked at him?

He nearly laughed at himself. He was starting to think

like the Foxworths apparently did, as even Lacy already seemed to be doing. Projecting human thoughts and emotions onto a dog.

He really would miss the visits. He'd always thought he'd never get a dog; no dog could replace having Sunny with him. But Cutter, while a very different dog, had him thinking about it, at least. Which is what he got for not driving him away in the first place.

And Lacy?

He would miss Lacy if he managed to drive her away completely. She was the good neighbor Gramps had said she was.

And that's all she is.

He thought it rather forcefully. Pondering getting a dog was one thing. Thinking about his long-legged, blue-eyed neighbor becoming more than just a neighbor set off alarm bells so loud even he couldn't ignore them.

But he couldn't quite forget how clearly appalled she had been at what Liz had done. And that made him feel… He wasn't sure how. Supported, yes. Warmed, even.

But when it came right down to it, he had the feeling he'd just learned everything he needed to know about who and what Lacy Steele was. But then, he'd thought he knew Liz, too. Had thought her tough enough—had thought she loved him enough—to get through his long deployments for the sake of the joyous return. But he'd been sadly wrong, and—

He'd never been so relieved to hear the revving motorcycle sound of his cell phone ring, because that not-to-be-trusted voice in the back of his mind was announcing that Lacy Steele would be as tough as her last name.

He found the phone under a sheet of sandpaper and picked it up. Saw the name. Grinned.

"He's on his way home," he said without preamble.

He heard a light, airy laugh. Yes, Quinn Foxworth was definitely a lucky man. "I hope he's not bothering you too much?" Hayley asked.

"Persistence won out," he admitted. "I'd miss him if he stopped."

"He's clever that way."

"I get the feeling he's clever in a lot of ways," Tate said, remembering that wink he thought he'd seen.

"More than you know," she said. "But listen, we wanted to talk to you about something. Are you free to come by the office this afternoon?"

Maybe they'd finally understood this was pointless and wanted to pull out. She could just tell him that now, and he'd be fine with it. He wasn't even sure why he hadn't followed through on having them quit himself.

Except there was Cutter. Hadn't Sunny taught him to trust the instincts of a clever dog?

And there was his faith in Gramps.

Decided now, he said, "Sure. It'll save me from having to look at paint colors."

Although after he'd grabbed a quick shower, changed and fired up the buggy, he thought he knew what he was going to do with that. Exactly what Lacy had said. It sounded right. He could even picture the room in his head with the color she'd suggested, which was strange enough for him that he thought it must mean it was right. Maybe he'd even pick up the paint on his way back from Foxworth. And try not to think about the fact that he was committing to living in a room that would now always be connected to her, even if in a small way.

He shook off the thought. Got back on track.

After paint, all that would be left would be furniture. An even worse decision to make. The rather ornate, curvy and curlicued bed Gram had favored had always seemed fussy to him, even as a boy. Not that he was glad it had been destroyed, simply because it had belonged to his grandparents. He probably would have kept it if not for the explosion. But it had been reduced mostly to large splinters. He'd just been lucky he hadn't been in it at the time, or he wouldn't have any decisions left to make, ever. They would have been picking up splinters of him.

He had had quite enough of close calls.

But this had been only a run of bad luck. It had to be.

He was going to tell Foxworth to let it go; it was nothing.

Funny how those decisions seemed easy compared to picking out a damned bed. He supposed asking the woman you were hot for but were intent on keeping just a neighbor to go bed shopping with you was not a good plan.

Lacy glanced at the clock again. Her current student lived in a rural area in eastern Europe where the internet was very spotty. Normally the rule of thumb on all her sessions was that if a dropped connection lasted beyond the scheduled end of session time, they canceled until next time. But Anna was so enthusiastic, and had made such great strides in both her English and reading, that Lacy gave her a bit more time when she had it. She could always find something to do while she was waiting at the computer for the connection to return.

And now she was staring at a search engine page, trying to talk herself out of doing what she'd begun to do.

It was prying, but there for anybody to find. She could almost hear her mother bemoaning the loss of any sense of privacy. Lacy usually just laughed, she'd grown up in the information age, after all, but once she had told her mother that she thought the ability to see if that babysitter you were going to hire was a convicted pedophile was a decent trade-off. Although she'd had to agree with her mom that the fact that that was even necessary was a sad thing.

And now here she sat, on the verge of typing a name into that search box, just to see what came up. And, in the end, she did it.

She eliminated a pro football player and a couple of inactive social media accounts right off. For that matter, there was no sign of him at all on social media that she could find. This didn't surprise her; he didn't seem the type even if he did have the time. She'd seen his laptop—a rugged, rubber-bumpered job that she supposed he'd had overseas—and he'd mentioned checking videos on wall repairs and shopping online, so she knew he wasn't phobic about it.

On the second page of her search she found three things. One was an old story that mentioned a University of Washington baseball player and was dated about the right time, nine years ago. She called it up, and seconds later Tate's image, younger but unmistakable, was in front of her in the familiar purple cap with the big *W*. The story was short—simply the highlights of a game that had occurred the night before, and mentioning that the lynchpin of a rare triple play had been second baseman Tate McLaughlin.

The second and third items were stories from two local media outlets about the same thing; local boy awarded Bronze Star and a Purple Heart. The two paragraphs about what he had done—striking out alone to take out a sniper who had already killed three Americans, saving the rest of his team and rescuing an entire large family of locals who had been taken hostage by the shooter—warmed her but didn't surprise her. Martin had told her he'd won medals, although he hadn't given the details. Too grim to dwell on, he'd said.

And now she knew the story of that scar above Tate's waist; he'd nearly died in that one.

And yet he'd gone back.

Gone back and ended up with another major scar.

She understood a little better why his girlfriend had run for cover. Because if he was hers, and he'd insisted on going back after the incident she'd just read about, she didn't know if she could handle it, either.

Teach you to be judgmental.

In the same moment the connection to her student came back she heard the buggy start up next door through her open window. She spared a brief moment to wonder where he was off to—to buy paint, perhaps?—and then closed her browser and went back to work.

"We've come up dry," Quinn said.

Tate nodded. "Not surprised." He'd expected as much. And told himself again that there was really nothing nefarious going on, even as he acknowledged that such thinking in a theater of war got people killed.

But this was home.

Before his brain could send him down memory lane, yet again, to what Lacy had said about that, he looked around. They were sitting upstairs this time, in what Hayley had called their meeting room. Cutter had once more greeted him outside, and he'd unquestioningly followed the dog upstairs. The large, open room held a couple of computers, a flat screen on the wall like the one downstairs over the fireplace and a large meeting table. But the centerpiece of the room was really the big bank of windows that looked out over the clearing behind the building, with a unobstructed view to the thick grove of big trees beyond.

"Handy doorman," he'd said, ruffling the dog's fur as they'd topped the steps.

"He makes himself useful," Quinn had said, ushering him over to the table.

Hayley spoke, snapping him back to the present. "No one had anything but good things to say about you."

"You didn't talk to everyone then," Tate said with a wry smile.

Quinn smiled back. "Guerra said you could be a pain in the ass over regs, but he'd want you with him in a fight. Carter said you beat him fair and square for that promotion, although it took him a while to admit it. And Alex Jordan said you deserved that spot on the Husky baseball team more than he ever did."

Tate blinked. They really had talked to everyone. And they'd gone way back.

"And," Quinn added, "they'd all like to hear from you, by the way."

"I— Wow."

"And if it's worth anything to you," Hayley said, her voice quiet, "Liz still feels guilty." He stiffened at that. Hayley shook her head. "Relax. She has no idea I have any connection to you."

"But—"

"Her social media profile. And we chatted briefly online. She thinks I'm in that same position, and she advised me to stick with my guy at least until he got home, because the guilt was horrible. That her ex was a really great guy, but she just hadn't been strong enough."

He sat back, a little stunned. He'd had no idea. And for a moment the memory of Lacy's shock and dismay at what Liz had done came back to him. And he wondered if knowing Liz's feelings now would soften her stance at all.

But he wondered even more at the fact that that mattered to him. It mattered to him a lot.

Uh-oh.

Cutter was suddenly beside his chair. The dog had been happily sprawled on his big, overstuffed bed under the window. Tate hadn't even heard him get up. He glanced down at the animal, who was looking up at him rather intently. As if he had sensed the sudden burst of inner alarm.

And for some reason he thought of the way Lacy had come running when she thought he might be hurt again. And he knew with a gut-deep certainty he couldn't explain that while she might let it go, might even forgive, she would never forget what Liz had done.

Neighbor, he told himself. *She's just my neighbor.*

And this was just a dog. A very clever one, true, who could sense moods as Sunny had, but not some mind-reading, thought-planting magician.

But as Cutter kept that amber-flecked gaze fastened upon him, he wondered if he was wrong on both counts.

Chapter 22

Tate was still floundering when Quinn said, in the brisk manner of a guy who knew that the person he was talking to didn't want to dwell on the subject at hand, "We checked out her husband, as well. He seems clear. Details if you want them."

Tate shook his head. The last thing he wanted was to hear about the guy Liz had married. Although the idea didn't have the sting it once had. "No, thanks. I'll take your word for it."

All of this could have been done on the phone. He studied Quinn, silently. Waiting for him to get to the real reason he was here. He didn't think his expression changed, but Quinn smiled.

"Since we came up empty," he said, "I'd like to call in someone else."

Tate drew back. He'd come here planning to tell them to stop, and now Quinn was talking about calling in more people?

"The names Accountability Counts or Sloan Burke mean anything to you?"

"Sure. Almost anybody in the service knows about her." The story of how the woman had dug and dug and faced down people in the highest halls of power to find the truth of what had happened to her late husband was legend among the ranks. "And most of them would nominate her for sainthood for what she does."

"I think Brett Dunbar would be among those," Hayley said with a laugh.

He was totally confused now. "Your detective friend?"

"And her significant other for a few months now."

He blinked. "She lives here?"

"Next town up the highway," Quinn said. "I'd like to call her in. As you can guess, she has a lot of military contacts, and many of them are different than ours. And she's a known quantity, trusted, so some people might be more willing to talk to her, given her reputation."

Tate frowned. "You really think this is connected to the Army?"

"More a case of we haven't eliminated the possibility yet," Hayley said.

Tate let out a breath. Gave a half shake of his head, more in puzzlement than negation.

"I know," Quinn said. "It's hard to think like that, that somebody you served with might be behind this. So let us do all we can to prove that false."

He couldn't have said anything better to convince him. Tate grimaced, but he said, "All right."

Almost on the words Cutter turned, ears and tail up, trotting toward the door and the stairs. As he went he let out an odd combination of yip and bark.

"That'll be Sloan," Hayley said.

Tate blinked. "What?"

Quinn laughed. "That's Brett's bark. Or it was. Now it's theirs."

Tate looked from Quinn to Hayley as Cutter headed down the stairs. An instant later he heard the sound of a car on the gravel drive outside.

"Wait. He not only has a different bark for different people, but he connects it to their...other half?"

"Yep," Hayley said cheerfully, getting up to follow the dog.

Tate knew a bit about trusting the gut and instincts of a smart dog. But this seemed in a whole different league.

He heard footsteps on the stairs and belatedly another, more important, realization hit him. He looked back at Quinn, who had just gotten to his feet.

"She was already on the way here. Am I that predictable?"

He heard a quiet laugh from the doorway. "If you'd said no, I would have quietly turned around and left."

Tate rose at the new female voice, turned.

Sloan Burke was maybe an inch taller than the woman beside her. Her hair, past her shoulders with bangs that fell over one eye, was a lighter brown, but as she stepped into the room and the sunlight from the windows hit her, he saw the same gold and red tones that made it so much more than just brown. And, like Hayley, her eyes were green, although a lighter shade.

What she didn't look like was a woman who had shaken the halls of power at the highest levels, demanding the truth about her SEAL husband's death, until they'd cringed to see her coming. And from what he'd heard, she still did, demanding the truth and, as the name of her organization stated, accountability.

He realized he was standing, in effect, at attention. He nearly saluted, and felt that if any civilian deserved it, this one did.

"Sloan Burke, Tate McLaughlin," Hayley said.

"It's an honor, Ms. Burke." And he meant it.

"The honor is mine," she said, holding his gaze. "And I thank you for your service."

"I'm sorry for your loss."

"Thank you. Jason was among the best of the best. His loss makes the world a poorer place."

Tate liked that, despite the fact that she had apparently found a new happiness with the Foxworths' friend, there was nothing but pure love, respect and sadness in her tone as she spoke of her late husband. She might have moved on, but she had not forgotten. He doubted she ever would.

He had a brief moment to realize he'd thought something similar about Lacy before they sat down at the table. Cutter settled in his bed, greeting and escort duties done for the moment. Quickly Quinn gave Sloan a summary of the events so far, and even Tate had to admit that hearing them like that again, laid out that way, had him thinking once more there was something going on. It was just too much to be coincidence.

Sloan nodded as Quinn spoke, taking an occasional note on the smartphone she'd put on the table before her.

"I'll start putting out some feelers," she said when he was done.

"I'm having trouble believing there's a connection," Tate admitted. And he still wasn't comfortable with this whole idea.

"Of course." She said it easily, as if it were obvious. "And let me assure you I'll approach this with the utmost discretion. I have enough data from Foxworth to correlate anything I might find with anyone you had contact with, without anyone knowing the inquiry is related to you."

That easily she addressed the fear he hadn't even really put into words yet. Accusing guys he had served with and trusted violated every belief he held. "Thank you," he said, meaning it sincerely.

"All right," she said, her tone businesslike now. "I've got the list of names Quinn gave me, but I'd like the name of anyone you interacted with over there or stateside. I know it's a lot of names, so we'll start by reverse pyramiding it from the ones you had the most contact with to the least. And whenever you think of a name to add, you call me," she said, handing him a card.

He looked at the business card with the saying *The first casualty of war is the truth* printed across an American flag. Beneath it was the name Accountability Counts and various forms of contact information. He wondered how her detective boyfriend felt about this organization formed out of love for her dead husband. Obviously he could handle it, which made him a stand-up guy in Tate's book.

"This could take a while," he said. "There were a lot of people. And some weren't military."

She nodded. "I want those names, too. You never know who might have heard something second- or thirdhand." She glanced at Quinn. "I know finding things that way isn't legally actionable, though."

"That's not really the goal," Quinn said. "Not to say that might not change, but right now we want to know first and foremost if Tate's in real or continuing danger, and secondly prove these incidents weren't negligence on the part of his grandfather. Right, Tate?"

He nodded, although it seemed odd to hear it discussed in such a professional manner. It made it more real somehow, as an investigation.

"All right, then," Sloan said briskly. "Since proving something isn't the goal, that gives me more leeway. And I'm not going in looking for anything specific, so hopefully any blip will register."

"Blip?" Tate asked.

"Things like a name that shows up in more than one place, gets mentioned by others. I'll start with the most recent and frequent, and work my way back and down that pyramid."

"I didn't realize what you did had become...almost like detective work," he said, beginning to see what she and this Detective Dunbar had in common.

"In a way. Finding the truth is different than finding a guilty party and proving it. Sometimes it involves simply looking for someone who knows someone who heard something, and then pulling on the right thread."

Curious, he asked, "What happens if you find something that's..." He wasn't sure how to say it, but Sloan got it.

"I have a network established now. People who believe as I do that the volunteers who protect us and their families deserve the truth."

"Sloan has built something amazing," Hayley said, pride in the woman who had clearly become a friend obvious in her voice. "Something that should have been in place all along."

Tate shifted his gaze back to the woman across the table from him. She met his gaze steadily, and he saw the strength it had taken to get her organization to where it was today.

"I didn't know him," he said quietly, "but I do know he would be incredibly proud of you."

She smiled then, and he knew those words, at least, had been right. "No more than I am of him."

He gave her every name he could think of and then she left to start her inquiries, escorted to the door primarily by a dog who seemed to exhibit the same respect they all did.

When she'd gone he looked at Quinn. "Your friend Dunbar must be quite a guy."

"He's worthy of her, if that's what you're wondering," Hayley said.

"Good."

Cutter, who had come back from seeing Sloan off, took up a position next to Hayley. Odd, Tate thought. He was nudging her hand, but looking at him. Hayley looked down at the dog, who shifted his gaze to her, then back to Tate.

"How's Lacy?" she asked. "I haven't seen her since you two came over for lemonade."

Well, that was a non sequitur, Tate thought. Or was it? Was Hayley implying something, after that talk of Sloan and their friend? Or merely asking him because as her neighbor, he'd likely seen her more recently?

"She's fine, I guess," he answered carefully. "Working, I think."

"It's wonderful, what she does. Not teaching, but leading kids to love reading."

"She's got a good mind," Quinn said, as if he were observing something obvious, like the weather. "Feel free to tell her where we're headed. She might think of something we haven't."

"I… Okay."

Hayley grinned. "We believe in all good brains on deck."

Well, Lacy certainly had that, Tate thought, suddenly feeling a little beleaguered.

"Tell her hello for us," Hayley added. "And that I'll call her later about lunch."

"Lunch?" Okay, more than beleaguered, left behind.

"We promised to get together."

"Oh."

He was back in his car and on his way to the hardware store for paint before he realized he'd somehow acquired several things on his to-do list, and most of them involved talking to Lacy Steele.

The image of Cutter nudging Hayley and then her bringing up his neighbor went through his mind.

Okay, now you really are losing it.

Still, he couldn't help feeling a bit coerced.

So you talk to her, deliver the info and then walk away. Simple.

Except nothing seemed simple where she was concerned. Not for him, anyway. He'd realized that last night, when he'd been moving through the trees in the dark, Gramps's old .45 in his belt. Because that was when he'd understood that half the reason he was still doing the so-far fruitless recons was because it would rip him apart if something happened to her because of…whatever this was.

Because of him.

And telling himself it was only that he didn't want to be responsible for an innocent bystander getting hurt, or worse, that he'd feel like this about anyone, wasn't working very well.

Chapter 23

"What do you think you would have done in his place, Mikel?"

The boy in the video window grinned. "I would jump right on that dragon's back!"

"What if the dragon didn't like that? Of all creatures, you don't want a dragon mad at you."

Mikel looked thoughtful for a moment. "I'd hafta make friends with him first, then."

"How would you do that?"

The thoughtful look again. Then a wide grin. "Hey! He likes cookies!"

Lacy grinned back at him. "Why don't you read that next chapter tonight and find out if our hero is as smart as you are."

After she'd closed out the video chat program, Lacy leaned back in her chair. She let the warm feeling of success flood through her.

"So that's how it works?"

She nearly jumped at the unexpected sound. She spun in her chair to see Tate leaning on the lower half of her back door, his elbows propped on the narrow shelf, the rest of him framed by the open upper half.

"Didn't mean to startle you. I tried to be quiet once I saw you were working."

"You certainly were," she said as she got up and walked over to the door. "I didn't hear you at all."

"Who's the kid?" he asked, nodding toward the computer.

"Mikel. He's quite fluent speaking English, but not so much reading."

"Second language?"

"Third, actually, which puts him above me. He's a smart kid." She hesitated, wondering what had stirred him out of his standard avoidance and brought him over here.

"I bought paint," he said.

She was fairly certain this wasn't it, either, but said only, "Did you? What did you settle on?"

He dug into his back pocket and brought out a strip of paint chips. One was circled. It was exactly the shade of slate blue she'd imagined. She smiled.

"I looked at some stuff online at the store. Rooms like you described, with one wall painted a darker color. I liked it, so that's what I'm going to do."

She couldn't help feeling flattered. "Well, the good thing about paint is it's fairly easy and cheap to change if you decide you hate it."

He nodded. And for a moment there was an awkward silence. He shifted on his feet. Normally she would have invited him in right away, but he had that tendency to misinterpret simple courtesy as having other intentions, which she did not. She most certainly did not.

No matter how damned sexy he was.

And there it was, what she'd been successfully denying until this moment when her guard was down, lowered by the ordinary, normal conversation. It certainly wasn't something she could deny any longer, not with him standing there framed in her doorway with his broad shoulders and tanned, strong arms crossed as he leaned at an angle that was somehow made even sexier by the way the cords of his neck stood out as he tilted his head to look at her. In that instant, she thought that she would carry this picture in her head forever.

Fine. So he's sexy. And then some. That doesn't mean you have to do anything about it. Besides, what would you do? Invite him in and jump him? Not your style, and you know it. Not to mention he's not the slightest bit interested.

She gave herself a mental shake.

"I had a meeting at Foxworth this afternoon."

She seized on the distraction. "Oh? Did they turn something up?"

"No, but some things are happening."

When he hesitated she said, "I have coffee on," leaving him to interpret that however he wanted. She assumed he had more to say or he would have left by now, but she wasn't going to prod him. She'd learned that much, at least.

"I… Sure. Thanks." He accepted the implied invitation. In fact, for an instant he almost looked eager, although she was sure she must be wrong about that.

She opened the bottom half of the door and he stepped inside. And told herself that he couldn't really, by that simple action, have sucked all the air out of the room. But when they almost brushed as he passed by her, it certainly felt that way. And when he paused for just a fraction of a second, within what seemed like an even smaller fraction of an inch of her, she wondered if somehow he'd felt it, too.

Chalking that thought up to temporary idiocy—at least she hoped it was temporary—she turned and walked into the kitchen. She got down a couple of mugs and filled them. She was trying a new brew, and so far quite liked it.

"I have a couple of flavorings if that's your preference."

"No, thanks. Strictly black."

She nodded; she'd expected that. "Outside?"

"It's nice," he said, apparently agreeing.

"Your place really is amazing," he said when they were seated in the chairs looking out over the garden. "You put in a lot of work."

"Effect and cause," she said. Then, with a smile, she added, "And a great neighbor who always let me borrow his tools."

He smiled at that. "I think he has to every one known to mankind."

"I had to be careful, though. If I wanted to borrow his shovel, he'd turn up with it and insist on digging the hole for me."

"That sounds like Gramps."

She nodded. "And most of the time I let him, if it wasn't too big a job. It made him feel good, I think."

He took a sip of the coffee, and leaned back before he spoke again. "Hayley said to tell you she'll be calling about lunch."

"Good," she said, meaning it. "I like her."

"So do I. I like them."

"Good neighbors to have," she said, "in many ways."

And that was as close as she was going to come to steering the conversation.

"They haven't found anything suspicious, so they called in reinforcements," he said after a moment.

She listened as he explained about Sloan Burke and her organization. She couldn't miss the pure respect and admiration in his tone, and felt a spark of something it took her a moment to recognize. When she realized it was a twinge of jealousy, she quashed it in a rush of self-censure and internal warning. She had no reason—or right—to feel jealous. He wasn't hers to feel jealous over. The fact that that knowledge made her feel a stab of regret was further warning. Funny how none of her self-warnings seemed to be very effective. They certainly didn't keep her from thinking of him in ways she shouldn't.

But then he told her the story behind the founding of Accountability Counts, and she found herself feeling exactly as he'd sounded.

"She sounds remarkable."

"She is. There's not a guy in uniform I know who wouldn't come running if she called. Which is what made Quinn think of calling her in. She has a ton of contacts. And people who won't talk to anyone else will talk to her."

"And he thinks what happened is connected to the Army?"

Tate shrugged, clearly still uncomfortable with the idea. "Hayley said it was more that they hadn't eliminated the possibility yet."

Lacy nodded in understanding. "It should be a lot easier to trust what they turn up when you know they haven't gone in with an agenda."

He gave a slight nod. "Exactly."

"So I assume she has the same list of names you gave them?"

"And a plan." His mouth quirked. "Something about a reverse pyramid of amount of contact and time passed."

Lacy grinned, she couldn't help it. "An organized woman."

He grinned back. It nearly took her breath away. She had to make herself focus on what else she was feeling, remorse for that stab of silly resentment. Sloan Burke had been tossed into hell and fought her way through it, and deserved every bit of his regard for her.

"Fortunate that she's here and that Quinn knew her."

He nodded. "He knew of her, but only met her through their detective friend. Hayley says they're serious."

The jab of relief she felt told her she hadn't been entirely successful in quashing that inappropriate jealousy.

Which was a yet further warning in itself.

Lacy savored the last delicious bite of her crab cake, looking across the round table at Hayley Foxworth. The day had been too nice to spend sitting inside the restaurant that overlooked the water, so they had chosen one of the outdoor tables. Besides, this allowed Cutter to be with them. He was currently plopped between their chairs, intently but politely watching the summer tourists pass by. Occasionally a child would run over to see the dog, who bore it all with calm equanimity.

"He's good with kids," Lacy said.

"Yes."

She gave her new friend another look across the table. "Planning on him having his own to play with someday?"

Hayley smiled. "Maybe. Life's pretty full right now, though."

In the nearly hour and a half since Hayley had picked her up, this was the first time they had gotten around to the current situation. Lacy counted that as a good sign for the friendship, that they hadn't had to rely only on work to keep the conversation going. She made a note of this restaurant in the neighboring town; the food had been excellent.

"I really admire what you do," she said.

"So do I," Hayley said with a wide smile. "Before I met Quinn I was kind of at loose ends. I needed some purpose, and Foxworth certainly provides that."

After lunch, as they walked through the waterfront park, Lacy remembered the story of how her new friends had met. It seemed straight out of the pages of a thriller novel, but Lacy didn't doubt a word of it. She'd met Quinn, after all.

Cutter, on a leash now in deference to the city ordinance, walked politely at her side. "He has very polished company manners," Lacy said with a smile.

"He does. He knows when the leash is on it's time either to behave or work."

"He acts very differently when he comes to visit."

Hayley smiled back at her. "You and Tate aren't company. You're friends he can relax around."

Lacy laughed, but had to admit it felt oddly flattering. Well, that or it was Hayley's linking of her and Tate. She told herself it was a natural way to refer to two people who happened to live next door to each other. And almost convinced herself.

"He's very picky. He—" Hayley cut off her own words as Cutter stopped in his tracks. She looked down at her dog, a slight frown on her face.

"Something wrong?" In the moment she spoke Lacy heard a low rumble coming from him, unlike any sound she'd heard the good-natured dog make before. "Is that a growl?" she asked quietly, glancing around for anything that might have caught the animal's attention.

"Yes." Hayley was watching intently as Cutter, head up, appeared to be sniffing the air in large, deep gulps. "And he never growls without good reason. And that's no coincidence," Hayley added as the dog moved from his usual spot at Hayley's right side to between them. As if he wanted to be close to both of them. Lacy got the strangest feeling it was a protective gesture, and her own senses kicked into high alert. Amazing how much she automatically trusted the dog's instincts.

There were lots of people around, too many to tell if he

was focused on one of them. "I don't see any other dogs around," Lacy said.

"This isn't a reaction to an animal," Hayley said.

Lacy didn't doubt her words; it was clear Hayley knew her dog well. Her friend was scanning the people in the direction the dog was facing. Cutter was practically humming, he was so tense.

"Someone you know, maybe?"

"It's not a reaction to a friend, either."

That gave rise to ideas that made Lacy uneasy.

"Do you have your phone handy?" Hayley asked.

"Sure, I—"

"Get it out and take a panning video of everything in that direction."

Even Hayley's voice had changed. The tone of it made her think of Quinn and his air of command. This wasn't her friend Hayley anymore; this was a Foxworth operative. And suddenly the crazy story she'd told about how she and Quinn had met, and what she'd done and learned since, didn't seem at all far-fetched.

Lacy grabbed her phone, activated the camera, switched it to video and started it. Trying to look like merely a tourist like the others she saw taking shots of the picturesque marina and inlet beyond, she began in the spot it seemed Cutter was staring—or rather smelling, which she guessed for a dog was more effective—and panned to each side until she'd covered about a hundred and eighty degrees.

When she'd finished, Hayley nodded. "Keep it out. Ready." Lacy nodded in turn. "All right, boy," Hayley said softly to the dog, "lead on."

Lacy half expected the dog to try to run, but he only set off purposely in the direction he'd been facing, head and ears up, nose flexing rhythmically. It was clearly the nose he was following, for he didn't look around at all.

He trusted those gazillion or so scent receptors Lacy had read about.

She just wished he could tell them what they were telling him.

"There's too many people," she muttered.

"I know. Can't tell who he's focused on. I doubt even he can see whoever it is, but his nose knows. It's definitely someone."

They went on a few more yards, then Hayley stopped.

"Something's changed... He... Lacy, grab a shot of that white car pulling out from the curb."

It only took her a split second to find it—it was her own model car, so she'd noticed it earlier—and she snapped the shot. "You think that was the person?"

"I don't know. It was just the only car leaving after he backed off."

And Lacy saw that the dog had indeed relaxed, and was back to his normal, polite, public-display self. The difference was obvious even to her.

"Wow. For an animal who can't talk, he sure does communicate."

Hayley, too, had relaxed. "That he does."

"Does he do that often?"

"When we're out casually? No. Never."

"I wonder why he reacted to some stranger like that, then?"

Lacy was merely thinking out loud, wasn't really expecting an answer, but Hayley had one.

"Maybe," she said slowly as she stroked the dog's head, "he wasn't a stranger. To Cutter."

Chapter 24

"There," Lacy said as the still photo she'd taken finished uploading.

Quinn nodded. "Now the video?"

She tapped the icon that would send it to the shared folder he had set up. That upload would take a bit longer, so Quinn opened the file to look at the single still shot. Even on the larger screen of the computer the image was sharp, but the car she'd been aiming at had been at an angle, the plate was only partially visible and the sun reflecting off the car window made it impossible to see the driver.

"Figures," Hayley muttered as she studied the picture. "Any other time of year and the sun wouldn't be a factor."

Lacy leaned in, squinting a little as she looked at the car's rear bumper. But then Cutter distracted them by suddenly getting to his feet and trotting toward the stairs.

"Must be Tate," Quinn said.

Lacy was surprised. When Hayley had called Quinn, once she'd described Cutter's actions her side of the conversation had lapsed into *yes*, *no* and *maybe*. Lacy hadn't really connected the dog's reaction to Tate and his situation. She had thought it was just… Now she wasn't sure what.

"You think this has something to do with him, with what's happening?"

"When Cutter's working, he's pretty focused," Quinn said. "And so far he's been a one-case-at-a-time kind of guy."

"Well, except for that time in the middle of a case when he paused to pull that little boy out of the water," Hayley said with a grin.

"There is that. He understands certain priorities."

Quinn's affection for the animal was clear in his voice. It warmed Lacy when she remembered Cutter had been Hayley's dog, not Quinn's, when they'd met. And then the subject of the conversation was coming back into the room, Tate beside him, scratching that spot behind his ear.

Tate didn't look surprised to see her as he greeted everyone, so she supposed Quinn had explained over the phone. But he did look a little surprised when Cutter leaned into his legs as they crossed to the table. The dog seemed to be pushing him, almost guiding him. She was smiling at this evidence of his herding heritage when she realized the dog was nudging him away from the chair next to Quinn and toward the empty chair beside her.

Again, she thought.

"That sticker on the bumper," she said, making herself go back to what she'd noticed just before Tate's arrival.

Quinn looked. Enlarged that section of the image.

"Rental," Hayley said. "Or a former rental someone bought."

"I think we'll stick with simple for now," Quinn said.

He hit a couple of keys on the laptop. The car image remained the same, but the flat screen on the wall came to life.

"We're on," Quinn said, and the red light on the small camera above the screen warned her this was now a two-way connection.

A split second later an image filled the screen, a young

man, obviously at an expansive workstation, with at least three large monitors she could see—and she suspected there were more out of camera range. He looked thin, with a wiry sort of quickness. Sandy brown hair that seemed to have a mind of its own, going every which way, topped a young face. When the image focused, he was scratching at a spot below his lower lip.

"Sticky in St. Louis here," he said.

"You shaved," Hayley said in surprise.

"Yeah, well." The scratching stopped. "Tired of it."

"Lacy, Tate, meet Tyler Hewitt, our resident tech genius," Quinn said. "Tyler, Lacy Steele and Tate McLaughlin."

"Hi," the young man said. "You're Cutter's latest, huh?"

"Tate is," Lacy corrected him.

Tyler grinned, shifted his gaze to Hayley. "They don't know yet, huh?"

"Don't even," she warned him. "Way too early."

"Yeah, yeah," he said, but he was still grinning. Obviously an inside joke, Lacy thought. "So whaddya got for me?"

Quinn answered. "Partial plate on a probable rental. Seen today. Just sent you what we have."

The young man glanced down at what had to be one of the other monitors she'd guessed at.

"Target's the person behind the reflection?"

"Yes."

"On it. Anything else?"

"Not yet. We've got a video to watch, we may be back at you then."

"Copy."

And without a farewell the screen went black. Lacy had listened to the exchange with interest. She'd known Foxworth had to be a big operation; after all, Hayley had spoken of all their offices and the headquarters in St. Louis, but still she was…not surprised but impressed by the professionalism. This wasn't just a hobby or whimsical quest to them, clearly it was a job they took seriously.

The video had finished uploading. This time Quinn hit some keys on the laptop and sent it to the big flat screen on the wall. There they watched as her video panned the arc from the marina through the waterfront park and out to the street. When it stopped, Quinn looked at Tate. He shook his head.

"I'm going to run it through again. Slower. Focus on the people, Tate. Watch for anyone who seems familiar."

Tate leaned forward, looking intently. He might not believe—or want to believe—that anything nefarious was really going on, but he was doing as Quinn had asked and giving this his full attention. She wondered if it was out of obligation, since he'd agreed to this in the first place, or if it was just respect for this man who seemed to effortlessly command it. To someone like Tate, fresh out of the service, that would mean a lot. Heck, it meant a lot to her, for that matter.

In the end, she decided it was both and made herself quit watching the man watching the video. She shifted her gaze to the screen.

"I'm sorry," Tate finally said. "Nobody rings a bell. But it's hard to tell."

Quinn nodded. "I know. In slo-mo we lose some resolution. I can have Tyler work on that. Maybe isolate some faces for enhancement. He's a wizard with facial software."

"You sure it's worth all that?" Tate asked.

"I try to keep him busy. Keeps him out of trouble."

Tate lifted a brow.

"Tyler's a reformed hacker of some notoriety," Hayley

explained. "We'd like him to stay reformed. He's essential to us."

"Does he know that?" Lacy asked.

Hayley looked at her, smiled. "We tell him regularly."

"That should help, then."

"He just needed a different path," Quinn said, as if offering that path were nothing out of the ordinary. Lacy was beginning to understand that, for Foxworth, it was not.

Quinn sent the video off with instructions. Hayley then suggested they decamp downstairs for some lunch.

"We had this nice new patio put in out back," she said, "and haven't had much chance to use it."

Hayley laid out chips and sandwich makings on the bar of the small but efficient kitchen and Quinn offered soda or iced tea. Soon they all had plates and glasses and were headed out onto the pleasant patio. Part of it was covered, either for shelter from the rain or the sun on those rare, actually hot days, but they walked out to a set of chairs around a metal-and-glass coffee table.

And once again Cutter began to herd them to where he apparently wanted them. Which was with Tate and Lacy sitting together.

"What's the deal, dog?" Tate protested.

"Once a herding dog, always a herding dog," Hayley said blithely. But Lacy couldn't help wondering if there was more to his question than puzzlement, if he simply didn't want to be forced to be close to her. It stung, and she hated that she let it bother her.

"You might as well sit," Quinn said. "He doesn't give up."

"I'm sure he's just linked us in his mind because he sort of met us together," she said. It seemed reasonable, and apparently it did to him, too, because he let it go. She sat, not sure why she'd bothered to give him that out.

They chatted about inconsequential things in the way of people brought together by something bigger but with nothing new to talk about. Lacy had just taken the last bite of her sandwich when Quinn's phone on the table chirped a very techno sort of sound. He glanced at it.

"We're up, enhanced," he said, and rose.

"Already?" she asked.

"Tyler's good and quick," Hayley said.

Moments later they were back inside, looking at the screen once more. Only this time it was isolated faces from the video, enhanced and sharpened so amazingly that Lacy said, "Wow, that's some software."

"It started out good," Quinn said, as he watched Tate inspect each face as it appeared. "Tyler made it better. A lot better."

Silence reigned for a few minutes until Tate said, "Wait. That guy looks like…somebody. Damn, I can't be sure at that angle."

Lacy looked and saw the figure of a man frozen in the act of walking past a blue building. The bookstore, she thought. He was of average height, looked a bit heavy around the middle under his loose shirt, with sandy brown hair and a stubbled jaw.

"It could be. He's in the right place," Hayley said.

"Could he have gotten to that car in the time between when I panned away from him and the car left?" Lacy asked.

Quinn called up the original and ran it in real time. Then they noticed the man by the bookstore had indeed started moving up the block, at a quicker than just strolling pace. The video ended and Quinn called up the still shot of the white rental vehicle, including the time stamp.

"Could be," he said.

"But we can't be sure," Tate said, sounding frustrated.

"No. He may not be connected at all. We have no way of knowing if it was this guy Cutter was on to. Or if that car has anything to do with him, or with Cutter's agitation."

"It's just another piece that may or may not fit this particular puzzle," Hayley said.

"This kind of work would drive me crazy," Tate said.

They went through the rest of the faces with little luck, and at last Tate got to his feet. Then he looked at her.

"Why don't you ride home with me? No point in Hayley duplicating the trip."

It only made sense, and she didn't want to impose on Hayley when this was clearly more practical. Telling herself she was being silly to feel slightly hurt that he hadn't liked Cutter herding them together, she agreed.

And besides, she didn't want to explain why she didn't want to be in a car alone with him just now.

She wasn't sure she could even explain it to herself.

Chapter 25

They were home, out of the car, and she was turning to go to her house—without a word, he noticed, just like the entire ride here—before he worked up the nerve to speak.

"I was just trying to figure out what Cutter was up to."

So he had noticed. She didn't look at him. "It's all right."

Tate let out a long breath. There was no easy way to explain this, no way that wasn't going to get him in one kind of trouble or another. But he'd been rude, he knew that, and it seemed imperative that he say something. Especially here at Gramps's house.

He took a step forward, lessening the physical distance between them, at least. He half expected her to back away, but she didn't.

"I admit, it's more than that. I'm not ready for..." He shook his head, then tried again. "Look, I'm a little gun-shy, after Liz."

"Why, Mr. McLaughlin," she said, her voice so light and airy he knew she was putting it on, but there was no amusement in her eyes, "I do believe you have misinterpreted."

"Misinterpreted?"

In a more normal voice with enough of an edge that it made him wish she'd continued in the light one, she said, "You seem to be under the impression that I am the one trying to push us together. Last I checked, it was a *dog*."

"I—"

"Did it ever occur to you that I have no more desire to be shoved on you than you have?"

You might be surprised at the desires I have. He quashed the traitorous thought. "Actually," he said, "that's always my first assumption."

She blinked. Drew back. "What?"

He shrugged.

"You always assume a woman's not interested? You're smart, great-looking and sexy as hell. And you volunteered to serve, to protect. Any woman with a brain would be interested."

He actually felt his jaw drop. He wanted to look away but couldn't, not when she was looking at him with such genuine puzzlement, after saying…that. And for a moment all he could think of was that she'd seen his scars and still said it.

"You," he said carefully, "have a brain."

"Enough of one to see that you're not interested."

He sucked in a deep breath. "Then I'm a better liar than I thought."

He hadn't meant to say that. But the words slipped out, and she was close, so close he caught that light, clean scent he had come to associate with her. It had taken him a while to realize it seemed familiar because it smelled like his grandmother's lavender plants when the spikes of purple flowers were blooming, as they would be soon.

And he was thinking of flowers when she was right here. Staring at him, as if she were trying to figure out if he'd meant it.

God help him, he had.

"Proximity," she said, sounding almost desperate.

"Maybe," he said. "I've tried to write it off as that."

She stared at him for a moment before saying, so softly it was like a feather tickling his spine, "So have I."

"Maybe," he said again, keeping his gaze locked on her eyes, those amazing blue eyes, "we should put it to a test."

He saw her swallow, and her lips parted. Too much. Just too much to resist. He leaned in. She didn't pull away. She tilted her head back in invitation.

Go on. Get it out of your system. Find out it's nothing special. Proximity, like she said.

It was his last rational thought. Because his lips touched hers, and every last bit of sanity seemed blasted out of him, along with any trace of common sense and the last hint of caution.

He'd been right about one thing. It wasn't special.

It was far, far beyond special.

His arms were around her then, pulling her closer. The feel of her against him, of her soft warmth, made him feel the need to gulp in air, but that would mean he'd have to break this kiss and no amount of air was worth it.

Instead he deepened the kiss, probing, tasting. Her mouth was yielding, soft, surely too soft to spark the fire that flared to life in him, racing along every nerve. His body responded fiercely, swiftly, and he only realized how numb he'd been now, when he was surging back to life.

She was kissing him back, and the delicate touch of her tongue on his nearly blasted him out of his boots.

He'd been wrong about another thing. Very, very wrong.

This was not going to get it out of his system.

How had he ever thought it was only proximity?

How had he ever convinced himself it was simply he'd gone too long without?

He'd better stop sanding this spot on the wall or it was going to need a whole new coat of primer. He stepped back, tried to focus on the job at hand, but his thoughts kept creeping back.

Tate's jaw clenched involuntarily. That made him aware of his mouth again, which brought back the searing memory of how hers had felt, tasted. A memory that was apparently so close to the surface it took next to nothing to bring it surging back.

She was the proverbial girl next door, for God's sake. He'd become a walking cliché.

And the look on her face, in her eyes, when at last they'd had to come up for air, that expression of stunned shock that he suspected had been mirrored on his own face, was etched permanently into his brain.

The brain that should have known better.

But what would have happened had her phone not chimed to remind her of a tutoring session? If she had not had that session scheduled, would that kiss have gone on? Would they have ended up, at some point, taking this to what suddenly seemed like an inevitable conclusion?

The thought of taking her to bed nearly put him on his knees. Until he looked around the room that not only wasn't painted yet but didn't even hold a bed. And while he would be perfectly willing—more, much more than willing—to pursue this anywhere that would work, including his makeshift bed in the workshop, she deserved better than that.

Get real. She deserves better than you, too. Why would she get involved with a guy who doesn't even have a job?

Get involved? He nearly groaned aloud at his own thoughts. Suddenly he was thinking long term? Like one kiss meant a relationship, ending in a ring, a house and kids? He'd wanted all that with Liz, or thought he had. Until she'd decided she didn't want it with him. He'd often wondered if she'd known he would be out of uniform and back home within a year if she could have waited.

That the thought didn't matter anymore was progress, right? Greg had told him it wouldn't, eventually. In the same session he'd told him not to fall for the first normal girl he was attracted to. Advice Tate was finding harder and harder to follow.

Especially when he was here in the house where he'd seen the only example of genuine, true love he'd ever had in his life. And he'd always told himself, once he'd gotten old enough to realize this was what he was seeing and how rare it was, that he would settle for nothing less. His mother had laughingly told him that likely would mean he'd die alone, and he'd barely stopped himself from telling her that would be better than what his father had.

His mother would not like Lacy. She was far too unpretentious and real for her taste. Which was what he liked about her. And while he was being honest with himself, he had to admit the fact that his mother would scorn Lacy was part of the attraction.

Well, that and the newly discovered fact that kissing her jolted him almost more than a hundred and ten volts of electricity had.

So buy a damned bed. A big one.

Or maybe a small one. So you have to stay wrapped around her. In her.

At that thought he sucked in a sharp breath. Was a little surprised he could breathe at all. And the fact that he was so revved up at just a thought was unnerving.

For a long moment he stood there, eyes closed, his body aching as images danced tauntingly through his head. Lacy, wanting as he wanted. Naked and beneath him. On top of him. He didn't care. He just…wanted. With a fierceness that went far beyond mere deprivation.

He tried to steady himself, to think logically.

Two options, he thought. Go for this, or not. Because going back to denial would assuredly not work. Not now. Trying to get her out of his system had been an abysmal failure in that respect. And cutting and running simply wasn't even on the table. Not only was it not in his nature, he wasn't about to give up this place Gramps had left him. So he was back to going for it, or not.

Of course, Lacy might have already made that decision for him. If she decided she wanted to dive back into denial—assuming she'd been there and had been jolted out of it as he had—there wasn't much he could do about it.

But how could anyone not want to explore that sweet, hot thing that had sprung to life here this afternoon?

Lacy wasn't one to indulge casually, he knew that about her, too. And he didn't want anything more than casual. Not now, not when his life was in such…chaos.

He remembered Gorilla saying, one night after they'd run afoul of fighters, that he couldn't wait to get home and be bored. Tate had laughed and agreed that boredom was underrated. Owen had scoffed at them both, saying the adrenaline rush was the only way you knew you were alive. Gorilla and Tate had merely exchanged the "new guy" glance everyone who'd been there more than a couple of months understood.

He was ready for that boredom.

What he hadn't been ready for was an explosion, nearly being electrocuted, and an interfering dog and his people.

And a woman who kept creeping into his thoughts despite his determination to keep her out.

Chapter 26

Lacy shut down her computer, her work for the day done. She'd had a full morning, as she often did on Saturday since weekends were the only time some of her students had free. With only a short break for some sleep, she had worked steadily since the session yesterday afternoon that had put an end to…whatever that was that had happened with Tate.

Just a kiss.

That was all it had been.

And if your reminder alarm hadn't gone off?

She hadn't seen Tate since that kiss. And just as well. She was tired, but used to it, since many of her international sessions happened at odd hours. Still, it wasn't the best condition in which to try to deal with…

With what? she wondered. What on earth did you call what had happened? *Just a kiss* didn't even come close. She'd never experienced anything like it. She'd always found kissing mildly pleasant, but nothing earth-shattering. For her it had always been an expression of caring, or attraction, a prelude, a step toward the deepening of a relationship. She had girlfriends who had warned her often enough that she was naive, that men tended to think of it as foreplay, aimed at getting a woman into bed.

For the first time in her life she understood how that

worked. Because despite the fact that she had never in her life gone to bed with a man she'd only known three weeks, she was now forced to contemplate the very real possibility that that was where they might have ended up if not for that alarm going off.

Talk about saved by the bell…

Problem was, she wasn't sure she felt saved. Maybe she was as naive as her friends said, but she'd never experienced anything like this. If this was what it was like for guys, no wonder they went into overdrive at a kiss.

And yet Tate had looked as stunned as she'd felt.

Her mind veered away from that image, and she determinedly busied herself around the house. Normally on a sunny, summer day like today, one of the unseasonable strings they'd had this June, she'd be happily out in the garden. But she couldn't quite bring herself to do it, and even chiding herself for letting emotions and confusion control her, she did a load of laundry that was almost too small to be considered a load, and hand washed the dishes from her hurried breakfast, squeezed in between Reykjavik and Fairbanks.

But by three, she'd run out of chores to do.

"You're hiding," she accused herself aloud.

Even as she said it she heard the now-familiar sound of paws on her deck. The Dutch door was closed—part of that hiding—but the dog didn't hesitate to scratch at it, albeit gently. A polite, soft woof followed.

It seemed too cold to ignore the dog, so she went over and opened the door. Her first warning was when he looked back over his shoulder and barked, as if he were telling a recalcitrant critter to hurry it up. She smothered a sigh when she saw Tate in the dog's wake. She wondered how the animal had managed it. Hayley had told her they had stopped trying to figure out how and just went with it. She was beginning to see the wisdom in that.

Tate stopped about a foot from the door. "Are you all right?"

"I'm fine."

"Oh. You weren't outside, like you usually are, and then he—" he gave the dog a scratch "—kept pushing me over here, so I was afraid something might have happened."

Something did. You.

She cut off her thoughts before they could veer into territory that would make her blush.

"I've been working all morning." She didn't point out that she'd told him before that Saturday mornings were busy for her.

"Oh." He looked down at Cutter. "False alarm, dog."

"Thanks for checking, though," she said, all the while marveling at the inanity of this formal conversation after that kiss.

"I didn't have much choice," he said.

Cutter, who had been standing beside Tate, moved back about a foot and sat. Then he gave a half bark, half growl that sounded so full of disgust Lacy almost laughed. As if he belatedly had realized how his words had sounded, Tate hastened to amend it.

"The dog, I mean. He wasn't taking no for an answer."

Cutter stared at him, unrelenting. As if he didn't like being used as an excuse.

"I wonder what's got him wound up?" she asked.

"I think he wants us to…get along."

Tate sounded as if he was afraid she'd find that silly, but she didn't. She shifted her gaze back to his face.

"And what do you want?"

Something changed in his face then, and she knew with certainty he was thinking about that kiss.

"You don't want to know what I want."

His voice was suddenly low, with a rough edge that sent a frisson of heat and ice down her spine in a faint echo of what she'd felt when his lips had met hers. And the sudden thought that perhaps he was just uncertain, too, that he wasn't sure what *she* wanted, hit her.

"Don't be so sure," she said, surprising herself. She saw his gaze narrow. Then he swallowed, as if getting ready to speak, but before he could Cutter let out a soft woof, as if to say, "That's better."

They both looked at the dog, who tilted his head at an angle and gave them a look of pure innocence.

"Sometimes I'd swear he plans all this," Tate muttered.

"I wouldn't argue with that," Lacy agreed.

And then the dog's head swiveled around to look over his shoulder. He leaped to his feet and turned to face the area between their houses, ears up and tail wagging. And then he took off at a run, forgoing the steps and jumping from the deck to the ground in a graceful and breath-stopping leap.

"Hayley? Or Quinn?" Tate said, his mouth quirking.

"Saturday. Both."

He looked at her then. He was smiling, and suddenly everything was all right, the ease returning between them.

"Of course," he said.

"They give me hope for the future of mankind," she said, only half joking.

"They're the best-together couple I've known since my grandparents," Tate said.

"I know how you felt about your grandparents, so I know the size of that compliment."

The smile he gave her then was even wider, and warmed her more than the sunlight that hit her as she stepped outside. The Foxworths' blue SUV was pulling into the drive, greeted ecstatically by Cutter. Hayley barely got out of the passenger side before she was enveloped in joyous tongue and tail.

"Sorry," Hayley said as they approached. "He took off in the middle of lunch like a dog with a mission."

"Don't apologize. He's welcome here," Lacy said, meaning it even though the dog seemed determined to throw her and Tate together. *Or maybe because of that*, she admitted in silent ruefulness.

"Does he ever just…play? You know, like a dog?" Tate asked.

"Sure," Quinn said as he came around the car. "And I've had the sore shoulder to prove it."

"Tennis balls?" Lacy asked. "I saw a basket of them by the back door at your place. Both of them, for that matter."

"Yep," Quinn said. He shifted his gaze to Tate. "Feel free to wear him out with one. Might do you good, too."

She remembered instantly the scar than ran up over his shoulder and the back of his neck. He never acted like it pained or even bothered him, but then she wasn't sure he would. His grandfather had been stoic about such things, ignoring them as long as he could keep moving, and she suspected Tate was the same way.

"Might," Tate agreed. "I'll pick up a couple."

"Don't bother," Hayley said dryly. "I'm sure there are at least a dozen in the car."

Lacy laughed. And her laugh deepened when Cutter, after inspecting the SUV as if to be sure nothing had changed since he'd last seen it, returned and placed himself dead center between the four of them, sat and tilted his head back far enough that he could see them all, and let his tongue loll crookedly—and obviously happily—out one side of his mouth.

"I liked it so much at your place the other day I've got

some lemonade in the fridge," Lacy said, "if you'd like to sit out on the deck for a bit."

"We actually have a reason to be here besides this scamp," Quinn said, ruffling the dog's ear.

Tate was suddenly alert. "News?"

"Not concrete. More questions, actually."

"Definitely lemonade, then," Lacy said. She headed back up to the deck—marveling as she went up the four steps at the leap the dog had taken without a second thought—with Hayley beside her. Cutter took the steps with them this time, sticking close to Hayley with obvious delight. She reached down to tickle his ear.

"Mission accomplished, eh, my fine lad?"

Hayley said it so quietly Lacy wasn't sure she was supposed to have heard. Nor was she sure what mission she was referring to. But then Hayley looked over at her, and something about the gleam in those green eyes told her. She knew perfectly well what Cutter had been up to in his visits.

"Someday, when it won't make any difference, I'll tell you about his track record," Hayley said.

Before she could explain, Tate and Quinn caught up with them. A few minutes later they all had cool, iced glasses and were seated comfortably on the deck. Except for Cutter, who trotted off to inspect the garden.

"He seems fascinated by that one spot," Lacy said with a laugh.

Hayley looked. "Let me guess…carrots?"

Lacy blinked. "Yes, why?"

"He loves them."

"Does he?" Lacy had never heard of a carrot-loving dog, but then she'd never met a dog like Cutter before. "I'll make sure I save some for him when they're ready."

"He'll be your slave," Hayley said as the dog came back and sprawled in the sun near Quinn's feet.

"I talked to Sloan this morning," Quinn said. "She came up with something I need to ask you about."

Lacy's breath caught in her throat. Quinn was focused on Tate, who just waited. When the question came, it was nothing she might have expected. But it opened up a whole new, and ugly, aspect of…everything.

"What do you know about a drug connection in your old unit?"

Chapter 27

"What?" Tate's response was instinctive, but even as he said it, a vague memory was tickling at the edge of his consciousness.

"One of Sloan's contacts heard something about an investigation. He—"

Quinn stopped when Tate held up a hand. His brow furrowed as he tried to pin down the memory, but it kept flitting away. Finally he closed his eyes, shutting out the world here to try to put himself back there. It was something he usually tried to avoid—he got enough of it in his dreams at night.

Even when he finally had the memory locked, it wasn't clear.

"I…think I remember getting asked about it. If anybody in my unit was using or even dealing. But I didn't know anything about it, so I just dismissed it."

"Do you know if they had a suspect?"

He shook his head. "It was right before I got hurt, and my memory of that time's pretty hazy."

"Who else did they talk to?"

"I don't know. And I don't have any memory at all from the morning before the explosion on." He grimaced. "I always figured I was better off that way."

Quinn nodded in understanding. "Some details are better not to have to carry around."

Tate frowned. "Do you think this is it?"

"We're not assuming anything. But it is the only thing we've come across so far that could explain all this."

"Explain it how? I didn't know anything about it when they asked, so—"

This time Quinn held up a hand. "We're just starting down this path, so I won't speculate. And we won't stop pursuing other angles."

After Hayley and Quinn left, Tate was more puzzled than ever. He turned the idea over and over in his mind, going through the members of his unit one by one, trying to hang the label of drug user or dealer on each of them. It didn't work. He couldn't believe it, just as he couldn't back then.

Or wouldn't.

"It must be awful, to wonder if someone you trusted to have your back could be behind this."

His gaze snapped around to Lacy as she spoke his very thoughts. Her voice was soft, understanding. In her face he saw a very real sadness. As if she truly did understand.

"Can't be," he said, shaking his head.

He expected her to point out the naïveté of that assumption. Instead she asked, "You really don't remember anything about that day?"

"No."

She studied him for a moment. "And you prefer it that way."

"Yes. I'm never happy when even a bit or piece comes back, so why would I want it all? I've seen the aftermath of an IED, so what I imagine is bad enough."

Her eyes closed, and he was taken aback at the genuine pain in her expression. "The things we ask of you," she whispered.

He knew she meant that in the larger sense of people in the service in general. And he couldn't doubt the depth of her emotion; Lacy Steele was many things, but phony wasn't one of them. Odd, he thought. The name he'd originally thought, and she had joked about being, an oxymoron actually suited her. She was beautiful and fine like lace, but beneath that was a core Tate suspected was steel strong.

He stood up abruptly. She rose as well, watching him.

"I've been thinking. About that…test we did."

He knew by the faint color that rose in her cheeks that she knew he was talking about that kiss.

"So have I. A lot." Her voice had taken on a husky note that felt impossibly like a touch, as if she had reached out and stroked her fingers over his skin.

"Once isn't really a fair test."

"No. It's not."

Taking that for permission, he reached up and cupped her face. She tilted her head back. She was watching him steadily, no shying away for her, not once she'd made up her mind.

That she'd made up her mind to this sent a shudder through him he had to fight to suppress.

The first kiss truly hadn't been a fair test. That had been a tentative, learning thing, and even then had nearly singed all his circuits. This one blasted them all to life in a way he'd never experienced in his life.

Her mouth was soft yet strong, tentative yet willing, and above all incredibly, impossibly sweet. Sensation exploded through him. He didn't want to just taste her, he wanted to explore, to learn, to know every intimate inch of her, and he wanted it now. It took everything he had to rein himself in.

And then she was tasting him back, probing, exploring, and his body nearly cramped with need. He pulled her hard against him and she not only didn't protest, she slipped her arms around him to add her strength to his until they were melded together from knee to head. He could feel the soft curves of her, yet at the same time sense the taut muscle beneath, and the contrasting facets of Lacy Steele once more nearly put him on his knees.

She made a tiny sound, a soft, needy moan that made him want to sweep her up and carry her off to—

Reality sliced through the haze of pleasure. Carry her off to his nonexistent bed?

Of course there was her bed, which was obviously closer, but it didn't seem quite right. It was one thing to choose—the old "Your place, or mine?"—but another when it was "It has to be yours because I don't have a bed."

With one of the greatest efforts he'd ever made, he broke the kiss.

Great time for pride to kick in. You're an idiot, McLaughlin.

But he couldn't step away, not when she was sagging against him as if her knees had weakened as much as his own had. Not when she was resting her head on his chest, and he could feel her quickened breathing, as if she, too, had forgotten about the need for air in those hot, swirling moments.

"Now that," she murmured, "was a test."

"Yeah." *Brilliant, McLaughlin.* "That's me," he muttered. "Always with the right words at the right time."

She leaned back and looked up at him. "You think I'd rather hear some smooth, practiced platitude that would tell me you do this all the time?"

Again she caught him off guard. And surprised him.

He remembered again her reaction to what Liz had

done. And despite having so misjudged the woman he'd thought he loved, he didn't doubt that he was right about this woman. She would never do that. Not that way. She would have stayed true until he got home, at least. She would never make someone she professed to care about deal with being dumped so far from home.

Of course, she would never merely profess to care; if she said it, it would be real and constant.

And the man she said it to would be a very, very lucky guy.

Something had definitely changed. Lacy wasn't sure if it was in her or in Tate, or maybe both of them. But the dynamic between them had definitely changed.

Gee, maybe it was the fact that he's kissed me twice now, and nearly accomplished what an explosion had not—burning down the neighborhood.

Even as she thought it, her fingers stole upward to touch her lips. Lips that had belatedly discovered their most powerful purpose, to send her pulse racing and heat rippling through her at the very thought of kissing him. Again. And again and again, if she had her way.

She knew he was wary. He'd meant it about being gun-shy, and she couldn't blame him after what his ex had done. But she'd lived thirty-two years without this kind of incredible feeling, and she wasn't about to turn her back on it because he wasn't ready for it. She wouldn't push, but she wasn't going to leave him alone, either.

Besides, he shouldn't be alone. For a lot of reasons. Something about the expression on his face when he was forced to contemplate the possibility that one of his former brothers in arms was trying to kill him had shifted something inside her. He needed to know he wasn't alone, she thought. Whether he liked it or not.

But he didn't seem to mind anymore. He didn't even mind when Cutter showed up and herded them together again the next day. Although when she turned away from adjusting the cage she'd placed around her newest tomato plant and saw him, Cutter not quite nipping at his heels, she couldn't stop her eyes from tearing up when she saw he was wearing Martin's old work shirt. It was a bit small on him, so it was unbuttoned over his T-shirt, but it was so preciously familiar with the various stains and the tear in one sleeve where it had caught on a nail.

He frowned the moment he got close enough to see her face.

"Lacy? What's wrong? Are you—"

"Fine. I'm fine." She waved in his direction. "It's the shirt."

He looked down at it, then back at her. "It bothers you?"

"No," she said quickly. "I think it's wonderful that you're wearing it. And so would Martin."

He plucked at one of the buttons. "It makes me feel… closer to him."

"Even better."

He changed the subject, although not so quickly she felt he was dodging away from his own grief. He gestured at Cutter. "I got the feeling I'd better do what he wanted or he was going to try to help me paint with his tail."

She laughed, bending over to scratch behind the dog's ears. "You'd look funny with a blue tail, sweetie," she crooned, planting a kiss on top of the dog's head. He gave her a string of canine kisses with quick flicks of his pink tongue. When she straightened she realized Tate was watching them intently, an odd sort of expression on his face and the slightest smile lurking at one corner of his mouth.

That mouth, she thought, and looked away before she

could betray the tiny burst of heat that threatened to blossom at the mere thought.

"Whatever you just thought, I'd like to hear it." His voice had gone a little rough, and the sound of it only intensified her reaction.

She wanted to dodge, to look away, to deny she'd thought—or felt—anything at all. But instead she found herself meeting his gaze.

"I think you already know," she said.

He stared at her for a long moment. She thought she saw him take in a deep breath before he said, his words almost rushed, "Go to dinner with me tomorrow."

She blinked. She hadn't expected that. "Is that a request or an order?"

"Whichever will get me to yes."

She didn't dare ask if that yes he was aiming for encompassed more than just dinner.

Chapter 28

It hit her as she was getting dressed that he probably felt he owed her for all the meals she'd fed him since he arrived—had it really only been three weeks ago? That idea helped her rein in emotions that threatened to gallop all over the place.

He'd told her they'd go someplace local but nice, and that he'd even put on a tie. Taking her cue from that she had gone to her closet, then selected her go-to, the proverbial little black dress. A sleeveless, scoop-neck sheath, it fit well and could be dressed up or down. She pondered for a moment, then added the delicate lace overdress with elbow-length sleeves, mainly because it was about three inches longer than the admittedly short dress. A pair of moderate heels—although with his height, she could have gotten away with the higher ones if her feet had felt up to it—finished it off. She left it at that, feeling any jewelry other than her small gold earrings would be overdoing it.

She was surprised when she heard the buggy start, and more so when she realized that he was actually driving it out of his driveway and into hers so she didn't have to walk across the grass.

"You raised him right, Martin," she whispered, glancing at the picture Tate had given her, which she had tucked into the frame of the mirror. The doorbell, that musical chime Martin had helped her install, rang and she headed for the door.

She'd been prepared for the tie. She hadn't been prepared for the way he looked in the dark blue suit coat that looked as if it had been tailored just for him. This was obviously his and made him look even fitter and more handsome.

But he was staring at her. Had she overdone it? Under?

"Wow. You look… Wow."

She could breathe again.

He gave a small shake of his head. "You make me wish I was better with compliments. A lot better."

Which was probably the best compliment he could give her. "You're just fine with them. 'Wow' will do nicely. And back at you, by the way."

He shrugged that off in a very male sort of way, but she thought she saw a trace of the same relief she'd felt. *What a strange dance we humans go through.*

She nearly teared up again when they arrived at the restaurant he'd chosen.

"This was Martin's favorite place," she said softly when he turned off the car. "We came here the last time we went out, for his birthday."

"I know. He wrote me about it."

She looked at him then, not caring if he saw the moisture welling up in her eyes.

"Would you rather not?" he asked quickly.

"No," she answered, even more quickly. "No, this is perfect. In his honor."

The slow smile and nod he gave her then warmed her in an entirely different way.

Yes, Martin. You raised him right. And nothing his idiot parents do can ever change the example you set for him.

* * *

He wanted, Tate realized with a bit of a jolt, more nights like this. A lot more. Simple nights, spent sitting across a table from this woman, who made a simple black dress look anything but simple. Who radiated class and genuineness and integrity. Just as Gramps had said.

I want you to meet her, Tate. She will remind you why you fight.

He hadn't quite understood what his grandfather had meant then, but he did now.

He'd been nervous about carrying on a couple of hours of conversation in such a setting, but it turned out to have been needless. While they started talking about what they already knew—his house, her house and landlady, then Cutter and the Foxworths—by the main course they were talking of other things, and Lacy seemed quite willing to just let it roll wherever it would.

They went from expected things like the menu and the weather predicted for the summer, which had now officially begun, to such esoteric things as sunspots and the aurora borealis, and the strikingly different art piece on the wall above their table—a piece of metal with intricate cutouts that reminded him of the lace on her dress. She loved the intricacy of it, the look of the strong metal made delicate, while he studied it trying to figure out how it had been done. Together the two approaches meshed nicely.

And it gave him another jolt that he'd never had a conversation like this with anyone other than Gramps.

The food was good, although he wasn't sure he gave it the focus it deserved. No, most of that was taken up by trying not to notice the glimpses he could get of bare skin beneath the lace. The dress was hardly provocative, just classy, but his mind went there, anyway. And then it careened off into some crazy Lacy in lace meme that was so beyond silly that he yanked his thoughts off that pathway before he mistakenly said something irretrievably stupid.

After dinner they walked along the waterfront. A sliver of moon was visible, even though sunset was still an hour away this time of year. Even as he thought it Lacy said, "I love this time of year, when I can read outside after nine o'clock without turning on a light."

"Have you always loved reading?"

"Always," she said. "It's let me live a thousand different lives."

"I used to read thrillers, but I kind of lost my taste for them while I was deployed."

"I can imagine. Must have seemed either too real, or too unreal."

"Exactly."

"If you're ready to try something else, maybe you need a good speculative fiction or historical saga, or a whopping big fantasy."

"Give me a list?"

She smiled. It was a great smile. "Happy to. You'd have to fill out my questionnaire, though."

"Okay." He found he was curious to see what she asked her prospective students. Obviously it worked, from what he'd overheard during at least one session.

An image popped into his head, of doing just what she'd said, sitting outside reading, sharing a quiet summer evening. He liked the feeling that just imagining it gave him. And as they walked and passed people who nodded and smiled, he found himself relaxing more and more, as if only now he was allowing himself to believe he was really home.

They passed a group of three guys carrying fishing gear. Tate saw them freeze as Lacy approached, saw their expressions change as their eyes flicked over her in that dress. *Don't even think it*, he silently ordered them. Three sets of eyes shifted to him, assessingly. And finally they arrived at the nod of greeting and kept going.

Good call.

Lacy hadn't seemed to notice. And he'd surprised himself with the sudden rush of possessiveness he'd felt. He supposed it was only to be expected. It had been a long time since he'd been regularly in the company of such an attractive woman. She wasn't flashy, like Cav's parade of willing females, and was far from plain like Gorilla's, who always said he preferred the shy, ordinary ones because they didn't cheat.

No, Lacy was her own kind. Maybe one of a kind.

Maybe that was why she scared him. So much that he'd pushed her away when what he'd really wanted was to pull her closer. Much closer.

On the way home it occurred to him that they hadn't talked at all about the one thing hovering, the thing he'd tried to put out of his mind, the thing he didn't even want to admit was a possibility, that someone was trying to kill him. It had been two weeks since anything had happened, and he very much wanted to believe it had been a run of inexplicable bad luck. A final kick from the universe, as it were, before he got on with the rest of his life.

But the possibility that the collateral damage every soldier dreaded in this case could be Lacy hovered like a black cloud of smoke. And so he kept going with his regular patrols through the thick trees, the old but scrupulously maintained Colt at hand. Gramps would understand. He'd be doing the same thing in his place.

For the first time in a very long time, Tate allowed himself to actually think about the rest of his life, about a future, to look beyond just getting through whatever came next. And he knew that the woman beside him had given him that, with her quiet presence, her support and even her anger on his behalf.

Not to mention what else she'd given him, he thought as he walked her to her door. Something he wanted more of. A lot more.

Just like, in this moment, he wanted to kiss her more than he wanted to keep breathing. He just had to taste her again and prove to himself she was really as sweet, as essential as he remembered.

And then he was doing it and finding he'd been wrong. She was much, much sweeter. She sent heat blasting through him until he was surprised he was still standing. And when she sagged against him as if she were feeling the same sudden weakness in her knees, he felt almost dizzy with it.

He'd forgotten to breathe again. But the moment he gulped in air her hands slid down his back, and that sucked the air right back out of him again. He couldn't stop himself from imagining her doing that over his bare skin. Even the thought of his scars couldn't derail the sensations that were building in him, because he knew with a bone-deep certainty they didn't matter to her.

In the moment he thought it, her fingers came to rest over the ridge of the scar above his waist. She held her hand there, not caressing, not rubbing, just…resting there, somehow warming that once-wounded flesh with the contact.

And then her tongue brushed over his and he let out a low groan at the need that made his entire body clench. He couldn't stop himself from sliding his hands down to her waist and pressing her against him. It only made things worse as his erection grew, straining toward the soft heat of her.

He knew he was fast approaching the point of no return. In the next minute, stopping would damn near kill him. And while Lacy had entered this kiss and his embrace wholeheartedly, he didn't know if she was ready for what he wanted next. Which was to get them both inside, naked, and to drive her as crazy as she was driving him. And he wanted it all now, in the next ten seconds.

"Lacy?"

It was all he said, all he could manage, but he sensed she knew what he was asking.

"I...I don't..."

She stopped, and her hands moved to lie palms down on his chest. She didn't push him away, but he read the signal. He released her and took a step back, sucking in a huge breath to try to steady himself.

It didn't work.

"I'm sorry," she began.

"Forget it."

His voice was harsh, rough, but he couldn't help it. Just as he couldn't help damning that idiot for going back to his ex when he could have had Lacy, and burning her so badly in the process. That gave her the right to caution, didn't it? But somehow that wasn't going to make the long night ahead any easier. He was almost glad when his cell phone rang.

"Too late?" a male voice asked.

"Quinn. No. I'm still up." *In more ways than one.*

"Good. Need to ask you something."

"You guys work long hours."

"Ty does his best work after midnight. And he came across something."

Tate went still, wondering what had been worth relaying at this hour.

"Tell me more about Eric Caveletti," Quinn said.

"Cav? I told you, he was my best friend over there.

We met up on the way to basic, so we kind of stuck together. He—"

Tate stopped suddenly. He supposed the haze kissing Lacy had put him in had slowed his thinking.

"Wait," he said sharply, "you're not thinking he had something to do with this?"

"You said he got sent back when you did?"

"Yes. He was hurt, too, same IED."

"But not hurt as bad as you were."

"He got out of the hospital a lot sooner, yeah. But I talked to him right after I got out. He was glad I was going to be okay."

It couldn't be, Tate thought, remembering that call. Cav had been genuinely happy he was on the mend, he was sure of it.

"Did you know why he joined up in the first place?" Quinn asked.

Tate frowned. "He only said it was the lesser of two evils."

"The other evil was going to jail. For possession with intent to sell."

Tate felt like he'd been double tapped, head and gut. "Drugs."

"Yes. Hard stuff."

What do you know about a drug connection in your old unit?

Cav?

No.

Please, no.

Lacy came back to him then. She put her arm around him and he leaned into her warmth because he didn't seem to have the strength to do anything else. Silently, no questions asked, she led him inside.

Chapter 29

"I don't believe it."

"Just because he got in trouble once doesn't mean he was the connection," Lacy said. "And even if he was, that doesn't mean he's behind this. Even Quinn said that."

Tate lifted his gaze to look at her. They were sitting in her living room, she suspected only because he'd been too stunned to resist after Quinn's phone call. He'd taken the glass of wine she'd offered—the last thing he needed on top of this was a caffeine hit—although he hadn't had more than a sip.

"You don't even know him, and you're defending him?"

"I'm just emphasizing facts versus possibilities," she said. "And he's your friend. Nobody wants to believe bad things of a friend."

"According to Tyler's search it wasn't just once. The dealing was just the final straw." He ran a hand through his hair.

"Always drugs?"

He nodded. "Why?"

"At least he wasn't out robbing convenience stores to support it."

His mouth quirked. "Well, now there's a bright side."

He said it so dryly she couldn't help but smile. "Sometimes," she said, "'It could be worse' is the only thing that helps you cope."

"And what taught you that lesson?"

"The accident that killed my father but that my mother survived."

He blinked. "God. I'm sorry." He looked very sheepish. "I know you never mentioned him, but I never asked. It's been all me."

"You," she said, "are the one with the overflowing plate right now. And the accident happened ten years ago."

"Still," he said. And she couldn't help but like that it bothered him. She studied him for a moment.

"I would guess part of the reason is that you don't like discussing your own parents, so you shy away from talking about other people's."

He grimaced. "That obvious, am I?"

She gave him the barest of grins. "Or they're that bad."

He let out a chuckle that, at that moment, was worth more than the biggest belly laugh. "Selection B," he said.

"I'm sorry. My mom and I have our moments, but I wouldn't trade her for anything."

"I really am sorry about your father. I know how much losing Gramps hurts, and he had a good, long run."

"He did, didn't he?" she said with a wide smile. "A good life, well lived."

"And we're back to me again."

But you're not fixated on your friend anymore.

"Tell me about your dad."

"It was a drunk driver. They were out for their twenty-fifth anniversary."

She saw him wince, but he said, "I didn't mean that. I meant him. Who he was."

That pleased her. "He was a quiet, soft-spoken but rock-solid man. He loved cars and fishing and baseball and

Mom and me." Her mouth tightened slightly as the words brought back how much she missed him. "In many ways, your grandfather reminded me of him. And that's the highest compliment I could give."

He held her gaze then. And after a silent moment he said, his throat obviously tight, "Thank you again for being there for him. Especially at the end."

"It was my honor," she said, meaning it and letting it show.

He reached out and brushed the backs of his fingers over her cheek. Then he turned his hand and cupped her face. She lifted a hand and put it over his, savoring the warmth they created together.

And that simply, she knew.

"Tate?"

"Mmm."

"That other yes you wanted? I think you've gotten there."

He went very still. He stared at her, hazel eyes locked on blue. She saw him swallow before he said, his voice rough, "You sure?"

"More than I've ever been. And for all the right reasons," she added, mindful of what he'd been afraid of before.

She wasn't sure what she had expected him to do, but it wasn't what he did. He twisted his hand around to clasp hers, turn it, and then he leaned in to press his lips to her palm. It was a simple, beautiful thing, an oddly gallant gesture, and it reinforced her certainty.

She leaned in herself, pressed her lips to his cheek, all she could reach. Even that innocent touch sent a new wave of sensation through her. But it was nothing compared to what swept over her when he grabbed her, pulled her close and his mouth came down on hers.

It was hot, fierce and nearly instantaneous. No slow,

lingering build here. But then this had been growing from that first night. Or perhaps even longer, when Martin had shared proud, loving stories of his heroic grandson.

Her heart was pounding in her chest until she could feel every beat, sense every pulse of her blood racing through her body. Nothing else mattered but the feel of his mouth, the taste of him, the heat of him.

He buried his fingers in her hair, pulling her even closer. She felt the sweep of his tongue as he tasted her in turn, and it was the most arousing thing she'd ever felt. And she realized with a little shock that she was feeling more now, with just a kiss, than she had ever felt with anyone.

His hands slipped down to her waist, but he never broke the kiss. Instead he deepened it, probing, lingering, as if she were the most wondrous thing he'd ever tasted. As he was to her.

Belatedly she realized they were standing, and she had no idea how or when. She only knew that the feel of his long, strong body against hers was fuel to the escalating fire.

She was nearly dizzy when he finally broke the kiss, as if she had truly forgotten how to breathe. She wasn't even sure what she was doing; knew only that she wanted more, wanted it all. She tugged his shirt free of his jeans, needing to touch skin, not fabric. When his hand slid up to cup her breast, she nearly cried out at the feel of the simple caress. His thumb slid over her nipple and she did cry out as the sensation shook her to the core. He did it again, and her back bent as her body arched toward him, pressing soft, curved flesh against his fingers.

She heard him swear, low and heartfelt.

He moved, pulled something out of his back pocket. Wallet, she realized. And then out of it a small foil packet.

"Parting gift from my physical therapist," he said when

she looked. "Unless you've changed your mind," he said, his voice soft. Honorable, she thought hazily. She would have expected no less.

"Way past that," she whispered. And this time she began the kiss, unable to resist the lure of that mouth, so close, so tempting. She didn't know if she was dizzy from the kiss or from forgetting to breathe when he finally pulled his mouth away.

"About that bed," he muttered.

"Due south," she whispered.

And then he moved, quickly, and they were a full step toward the hallway before he swept her up in his arms. He was carrying her, as if she weighed no more than a child. She thought of his wounds, and the grit and determination it must have taken to go through that and still be this strong.

He put her gently down on her bed—she spared a split second to be glad she'd tidied up this morning—and knelt beside her. For a moment he just looked down at her. And then, jaw oddly set, he pulled off his shirt. She didn't understand at first why he just stood there, why he wasn't down here with her. For that matter, she didn't understand why they weren't both naked by now and easing this ferocious need.

A possibility struck her. She sat up. Leaned over to him and pressed her lips against the gnarled end of the scar that wrapped around his waist. At the same time she slid one hand up his back, finding the other scar, the newer one, gently tracing its path up to his neck. His head fell back, and she heard a long breath escape him. Looking up at him, at the contours of muscle and sinew and the cords of his neck, she thought she'd never seen anything so beautiful.

"These make me think of your strength and your courage," she whispered. "To me they don't make you less, Tate. They make you more."

He came down to her in a rush then, and she knew she'd somehow found the right words. With fierce urgency they tugged at each other's clothes. When she was free of them his hands, his mouth, seemed to be everywhere, and sensation rippled out from every place he touched. She clutched at him blindly, stroking, hungrily planting kisses wherever she could reach. She wanted everything, all at once, and in the instant she thought it he muttered, "We'd better slow down, I'm—"

"Next time," she said, cutting him off as she slipped her hands down his body and curled her fingers around rigid flesh that told her he was more than ready. He made a harsh, guttural sound as she stroked him. And then he moved, parting her, probing. She guided him, felt the first touch, and her body nearly cramped with need. And then the delicious invasion, slick and yet with a perfect tug of friction, began to fill that place she hadn't realized had been so empty. She thought she couldn't possibly, but he was there, stretching her to an exquisite fullness that made her feel she was whole at last.

He whispered her name over and over, hot and breathless beside her ear as he began to move, stroking her from within, her own body's response surprising her yet again with its ferocity. The rightness of it blasted through her. But then his hand crept between them, his fingers reaching that place where they were joined, and he began a small, circular caress that made every muscle tighten as she arched toward him. She could no longer think, could barely breathe.

She had just enough breath to gasp out his name as her body clenched then exploded in a riot of sensation that left no part of her unshaken. She felt his hands slip under her shoulders and curl back to brace her, felt him drive hard and deep one last time and then felt the pulse of him inside her. He nearly shouted her name in a deep, wrenching tone that made her tighten around him once more.

And when he collapsed atop her, his breath coming in harsh pants, when she heard a simple oath muttered in a tone of complete wonder, she felt moisture well up in her eyes at the sheer beauty of what they'd found.

Chapter 30

"Have you noticed," Tate said as he stretched lazily, "Cutter hasn't been around as often lately?"

Lacy snuggled up against him. In the last three days they'd spent much of their time here in her bed. They'd explored each other and the heat they kindled together, sometimes a low, warmth-giving glow, more often a blaze that turned into an inferno. He smiled inwardly at himself, usually the most prosaic of men, thinking in metaphors.

And smiled more at the most amazing thing—well, after the incredible sex—that they'd spent so much time talking in between. It hadn't been a strain at all. It had just flowed, often in strange, funny or even philosophical directions. It was unlike anything he'd ever done with a woman before, and time passed so quickly it startled him when he noticed the clock when he'd headed home for a brief interval during one of her tutoring sessions.

Of course, the first twenty-four hours he'd never set foot in his own place, which made him think of the shower they'd taken together. He'd never quite realized how erotic the feel of wet skin was, or how sweet the taste of water as he licked it off her or watched it as it streamed over her breasts and parted around nipples taut and aroused from his mouth.

And there he was, ready all over again just from thinking about it. It was a while before they got back to his question.

"I noticed," she said when he repeated it. She sounded deliciously satisfied and looked it, as well. That made him wonder what the hell had taken him so long. She made him feel… He couldn't even list all the ways she made him feel. "Judging from what Hayley said, he probably thinks his main job here is done."

Since there had been no developments in the case, if you could even call it that, he wasn't sure what she meant. "You mean he thinks it's over?"

"Hayley says he's an inveterate matchmaker."

Tate blinked. "What?"

"His pushing us together all the time was intentional."

"You're saying that dog wanted…this?"

"Quinn says it's a side effect of the cases they work. Hayley thinks deep down it might be Cutter's main reason for finding the cases he does." She looked up at him with a smile. "And by the way, she knew the minute she saw me at the market yesterday. Before you even appeared out of the cookie and cracker section."

They'd had to make a food run because her cupboards were getting bare. "Hey, we've been burning up a lot of energy."

"Indeed we have. But I'm still sorry we had to get out of bed to do that," she said, stretching in turn. He loved when she did that, loved just watching the way her luscious body moved.

He grinned at her. "It's nice to be *in* a bed."

"Well, if that's all you wanted," she said, in clearly mock outrage.

He liked that she felt sure enough now to tease him. Liked that she liked to tease him. Liz had wanted high drama and perfection. Lacy could laugh at the beginning awkwardness as they found their way.

"All I want," he said, utterly serious now, "is you. I don't care where."

"I can live with that," she said.

"Although I probably really should get a bed for that room."

"Yes."

His earlier thought came back to him, and he lifted a brow at her. "Want to help me pick one out?"

She drew back slightly. "You want me to furniture shop with you?"

"Well, you do have a vested interest. In the bed, I mean." *Damn, that sounded bad*, he thought. "I just meant—"

"I do have a serious interest in you getting a bed," she agreed easily. "I'd say that's fair."

God, she made this so easy, he thought. And less than an hour later they were on their way to bed shopping, in the buggy, although he wasn't sure if a bed would fit in it if he bought one that he could actually cart home. Because he wanted a big bed. After all, they had proven they could and would utilize every bit of it.

Once last night he'd awakened sideways, but with Lacy still tucked tight against him. It felt so good he'd just stayed there, savoring the warmth of her, the feel of her, until she'd awakened on her own and turned to him with a sleepy sweetness. He ached for her inside as much as he ached for her outside.

"You've got a lot of decisions to make," she said as they pulled out of the driveway.

He shot her a glance, startled.

"You'll need a mattress, too, obviously, and bedding."

"Oh." That kind of decision. He'd thought she meant... His own thought broke off as decisions about them didn't scare him as much as they once had. Because he wanted this to go on, and on.

"Sheets and blankets are easy enough," she continued, "but you'll have to really like the top layer, since it will be visible. Should probably pick it first, and then the sheets can go with it. Unless you're a traditionalist and want to just go for white."

"Easier" was all he could manage. This was deep water for him. His brain hadn't gone any further than picturing a king-size bed, maybe with big, square posts at the corners.

"You could always start with a set of white, then get another set in a color once you've settled on a comforter or whatever." She was looking at him, he could feel it. "And as a practical matter, life's easier if you don't have to wash them and put them right back on every time."

"Sure."

"So let's see, we can hit two or three furniture stores, more if you don't find something you like." He pulled to a halt at a stop sign but didn't look at her as she rattled on. "Then a mattress store. There's only one of those locally, so that's easy. Then a bed and bath place or two. Or three, depending on how far you want to go."

In the moment he saw his hands had tightened around the steering wheel, Lacy burst out laughing. His head snapped around and he stared at her.

"Take a breath, ye of the one-word answers. I'm just ribbing you."

He blinked. "What?"

"You hadn't thought a step beyond a bed frame, had you?"

She nailed it so accurately he couldn't do anything but smile ruefully. "No."

"Well, unless you want to sleep—or do other things—on slats, you'd better think about it."

He liked the "do other things" part. But if he thought about that now, the temptation to turn around and go back, to explore those things some more, would be too much. And then a car pulled up behind them and he had to turn his attention back to driving.

"Do we really have to go to all those places?" he asked. It sound perilously close to a whine even to him, but the prospect seemed daunting. "I'm more of a one stop kind of guy."

"I'm getting that," she said. "I'll bet you can stick to a shopping list, too."

His brow furrowed. "Well, yeah. Why else make one?"

"So you don't forget anything. Not as a limitation."

He gave her a wry glance. "Is this one of those male-female things that are never going to meet?"

She laughed again. "Maybe so. But how boring would it be if there was never anything to figure out?"

He found himself grinning at her. There was no doubt that he'd laughed more in the last three days than he had in… He couldn't remember the last time. And it had nothing to do with that knock on the head. On the heels of that realization came another—he hadn't had a headache, either.

Stress is a trigger…

The doctors had repeated that, but he hadn't quite believed it. They told him that was typical, to resist the idea that you were stressed by anything, but he'd better admit to it and deal with it if he wanted the headaches to stop eventually.

He thought he'd found a pretty damned good way to deal with it.

"I have an idea," she said.

Oh, so do I. He bit back the words. "What?"

"If you don't mind going farther, you might be able to find everything in one place."

"If it will save a half a dozen stops, I'm all for it."

"It's on the other side," she said. "So we're talking commuter hour ferry."

"I'll deal." They were pulling up to one of the two stoplights in town, the one where they had to decide which way to go. "Do you have the time?"

"I'm clear until four."

"If we're not done by then, I'll be slitting my throat," he said dryly. And made the turn toward the ferry.

The ferry holding lanes were already nearly full; it was, as she'd said, a morning commute. There was a blast of horns, unusual in this land of polite drivers, as a car cut into the line a couple of vehicles behind them. They made it onto the boat by about a dozen cars, at the tail end of the outside lane on the starboard side. The vessel was packed with walk-on passengers, as well, and since it was a clear, summer day already, the upper outside decks were crowded as Northwesterners savored the sunshine. After grabbing a cup of coffee from the busy vending area inside, they found a spot at the rail to watch their wooded home county grow smaller behind them and the city side get nearer.

"I swear, you can feel the city tension start halfway across," Lacy said.

He looked down at her, reached out to tug a lock of hair, blown by the wind of their passage, out of her face. Remembered twining those silken strands through his fingers as he drove deep into her body, and the sound of her gasp of pleasure as he did. And that quickly he was at a boil again. He tamped it down with a promise that he would hear her cry out his name like that again soon. He wanted to kiss her, but wasn't sure how she'd take it, here amidst a couple of hundred or so people milling about. So he spoke instead.

"Flip side is that you can feel it fade away halfway across on the way back."

She smiled at him. That smile that had changed his mood, his outlook...his life.

Someone in the crowd brushed against his back, and he took a step to get out of the way. Since it brought him even closer to Lacy, he didn't mind. But then he sensed the person bending over, and thought maybe they were ill. It was hard to get seasick on the broad, steady ferries, but—

He felt another bump from behind them.

Lacy screamed as she went over the rail toward the dark, deep water of the sound.

Chapter 31

Tate yelled her name. Grabbed at her. Caught one arm. She was scrabbling, trying for anything to cling to. It made it harder to hold on to her. Her sleeve slipped. He grabbed with his other hand and caught her bare wrist. Her legs windmilling desperately over the drop, she looked up at him. He could see the fear in her eyes. It stabbed at him like the blade of a combat knife.

She dangled over the water of Puget Sound, over nine hundred feet deep here and less than sixty degrees, even in summer. He was within a whisker of going over himself. His brain slammed into high gear, assessing, quantifying possibilities. There was really only one decision to make. This was Lacy.

"Hold still," he yelled over the chaotic noise of the wind and people still crying out in shock. "Quit struggling. Give me three seconds."

He saw her doubt.

"Trust me." And because he couldn't bear that fear, that doubt, he winked at her. *Easy peasy, girl.*

That quickly her expression changed. Became calm. She quit moving and trusted him.

As he went over the rail, he knew he would never, ever forget that look. He got a toe on the deck through the tiny gap at the bottom of the safety screen. It was dicey, hanging on to her with one hand while he kept his own grip on the railing with the other. He felt the damaged muscles of his back announcing their presence. He ignored them. There were onlookers there now, calling out, but he ignored them. He'd asked Lacy to trust him and she had. He wasn't about to betray that trust.

He bent himself double, toward her. Pulled her up. The muscles of his right arm strained, bulged. Lifted her. Slowly.

"Around my neck," he called to her. "As soon as you can reach. Climb me if you have to."

She saw the intent instantly and grabbed at his arm with her free hand. She had some arm strength of her own, from all the shoveling and moving bags of soil. She gained a little. A little more. He saw her reach for his leg. She could have done it, but she changed her mind. He was glad because he was barely able to keep his foot in that spot on the tiny lip, and the people clustered along the rail weren't helping, even though some seemed to be trying to.

"Waistband," he called to her. She tried, but couldn't quite reach.

He gave it everything he had. Got her another inch closer. Felt her fingers at his hip, felt the tug on the other side as the denim dug in. Felt the slightest easing of the weight in his right arm.

It was just enough. He flexed his arm, lifting. And then she was there, an arm around his neck. The load eased. He lifted the arm he held to his neck.

"Grab your other wrist and hang on. We're almost there."

He couldn't even think of the amount of nerve it took for her to let him release her arm, but she did it. She locked her arms around his neck, clinging to his back.

The onlookers were clustered along the rail now. In the

moment when he heard the shouts of two ferry workers trying to shoulder their way through to get to them, one of the well-meaning passengers hit his foot with their own. Knocked it off the deck.

Both he and Lacy dropped. He barely managed to keep his grip on the upper rail. His left hand protested fiercely. The jolt of their combined weight made his shoulder and back scream, as if the scar was burning.

Do not *give out on me now, you son of a bitch.*

"Hang on, Lace. We're good."

"I know."

Her voice was so calm, so confident, it seemed to flood into him through her. He swung slightly sideways, then back. Her weight changed the dynamic, and it took him two tries to get the extra two inches he needed to get his other hand on the rail.

And then he had it, and he knew they were all right. As long as no one else tried to help and knocked his hands loose.

Slowly he pulled up. Spared a split second to thank his physical therapist—and his drill instructor, for that matter—for all those pull-ups under a full pack. And thanked them again as his strength held out.

He felt the instant when Lacy was able to get a foot on that lip of the deck under the screen.

"Going right," she said to him, somehow realizing despite it all that an unannounced sudden shift could cause a problem. The weight lessened. The screaming in his back eased. And then two ferry crew members were grabbing, tugging, pulling them over the bright green railing.

They were back on the deck. Lacy sagged against him, and he could feel her trembling. He held her, his own arms a bit unsteady. If he'd stopped to think about deadlifting over a hundred pounds with one arm…but he hadn't stopped to think.

Trust me.

We're good.

I know.

He thought it would take him the rest of his life to truly grasp the size of that gift.

He talked to her, soothing words he wasn't sure made any sense, but the horror began to fade. She clung to him, her arms around him, as if she wanted to keep him that close forever. Just the thought sent his heart racing all over again.

He answered questions from a uniformed crew member, guessing he probably had to file some kind of report. But through it all he was hyperaware of Lacy's head resting on his chest, savoring the way she hung on to him still. It was the only thing that kept the awful image of her plummeting toward the water at bay.

But something an excited, young, male voice was saying snapped him to full attention.

"—crazy, man. That guy just crashed right into you. You wanna sue him? I got the whole thing on video, man."

Tate went still. "You did?"

"Yeah! I was shooting the seagulls flying alongside when she went over."

The kid held out his phone for Tate to see. He had to shade it with a hand to see it in the bright sunlight. Lacy didn't look; he guessed the last thing she wanted to see right now—or ever—was a replay of those horrific moments.

"Can you send me this?" he asked the kid.

"Sure."

They had to wait until they were closer to the terminal, for a stronger signal, but once there the transfer took only moments. Tate thanked the boy, then turned to the ferry crew member who had come up to them.

"That was a hell of a thing you did," the man said.

He looked at Lacy. "No. Her trusting me enough to let go, that was a hell of a thing."

She met his gaze. Managed a smile in return. "I do trust you."

Something in her voice told him there was more than one layer in those words. And then he nearly laughed at his own thought.

This is Lacy. Of course there is.

He once more thanked the other passengers who had helped, then guided her toward the inside stairway to head back to the outer car deck.

"Good thing we're last in line," he said as they got to the buggy. Other drivers were already getting into their vehicles as the boat docked.

"Why?" she asked, although she got in without demanding her answer first.

"Easier to get the car turned around." He slid into the driver's seat and looked at her. "Because we're going back."

"We are?"

"Yes."

He pulled the door shut and then called up a contact on his phone. She didn't ask, simply waited, and Tate guessed she was glad she was finally sitting down. Perhaps she was realizing how shaky she was. An adrenaline crash was like that. He was experiencing a bit of it himself.

"Quinn? Tate. Something I'd like you to see."

"At the office."

"On the way."

And that quickly it was done. No questions asked. He liked that.

He spoke little on the way back, or once they were back

on the road. But he reached out and took her hand, held it, and that was enough. He needed that contact, the feel of her, alive and well.

When they arrived at the Foxworth building, tucked away in the trees, she saw Cutter bound out in his usual manner to greet them. But the dog skidded to a halt several feet away. His head came up, his tail went straight out, the friendly manner vanishing. He went straight to Lacy and looked her up and down, then walked behind Tate and did the same. She had no idea what the dog was sensing, but clearly he knew that something had happened.

Cutter gave Tate another sniff, as if he weren't sure, but then he walked around and gave Lacy a comforting nudge, leaning into her in that way he had.

"Aren't you the cleverest boy," she crooned, bending to plant a kiss atop his head. When she straightened she saw Tate watching her. She read concern lingering in his gaze, and added, "I'm fine. A little drained, but fine. I'm more worried about you."

"I'm fine."

"Your back? Shoulder?"

Another time, someone else, he might have bristled at the implication he might be in less than optimal condition. But what he saw in her face made that impossible.

"Not happy, but fine."

"Maybe I can work on that for you later."

Every ache in his body seemed to suddenly coalesce in one low, deep spot at the thought of her working on him in any and every way.

"I'll hold you to that," he muttered as they followed Cutter.

When they got inside both Hayley and Quinn were there. Tate didn't explain, as she'd expected. Instead he handed over his phone to Quinn, with the video loaded, and asked him just to watch it. Lacy watched as he did, his expression intent, focused. Much as Tate often looked when he was concentrating on something. And she couldn't explain why it appealed to her so much, that ability to isolate against anything but the problem at hand. Except that it seemed to her that was how those problems got solved.

The video ended. Quinn's head came up. He looked at Tate, who met his gaze steadily. But neither man spoke. Which was carrying the strong, silent bit just a little too far, Lacy thought.

Then Quinn said, "Let me send this to our system. I want to watch it again on a bigger screen."

Tate nodded. And a few minutes later the flat screen on the wall came to life. Lacy wasn't sure she wanted to watch this again, and doubted her ability to do so without screaming just as she had then. *Only till it happens*, she told herself, then she'd look away.

The wind of the ferry's passage permeated the video, along with the occasional sound of someone speaking loudly enough to be heard over it. The gulls that the kid had mentioned, three of them, were there, seeming to be pulled along effortlessly by the boat itself.

The scene shifted slightly. The boy had apparently moved so that he could include a pretty girl with long, blond hair in his shot. She nearly smiled at that. But then she saw that they—she and Tate—were clearly visible on the other side of the girl. In the moment she realized that, she realized something else. She had been also watching the gulls sail beside them.

But Tate had been watching her.

It was the briefest of moments, but in those seconds it seemed all his guards were down. She saw doubt there in his expression, but also an awed touch of wonder. As if he were afraid to believe it—they?—were real. She saw his hand come up, toward her. He'd been going to touch her, she realized, and—

A man in a heavy jacket careened into the frame, and right into Tate's back. He made a jerky downward movement as if trying to regain his balance by touching the deck. In that moment she saw he had a scarf pulled up over his lower face and a knit cap pulled so low that all that was visible were his nose and eyes. He was dressed as if it were winter, not a bright, sunny summer day.

It happened so fast she didn't have the chance to look away as she'd planned. She saw herself go over the rail. Heard her own scream. She smothered a cry of protest as she jerked her head to the side, not wanting to see any more. The others continued to watch, but Tate again reached out and took her hand. She curled her fingers around his, trying not to think about how close she had come to disappearing in those cold waters.

"You are in pretty damned good shape for a guy who just came out of four months in a hospital and rehab," Quinn said with a grin at him.

Tate grinned back. "My physical therapist used to be a drill sergeant."

Lacy could breathe again. And her smile at the exchange wasn't just at how much Tate had opened up, but also at the very private thoughts of just what kind of shape Tate McLaughlin was in, in more ways than one.

Quinn ran the video back to just before the man who had nearly knocked her into Puget Sound entered the frame. This time he played it in slow motion.

And Lacy saw what she'd missed before.

A gasp escaped her. Quinn froze the image at the point where it happened.

Realizations tumbled through her mind, that the man

hadn't been an out-of-towner from a warmer clime bundled up against a Northwesterner's idea of balmy; he'd been hiding his face. And he hadn't merely stumbled, nor had he just been trying to regain his balance when he'd bent down.

She sat staring at the unmistakable image of the man's arm purposefully sweeping at their feet in the instant before she went over the rail.

Chapter 32

Lacy was staring at him. Tate could see by her shocked expression that awareness had dawned.

"You knew," she said.

He didn't lie to her. He may have known her for less than a month—God, could it be?—but he knew she didn't need nor would she want to be protected in that way.

"Suspected. I felt him shove at my ankles. He hit the front, not the back, where he would have if it had just been a guy trying not to fall. He just didn't hit me hard enough."

He fought down a burgeoning rage at the knowledge that while the man hadn't managed to lever his heavier weight over the rail, he'd sent Lacy over. But his anger wasn't reserved solely for the man in the concealing scarf. A big chunk of it was aimed at himself. He should have believed from the beginning, and now she had nearly paid the ultimate price for his denial.

He didn't dare speak, not at that moment, and he saw by Quinn's expression that he knew quite well how he was feeling. Quinn ran the video back to that moment where the man's eyes were visible. Then he paused it, and the image sat silently. So did they. He could guess at the man's height, but build was anybody's guess in that heavy jacket. The knit hat was pulled down too far to get even a glimpse of hair color or even the shape of an ear. And the scarf, tightly wrapped, hid his chin, jawline and mouth. All by design, obviously.

Tate stared at those eyes. The nose was nothing distinctive, but those eyes… Something once more tickled at the edge of his memory, but the harder he tried to seize it the faster it flitted away.

He swore under his breath. "There's something, but I can't pin it."

Quinn only nodded. He opened the laptop on the table before him. He tapped the pad and then a couple of keys. The screen on the wall split into two images, one the frozen video, the other an empty workstation. It was the tech guy, Tyler. In that same moment he heard a sound that reminded him of the video game some of the guys had played whenever they'd had the chance in the makeshift rec room they'd set up in camp.

"Be right there."

The voice came over the speakers, but as if from a distance. And then a blur of movement and Tyler was there.

"Sorry," he said. "Charlie's on a roll."

"My sympathy," Quinn said dryly.

"What's up?" Tyler asked.

"Sending you a video," Quinn said. "I need you to take what you can see of a face and run it against the image from the earlier video. I need the likelihood it's the same guy."

"Which face?"

"Guy in a hat and scarf. You'll know when you see him."

"On it," Tyler said, and his side of the screen abruptly went dark.

"He's not much for the niceties," Hayley said.

"Small price to pay," Tate said.

"Exactly," Quinn agreed. He leaned back in his chair. "You didn't report it, beyond the crew?"

Tate shook his head. "I wasn't positive enough it wasn't an accident until I saw this on the big screen. I wasn't sure they'd believe me, anyway."

"Maybe," Quinn said. "But you're building up a very long string of bad luck and 'accidents' to just write it off. There's intent here, Tate. I know you don't want to see it, and I understand why, after all you've been through—"

"I see it," he said, his teeth on edge. "And I've had more than enough of it. Lacy could have been badly hurt, or…worse."

Tate saw in Quinn's eyes the acknowledgment that it had been the danger to Lacy that had done it. And he also saw that the man understood completely; Tate was certain he would feel the same way if something to do with Quinn endangered Hayley.

"'Beware the fury of a patient man,'" Quinn quoted softly. "Lacy's right. You should be safe here, at home. You were rightfully expecting to be. To be out of it, away from it."

Tate grimaced. "There, I would have known what to do. I could take action. But here, when I don't even know who the enemy is…"

Quinn nodded in understanding. "I get it." And Tate knew he did. "That's why we're here. It's taking longer than I'd hoped, but we will ID him."

Lacy was staring at him. "I never thought of that aspect," she said when he lifted a brow at her. "I can't imagine how that must grate. I guess the price of civilization versus war is giving up the pleasure of instant karma."

Lacy was right about many, many things.

And, he thought sometime later when they were driving back home, he still had no bed in which to show her how much he appreciated that fact. He doubted she would appreciate that observation, however, so he didn't say it.

"Maybe you really are meant to order a bed online," Lacy said.

He blinked as she said exactly what he'd been thinking.

"Maybe," he agreed. And smiled despite himself. With Liz, if he had tried to guess at what she was thinking and had been way off, he'd gotten a chilling glare. And she'd blamed him for it, as if he were supposed to be able to read her mind.

Lacy usually just smiled and said something about her mind having veered in a different direction.

Everything with Lacy was different.

Everything with Lacy was better, he admitted. Not just the sex, although that alone was enough to have him thinking things he'd never expected to be thinking about again.

And you're thinking too much now, he told himself, shifting uncomfortably as he drove.

But he was still thinking later, when he had finished the last coat of paint in his bedroom. He pounded the lid down on the paint can with more force than was needed. He turned, scanned the empty room, hoping seeing nothing but walls and the repaired floor would cool him down. He was still a long way from having a room he'd want to bring a woman into.

Your grandmother never cared. She always said her home was me, not a house. But I always wanted her to have the best I could give her.

Gramps's words, spoken to him years ago, echoed in his head now. He'd decided then and there that when he grew up, if he ever got married, it would have to be to a woman like that. Who would say *he* was her home, not a place. And who he could say the same about in return.

He'd forgotten that vow. And he realized now that Liz

would never have said or felt that. And for the first time he thought himself lucky to have escaped trying to give her what she wanted.

But Lacy would. He knew it on some gut level he didn't question. She was that kind of woman. And no amount of telling himself he'd been wrong about Liz seemed to shake that certainty. Nor did reminding himself of his plan, that he'd intended to settle in here, find a job, maybe look up some old friends before he ever went looking for any female companionship.

You didn't have to go looking. She was right next door.

He tried to ignore that little voice. But he felt the fighter within him, that part of him that had been in hiding since he'd gotten home, was stirring. And he knew he had his answer. The only answer possible. The answer he'd been avoiding.

In truth, it had been unavoidable since that moment he'd said *Trust me*, and she unhesitatingly had done so. That look in her eyes…

I do trust you.

And he finally let the thought form. The realization that one of the layers in those words had been love.

He drew in a long, deep breath. Let it out slowly. Let the wonder of it fill him.

And knew he was going to go for it.

He picked up the paint can, the roller tray, and the used roller and brushes. He headed out to the workshop, put the paint on a shelf and started on the brushes. Gramps had never skimped on certain tools, and paintbrushes were one of them, so Tate took care to get them as clean as he could. When he'd finished, he hung them up to dry. He noticed the shovel Lacy had brought back leaning against the wall. Remembered when she'd handed it to him, and the way she'd lovingly run her fingers over the handle, well worn and rubbed by his grandfather's hands over the years.

"It makes him feel closer," she'd said. And her words had made his chest tighten, as she echoed how he'd felt wearing his grandfather's shirt.

And suddenly he had to see her, right now. He set down the shovel, spun on his heel and raced out of the workshop.

He found her in the kitchen, where something already smelled delicious.

"Roast beef," she said when he asked, coming up behind her and slipping his arms around her. "It will be ready in an hour. Interested?"

"Very," he said huskily against her ear.

She laughed, that light, lovely sound that seemed to brush across his skin.

"Sorry, session in five minutes. But hold that thought."

"Oh, I will," he said.

And he did, every step of the way when he made another trek through the trees, Gramps's pistol in his hand, looking for any change, any sign someone had come back. His every sense was on alert, and he was even more determined now than he had been when he'd been in uniform and it had been his job. Keeping Lacy safe had become more important than even his own safety, and at last he didn't mind admitting that. Nor would he skimp on whatever he could do.

Still, he got back in time to hear the end of her lesson. He enjoyed hearing how she had coaxed this particular student into trying something she never had before, and ended up creating an enthusiastic reader looking for more.

"I started reading one of Gramps's mysteries the other day," he told her later, over a plate of the rare beef that was as good as it had smelled.

"And?"

"I like the puzzle aspect. Trying to guess."

She nodded. "I can give you a great list." Then she stopped and grinned. "Wait, never mind. I gave him the list, and I think he got most of them."

He laughed. "I should have known. And, yeah, there's quite a stack. And I found an e-reader with more. It'll take me a while. Then I'll come running."

"Do that."

Her voice was different, and he understood that she wasn't talking just about books. He lowered his gaze to his plate, wishing he was better at saying things, at coming up with the right words. He was thankful when his cell phone signaled a text coming in, then hesitated, not wanting to be rude on top of everything else.

"It might be Quinn or Hayley," Lacy said. "You should check."

And just how many times did he need to be reminded that Lacy wasn't Liz? he wondered as he reached for the phone.

It was indeed Quinn. And the message was Quinn-short and to the point: 89% chance guy in both videos is the same.

Tate texted back a quick Copy. Then he told Lacy, without even thinking about whether he should. She was part of this now.

She was part of him.

And that was somehow more important even than the knowledge he was being hunted.

Chapter 33

He ate too much, and Tate wondered if the close call with the chilly waters of the sound had sparked his appetite. Or if it was simply that he was sitting here with the woman who had changed his life.

Because he could no longer deny it was true. She had changed it, and in ways he suspected he didn't even know yet. She'd changed it despite the fact that he wasn't sure what this new life was going to be. Except that he wanted her in it. But he had no right to ask her to share it with… whatever this was hanging over him.

In fact, if he was smart, he'd get out of here. Leave, and hope whoever this predator was would follow, since it was Tate he was after. That way, at least Lacy would be safe.

His appetite for food more than satisfied, he stood up to help clear the table. This act of doing something so… domestic together seemed both simple and impossibly complex. But he concentrated on it as if it were crucial, trying not to think about the other appetite that was building.

Not that he needed any help sparking his appetite for Lacy. He was almost afraid to look at her, for fear she would see the need already raging in him. And as soon as he thought it, he heard her say softly,

"About that thought you had…"

It flared as quickly, as hotly as it had from the first

time he'd touched her. He had no thought of explosions or electric shocks or near dunks in the sound in his head. There was only room for Lacy and the feel and taste of her. And that precious moment when, straining to hold back, he felt her body clench around him as she cried out his name. When he let himself go and exploded into her with a ferocity that took his breath away.

He awoke before dawn with a jolt, after a dream in which he had frozen, watching Lacy pitch over the rail, unable to stop it or help her. She had disappeared beneath the chilly waters and never surfaced again. And a voice behind him, from a man wrapped mummy-like in a scarf, announced there was more than one way to kill a man.

The truth of that gnawed at him, just as the image of her slipping out of sight haunted him. He got Gramps's Colt and made another circuit, on the distant chance something other than that dream had awakened him. He found nothing, but the visuals hung on. It was all he could do to wait until a decent hour before texting Quinn for a meeting. He felt guilty not telling Lacy what he planned, but he knew she would not want him to do what he thought he had to do. Quinn would understand. It didn't take a genius, or even a particularly perceptive person, to see that the man would move mountains and more to protect Hayley.

When he arrived at Foxworth, Quinn's vehicle was there, but there was no sign of anyone. Nor did Cutter greet him as before. But the moment he registered the dog's absence, Cutter came racing around the side of the building and headed straight for him. The dog greeted him effusively, making him smile despite it all. And the moment he started scratching behind the dog's ear he felt that easing of tension he'd noticed before. He wondered if it was an effect of all dogs, or just a special few, like Cutter and Sunny.

A minute Quinn, with a tennis ball in hand, appeared from the same direction.

"Morning," he said. "What's up?"

"I have to leave," Tate said without dissembling, knowing Quinn wouldn't mind the blunt opening.

Quinn always had that air of watchfulness that the best of his team had had, but now it shifted from a general sort of thing to a tight focus, and the difference was almost palpable. Just like the change in Cutter when he went from being just a dog to...whatever it was he became.

"She could have died yesterday," he said.

Quinn lifted his head slightly. "And you think you need to get away from her, to keep her safe."

He was a little relieved that Quinn had gotten there so quickly. "Yes. If this guy, whoever it is, is after me, then if I go, he'll follow."

"And then what?"

He hadn't really thought that part through completely yet, that damned dream had him too rattled. It would have been bad enough if any innocent had been hurt because of him, but Lacy... God, Lacy...

The bottom line was obvious, to him at least.

"Lure him out. I've had enough of this sneak attack crap."

"Using yourself as bait?"

"I'm what he wants, right?"

"Safe enough assumption," Quinn agreed.

"So if I'm not here, Lacy will be safe. I know it sounds like running, but—"

Quinn cut him off with a shake of his head. Then, quietly, he said, "Running's not in you. And I know if it was just you, you'd never even think about it."

Relieved, Tate nodded. "I couldn't live with it."

"And that I understand completely," Quinn said. "But if you do go, then he'll know you're on to him."

Tate frowned. "Wouldn't anybody be on to him by now?"

Quinn smiled. "One of the things I've learned since we started Foxworth is that guys like this often think they're smarter than everyone else. Besides, don't forget he's been trying to make this look like an accident every time."

"Lucky for me," Tate muttered. "But then again, if he had the balls to come at me head-on, this would be over by now."

"And that," Quinn said with a grin, "would be an epic fight worth watching."

He appreciated that assessment, coming from this man. But none of this changed the crux of the thing. "I can't keep putting Lacy in danger."

"I get that. Look, by tomorrow I'll have a couple of guys back who can start keeping an eye on her place, round the clock. I'll do it in the meantime—"

"I can," Tate said. "I've been doing recons, but I'll step it up."

"He went after you on that ferry, a very public place with lots of possible witnesses. You've already driven him to that."

"Then he does know I'm on to him."

"Maybe. Could be he's getting desperate."

Tate swore under his breath. "Why can't I remember? There's not a damn thing I can think of that would explain this."

"Then we have to assume either it's in that patch you lost, or it's something he just thinks you know."

"I don't even know him." Tate shook his head in frustration. "That still doesn't change the bottom line."

"Lacy."

"Yes. I can't let anything else happen to her because of me."

"Somehow," Quinn said thoughtfully, "I don't see her as the running type any more than you."

"She's not. But I brought this down on her—"

"You did not. The responsibility for this belongs to one person only, and it's not you."

"But if she hadn't... If we hadn't..."

Quinn grinned then. "Yeah, but think what you would have missed out on."

Tate blinked. Then he gave a rueful smile. "That obvious, huh?"

"Only to a man who's been there. And since I have, let me point out that any guy who has a woman like Lacy in his life is a very lucky man."

"Even if somebody's trying to kill him?"

The grin widened. "Even if." Then he glanced from Tate to Cutter and back. "Feel like dog sitting?"

Tate blinked. "What?"

"Best burglar, prowler and trespasser alarm there is," Quinn said with a nod at Cutter.

"You mean...keep him at my place?"

"Just until we round this clownhat up."

"I... You sure you want to risk him?"

"He can take care of himself. And help you take care of Lacy," Quinn said.

Tate looked down at the dog who was suddenly watching him intently, as if he knew what Quinn was saying. Hell, maybe he did.

"He might not like that."

He was thinking fast. Would Lacy mind? After all, he was spending most of his nights with her. Then he remembered her crooning over the dog, planting kisses on his head, and knew she wouldn't.

"He's done it before," Quinn was saying. "He knows it's sometimes part of the job."

For an instant he wasn't seeing Cutter, but another, sunny yellow dog who had also known what was part of the job. He felt the familiar tug, but was brought out of it by Quinn's voice.

"I'll get his stuff."

Quinn walked over to his SUV and opened the back. He pulled out a small backpack and carried it over to Tate.

"Bowls, food enough for a week, chew bones and some treats if he earns them. Oh, and a couple of tennis balls," he added with a grin.

"You keep a go bag for a dog?" Tate couldn't help smiling as he took the pack. Cutter watched the handover and was suddenly on his feet, ears up, alert.

"He's one of the team."

"You're sure you trust me with him?"

Quinn's grin vanished. "If you weren't the kind of person we would trust with him, we would never have taken the case."

Tate felt a sudden jab of…not envy, he liked the guy too much for that. More like admiration, that he'd managed to arrange his life to only work with people he liked and trusted.

"You're with him," Quinn said to his dog. "Guard."

Cutter gave a low woof that was clearly an acknowledgment. And even knowing how clever the animal was, Tate was still a little surprised when the dog turned and sat beside him, so close he was touching his leg.

As Sunny used to do.

Damn, this was going to be harder than he'd thought.

"It's Lacy who needs guarding," he said, trying to fight down the stab of missing his old partner.

"He knows she's part of you. He put you two together, didn't he?"

Tate's gaze shot back to Quinn's face. He might be smiling, but he also looked dead serious.

Hayley says he's an inveterate matchmaker…

"You believe that."

"His track record is hard to ignore," Quinn said. Then, briskly, he added, "Food morning and night if you can manage it, although he's not manic about it. And he'll take orders from you, unless he thinks they conflict with getting his job done."

Tate almost grinned himself. "And if he does think that?"

"He'll ignore you."

"Because he's obeying you first."

"Exactly."

Cutter jumped into the buggy without hesitation. Tate glanced back at Quinn, who had taken out his phone.

"Better let my wife know I just loaned him out again," he said with a grin.

Tate drove home with Cutter beside him and the image of a man crazy in love with his wife in his mind.

Chapter 34

"I know Quinn said you came like this, dog, but you must have had some training," Tate whispered as he and Cutter made their way through the trees.

They'd almost finished the circle around both his and Lacy's houses. The dog had paused once or twice to investigate something, including the spot where someone likely had been hiding that first night, but he'd never alerted on anything new.

When he'd started doing these recons Tate felt odd, but no more. He had told himself it was the continuation of the threat that had changed his feelings, but he knew it was more than that. It was Lacy. Any threat to her was intolerable. A McLaughlin protects his own, Gramps had often told him. It was why Martin had enlisted the day he turned eighteen. He'd wanted to the day after Pearl Harbor, but he'd been too young.

And Lacy was his, in that undeniable, forever way that his grandfather had felt about his grandmother. It seemed fitting somehow that the sidearm he carried now had been Martin's.

Thanks, Gramps. For everything.

Cutter snapped to attention, stopping dead. Tate froze. He saw the clear difference in the animal's posture and manner. He made no sound, but his nose was working hard, his sides flexing rapidly as he sniffed and sorted the smells.

When he headed down the trail away from Lacy's house, Tate almost called him back. Then Quinn's warning echoed in his mind. *He'll take orders from you, unless he thinks they conflict with getting his job done.*

He followed the dog. It wasn't the first time he'd put his trust and his life in the paws of a working canine. And Cutter was quite obviously working.

A few yards later the dog veered off the trail to the left, nose still down and clearly intent. It was rough going, the underbrush and ferns were thick on the forest floor. But Tate decided that if someone were actually here at this moment, the dog would be acting differently, so he focused more on keeping up than silence.

On some level he was aware this was all too familiar. Following, trusting a dog in the night was something he did instinctively, although it felt different doing it in this cool, green forest of tall evergreens. A far cry from desert sands, but in its own way even more dangerous simply by virtue of there being more places to hide.

When they broke out of the trees they were at the road, seventy-five feet or so from the edge of Lacy's property. There was a wide shoulder there, and Cutter went straight to it. He stopped, then started casting about, sniffing at the dirt and gravel. Tate looked carefully around, but didn't expect to see anyone, not the way the dog was acting. Finally the dog walked back to where he'd stopped for that moment, and sat. Tate joined him.

"Where it ends, eh, boy?" he said softly.

Cutter whined, clearly very unhappy with the abrupt ending of his scent trail.

Of course, it could have been somebody just out for a summer hike. But Tate didn't think so. Not the way Cutter had reacted. He trusted what Quinn had said, that the dog had a narrow focus when he was working. One case at a time.

He played it down a bit with Lacy when he got back to her place. Some of the tension lingered, in a too-familiar way. Especially when Cutter wouldn't settle for the longest time, pacing and constantly wanting to go outside to sniff around.

"What's bothering you?" Lacy finally asked when they were cleaning up after dinner. "I know he's acting differently, all the pacing and restlessness, but you're watching him like you've never seen him before."

Tate had been staring at Cutter. But his mind had been thousands of miles away.

He looked at Lacy. And something in her steady gaze told him she'd understand. So with faith he was right, as he had been about her unhesitating welcome of the dog into her home, he tried to explain.

"I think he's just on guard. As ordered. But out there with him tonight," he said, "it was...familiar. A partnership, a team."

She got there instantly. "Like you had with your Sunny."

He nodded. Looked back at Cutter. "I'm going to miss him when this is over."

She started to speak, then stopped. "What?" he asked.

"I was going to say you could always get a dog now, but...it wouldn't be the same, would it? Your average pet isn't Sunny. Or Cutter."

The dog looked up as she said his name, his tail waving a couple of times in acknowledgment. But Tate was focused on Lacy.

"Is there anything you don't understand?" he asked, not even trying to hide the wonder in his voice.

"Yes," she said, turning to slip her arms around his

neck. "Why we're doing this when we could be doing… other things."

And that quickly it began again. They knew each other now, knew where to touch, to kiss, to stroke, and yet it was still new and wondrous. At the same time he sensed something he never had before, a core, a foundation as solid, as strong, as unwavering as Lacy herself.

He awoke much later. He lay in her bed in the darkness, toying with a lock of her silky dark hair. Her hand was resting on his chest, and he closed his eyes, oddly remembering those long, slender fingers as she had stroked the handle of that shovel, rubbed smooth by his grandfather's hands. Remembered again that she had been here for Gramps when he couldn't be. How much she had cared for an old man she wasn't even related to. How he could never thank her enough for that. Or for caring about him, for that matter.

The only things he could think of to do for her were too small, too simple. Washing her car or taking her out to dinner again were nothing, even if she did love that metalwork art at the restaurant they'd gone to.

The memory hit him of how she'd reached up to touch the delicate yet strong piece in wonder. She'd traced the curve of the intricate, lacy pattern with the same fingers that he'd now felt trailing over every part of him. And it had given him a sense of humbled awe when she looked at him in the same way, as if he were some creation that sparked wonder in her. He'd never felt that way in his life.

It was then he was struck with what he thought had to be the stupidest idea he'd ever had. Yet it lingered, and he turned it over and over in his mind. He was sure Gramps would have all the tools he needed. There was little he hadn't worked on or with in the course of his ninety-three years. Tate doubted he could pull it off, or if she would like it if he did, but it wouldn't leave him alone.

After lying awake for nearly an hour he finally slipped out of bed, pausing only to tuck the covers around Lacy, who stirred but didn't awaken. He was grateful, because he didn't think he could explain. She'd see soon enough. If it worked.

He grabbed up his clothes from the floor where they'd landed, wondering for a moment where his shirt was before he remembered it had hit the floor out in the living room. Or maybe the kitchen. While he was at it, he gathered Lacy's clothes as well, brows furrowing slightly as he picked up the bra and saw it was still hooked. For the life of him he couldn't remember how that had happened. He was grinning into the darkness as he let the silky fabric slide through his fingers, putting the garment on the bed with the rest. It was nothing compared to the silk of her skin.

Cutter was on his feet, restlessly looking from him to the bed where Lacy still slept.

"Stay with her," he whispered. "Guard."

He hadn't been sure the dog would do it. But after a moment Cutter turned and went back to plop on the floor on Lacy's side of the bed, as much as announcing no one would get to her without going past him, and good luck with that.

Tate dressed quickly in the hallway, then headed out and over to the workshop. He approached the idea systematically, as Gramps had taught him, doing some research first. He smiled as he checked various blogs and videos on his phone, remembering how amazed Gramps had been at what you could do on such a small device. But he'd taken to it, and Tate had always thought his efforts to keep up with changing technology had done a lot to keep him going so long.

When he thought he had a handle on the process, he began to gather the tools he'd need. It took him a while to find them all—he was distracted a bit by his makeshift bed and the thoughts it brought on—but when he had everything he was left only with the need for the actual material for the project. And he knew what that would be.

He nearly grinned at how perfect it seemed, while at the same time shaking his head again at the whole idea, wondering if she'd think it ridiculous. But then he answered his own question.

No, she wouldn't. Lacy Steele wasn't one to think any serious effort ridiculous.

He walked over to the rack of garden tools and picked up the shovel. It would need a good cleaning, but otherwise he would leave it as it was. It had some dings and scrapes acquired over long years of use; that was part of the appeal. Those marks had been put there by his grandfather, and perhaps by Lacy herself. That thought made it seem even more right.

He would check it structurally first and make sure the handle was solid, all the fittings secure, and clean it thoroughly. Then—

"Missing your air mattress?"

He spun around as the teasing inquiry came from the workshop doorway. Lacy stood there, Cutter at her side, still following orders. She was in the T-shirt and loose-knit pants she'd had on for that tutoring session before dinner. He remembered her student from halfway around the world saying, "Miz Lacy, you look so happy!"

And that, too, had made him feel like he never had before.

"Only thing that air mattress is missing is you," he said.

She came in then, a smile on her face that did impossible things to him so quickly it took his breath away. He was a little astonished at how quickly having her beside him had become imperative. He barely noticed when Cutter plopped down by the door like a furry blockade.

"We could fix that," she suggested as she reached him, and ran a hand under his shirt and over his abdomen.

"It's not a bed," he said, his muscles tightening at her touch, heat arrowing straight downward to that part of him that didn't care anything about where, only now.

"Better than the floor," Lacy said, her hand slipping down to the waistband of the sweats he'd thrown on.

And that quickly she shattered the last of what was left of his ideas about where he wanted her. He just wanted her, and he didn't care where. Although the thought of outside in the grass on a warm summer night suddenly appealed. But for now, this would do nicely. And clearly Lacy didn't care.

Your grandmother never cared. She always said her home was me, not a house. But I always wanted her to have the best I could give her.

He understood now, in a way he never could have before. Before Lacy they were just words, words that made him long for something he didn't really think was possible in this crazy world anymore.

Her hand slipped lower, caressing him. The fire that had only been banked flared instantly, and she wrapped her fingers around his rapidly responding flesh. And yet for a moment he only held her, savoring the feel of her in his arms as much as the fiery stroking.

And when they went down to his makeshift bed he knew it was possible. And he dared to hope that his luck had finally turned.

* * *

It was a good thing it was almost summer, Lacy thought sleepily, or it would be too chilly to sleep out here unless you kept the heater on all the time.

Well, unless you had a personal heater like Tate wrapped around you.

Which she did, and she snuggled against him. He stirred slightly, but only to pull her closer into the curve of his body. The single blanket was more than enough with him here. For a moment she thought of the man she'd first met and the man he was now, and with a smile she hoped she'd had a part in the change.

You, too, she added as she lifted her head to see Cutter curled up a couple of feet away.

The night was dark and still, and she drifted back to sleep. But the smile remained, for she was quickly dreaming that Martin had come into the workshop and found them, but rather than expressing embarrassment or awkwardness he merely smiled down at them in obvious satisfaction.

A crashing boom that was as much a physical jolt as sound brought her jarringly awake. The ground beneath them had actually jumped, she thought, groggily trying to focus. Tate was having no such trouble. He was already on his feet, racing for the door. Cutter was at his heels, letting out a furious tirade of barking.

Another explosion.

It hit her then, and anger flashed through her. It would have been fear had they not been together, so she'd known he was all right. The hit of instant wrath scattered all trace of sleep, of grogginess.

"Stay with her," Tate yelled as he raced outside.

It took her a split second to realize he was talking to Cutter. She grabbed at her clothes and tugged them on, then scrambled to her feet. She picked up Tate's sweats. Much as she loved the sight of him naked, she wasn't sure he'd appreciate his own state when others inevitably started to arrive. She ran after him, the protective Cutter close on her heels.

As soon as she was outside she instinctively looked at his house. The realization that she thought of it that way now, his house, darted through her mind, but was vanquished at the sight of it, sitting quiet and whole in the dark.

It took her a split second. And then she turned.

It wasn't Tate's house shattered, burning this time.

It was hers.

Chapter 35

Lacy could have been right there, Tate thought as he stared at the wreckage of what had been her bedroom. She would have been, had she not come out to the workshop looking for him.

And if she had been at home, there was no doubt, looking at the destruction, that she would be dead.

Lacy, dead.

Just formulating the thought made every nerve he had curl up and scream in protest. But he knew with a deep, complete certainty that if Lacy had been killed, or if she'd been so much as scratched, he would have hunted down the one responsible, and when Tate finished with him there would be nothing left for the law. His own probable death along with hers, had this happened two hours sooner, meant little to him compared to the mere thought of trying to go on without her.

And then she was there, beside him, alive and breathing and precious. He grabbed her, wrapped his arms around her, needing to feel her, as if he wouldn't believe she was truly here and okay until he could feel her heartbeat and her breath against his chest. He acknowledged what he had known on some level for a while now.

He loved her.

He hadn't wanted to, or expected to, but in her quiet, supportive way she'd gotten past all his defenses.

It was a moment before he heard her mutter, "I don't even have a propane tank."

His jaw tightened. "This was not that. This was an explosive."

She tilted her head back to look up at him. But she didn't question his conclusion. He was grateful. He didn't want to explain that this was all too familiar. The kind of destruction, the pattern, the smell, he'd seen it before, in that hot dry place so far from here in so many more ways than distance.

He'd done it before.

"Here."

He jerked his attention from the smoking ruin before them to what she was holding out to him. Only then did he fully realized he'd bolted out here stark naked. With the reason he'd been in that state standing beside him, he wasn't too concerned. Any guy would realize and envy him. But he hastily pulled on the sweats she'd thought to bring. Then he started toward her house.

"Tate—" she began.

"See if your water's still working. Should be. Let's make sure what fire there is doesn't spread. Cutter, guard."

The dog seemed as unsettled as he felt, but he stuck close to Lacy and that was all Tate cared about. He grabbed the main hose she used for the garden and headed toward the house. Lacy ran to the upright yard hydrant that stood near the closest raised bed and flipped up the handle all the way. Water immediately started at the nozzle and he sprayed the spots where the most smoke was rising.

Something burst out of the dark toward him. He whirled. Held the hose. It wasn't much, but might give him an edge of surprise if he hit an attacker in the face with it. Then he saw, and shut down the spray at the nozzle.

Cutter. Who was supposed to be guarding Lacy.

He'll take orders from you, unless he thinks they conflict with getting his job done…

He threw Tate a look and a growl as he raced past and headed for the woods, tail out straight and head down, a snarl unlike anything Tate had ever heard issuing from the dog's throat. It hit him then. He'd been so thankful Lacy had not been in there, his brain had malfunctioned.

He was here. The damned guy, whoever he was, was here, maybe hiding in those trees, watching. Far enough away that Cutter hadn't heard or scented him, but close enough to watch the result of his handiwork.

Tate had nothing, no weapon with him, but he didn't care. His bare hands would do. He started after the dog. The moment he did the snarl ceased, as if Cutter had only needed to be sure Tate understood and was following. Or as if he didn't want to give his quarry any warning.

"Tate, wait!" Lacy yelled. "You know Quinn will be here—"

"He'll escape by then," he called back.

He broke into a run as Cutter reached the trees. He had to keep the dog in sight. He ignored the occasional jab of a stone or downed branch to his bare feet, at the newly healed cut. He wanted this guy with a white-hot anger unlike anything he'd ever known. In uniform he had occasionally hunted, but it had been his job, the job he'd volunteered to do. So that people like Lacy could live in peace and safety.

She will remind you why you fight.

He dodged a low-hanging branch. Yes, she did. Only now it was much, much more personal. Now she was why he kept breathing.

He knew he was closing in. He could only hear Cutter now, but he caught a whiff of…something on the air as he leaped over a bunch of ferns growing on the tree-shadowed forest floor. His sense of smell had sharpened overseas when a trace of certain odors lingering could mean life or death, but this was the first time it had happened here. He was back in warrior mode as much as he had been then. Only this time for a much more personal reason.

Lacy could have been killed.

That he likely would have been there with her, as he had been every night since his world had been changed forever, didn't matter a bit next to that.

Up ahead Cutter suddenly darted left. The dog gave a sharp yip, as if to notify Tate of the change in direction. It was the same path they had followed last night. Toward the street. Maybe that was when someone had planted the bomb. The presence of the explosive could be why Cutter had been so anxious when the trail had ended. And had refused to settle afterward. He wasn't a trained bomb dog, but he'd still known something was wrong.

He was trying to tell you, you idiot. Didn't Sunny teach you anything?

If the guy had a car parked out there, like before, they'd lose him. He was too far ahead.

But maybe not for Cutter. And a new worry slammed into him; if the guy was trying to kill him and was willing to take Lacy out, too, then he surely wouldn't hesitate to kill a dog. He felt a new knot in his stomach, the one he'd always felt when Sunny had gone ahead to protect them.

His feet were taking a beating but he kept going. He felt the scrape of branches as he barreled through the thick trees. Only barks from Cutter—coming oddly spaced at about every fifteen seconds, as if he knew Tate would need the guidance out here in the dark, lacking the keen canine ears and nose—kept him on the trail.

And then he heard the snarl again, in the instant before he broke clear of the trees. He nearly stumbled at the drainage ditch that ran alongside the pavement, but he managed to jump it at the last second. Landed. Saw Cutter ahead, heading north. A person, barely two yards ahead of the dog, dove for the car parked at an angle on the shoulder.

He made it. The door slammed the instant before Cutter got there. There was no trace of the amiable, clever, sometimes goofy dog now. He was furious, snarling, snapping at the man in the car. If that window had been open Tate had no doubt Cutter would have jumped right through it and gone for a piece of the man. Tate calculated the distance, wondering if he could get there before he took off, if there was a chance he hadn't locked the door, if he could break the window to get to him, if—

The car wouldn't start.

Tate could see the man trying, saw him pound the steering wheel when nothing happened. And then he was there, yanking at the door, hoping that since the car hadn't started, no automatic door locks had engaged.

The door opened. The man recoiled as Cutter lunged at him. Threw up his hands in an effort to protect his throat. The likely instinctive movement allowed Tate to grab his arms and haul him bodily out of the car. The man struggled, but Tate's blood was up. He flattened him with an elbow to his jaw, putting every ounce of force and momentum he had behind it. The man's scream as he went facedown in the dirt gave Tate a snap of satisfaction. But not enough. Not nearly enough.

He dropped a knee on the man's back, over his kidneys. Cutter was right there, and Tate thought anyone who ignored that snarl deserved what he got. He leaned in, caught the man's neck in the bend of his elbow. The temptation to pull, to twist, to hear that snap as his neck went was fierce. Tate tightened his grip. Heard a gurgling sound as the man tried to scream again.

"Tate."

The sound of her voice yanked him back from the edge. He looked up. She was kneeling beside him, understanding in her eyes. It was that look that undid him. And he knew he couldn't give her that memory to carry, of him killing a man who was already subdued, a man he didn't have to kill.

He eased up. The man gasped for breath. Tried to pull away. Froze when Cutter growled a warning.

"Move," Tate said, "and I won't stop him."

"I called Quinn. They were already on the way," Lacy said as she turned on the flashlight on her phone and shone it toward the man on the ground. Tate's brow furrowed. The guy looked vaguely familiar, but he didn't recognize him, at least not at that angle. He eased off the man's back, watching for any sign he was going to try to get up. Then he shoved him over on his back so he could fully see his face. Lacy moved the light. The man blinked, squinted as the bright light hit his eyes.

"Owen," Tate hissed out. "I should have known it would be you."

The man's lip curled. Cutter growled. He subsided.

"It was you, wasn't it? You're the drug connection they were investigating."

Bart Owen's bushy eyebrows lowered. "Don't play dumb, McLaughlin. I know you were there. I know you saw everything."

Tate started to ask what he was talking about, but caught

himself. It might be best if Owen thought he did remember… whatever he thought he'd seen.

"You're going down, Simpson," he said instead, using the nickname they'd given him.

The man snorted. "Go to hell, McLaughlin."

"Already been." He looked at Lacy. "Heaven's better," he said softly. Her smile was brighter than the shine of the flashlight.

Cutter's head came up. A pair of headlights illuminated the road as a car turned the corner. Tate saw the dog's tail begin to wag. Then came the happy bark that said the Foxworths had arrived.

It was over.

He slipped an arm around Lacy, pulling her close.

"It's over," he said.

"Yes."

"What are you doing out here?"

"I remembered what you said about him probably having a car parked up the street, so I went to look."

"You should have stayed back there, safe."

She leaned back, gave him a pointed look. "Really?"

She held out a hand, uncurled her fingers. In the glare of the approaching headlights he saw what she held. His gaze snapped to her face.

"The same model car as mine. Did you think it was just dumb luck it wouldn't start?"

He burst out laughing as she grinned at him, still holding the handful of fuses that had turned the car beside them into a useless pile of parts.

"You know," Quinn said, sounding utterly satisfied as they all sat downstairs at the Foxworth building, "it was almost worth it to see the look on Owen's face when he realized it was all needless."

Tate shook his head. "I still can't quite believe I can't remember."

"I'd say if last night didn't bring it back, that memory's gone for good," Quinn said, and Tate appreciated his honesty. Not to mention the way Foxworth had stepped in to coordinate between the sheriff, the fire department and the military police who eventually arrived to take custody, since Owen had been AWOL since being recalled after his own relatively minor injuries from the same IED that had landed Tate in the hospital.

"Fine with me, as long as he goes down, anyway."

"Oh, he will. They only needed the name to start tying it all up. They've got parts of the bomb, including the timer. They'll find something."

"Cutter tried to tell me," Tate said ruefully. "I just didn't see."

"You're used to a trained bomb dog," Quinn said. "Cutter's beyond clever, but he doesn't signal the same way. Oh, and Brett had them do a search, and they found that hat and scarf in one of the trash bins on the ferry. There'll likely be DNA on it, to match to his."

Tate nodded.

"So he thinks you saw him actually dealing drugs?" Lacy asked.

"Apparently I did see him," Tate answered. "Picking up a delivery. The morning we hit the IED. Which wiped out the memory."

"But Owen didn't know that," Hayley said. "So he came after you."

Lacy shook her head. "Committing murder to avoid drug charges?"

"Not unheard of," Quinn said. "Or even unusual."

He studied Tate for a moment. Tate sensed there was something else, something Quinn wasn't sure about saying.

"Tell me," he said.

"Sloan's been busy, now that we have a name. One of her contacts told her that Owen had put on quite a show of concern about you while you were still in the hospital."

"Let me guess," he said dryly. "He wanted to know when I might be getting out."

"Not just that. He seemed very interested in whether you were diagnosed with PTSD."

Tate pulled back slightly, puzzled. But Lacy let out a little gasp. Quinn shifted his gaze to her, seemed to read something in her face and nodded.

"What am I missing?" Tate asked.

Lacy's voice held that incredibly soft, emotional note when she spoke. "The current suicide rate for veterans is about twenty-two every day."

He blinked. It took him a moment to get there. "You mean…if I'd been diagnosed…"

"He might have tried to make it look like a suicide," Quinn said. "I'm a little surprised he didn't anyway, given when the symptoms show up is unpredictable."

"You should have let Cutter rip his throat out." Lacy said it so grimly he stared at her. She refused to back down. "That aspect makes him even more despicable."

Tate couldn't argue with that. Didn't even want to. He sank back on the sofa. "He really…planned this."

"Yes," Quinn said. "I'm sorry."

Tate gave a half shake of his head. "I barely knew the guy."

"Better him than Cav," Lacy said.

He couldn't deny that. And at her use of their nickname for his friend, he had the thought that he couldn't wait to introduce them. He had no doubts Lacy could keep up with the guy's wicked sense of humor.

"You may still have to testify," Quinn said. "Not about the drugs, since you can't, but about what's happened here."

Tate nodded.

"We've got repair crews lined up, ready to go," Quinn said. "Your house will be back in shape soon."

Lacy nodded. "My landlady will be glad to hear it."

"Guess we'd better resume that shopping trip so you'll have a place to sleep in the interim," Tate said. Lacy looked at him, and he liked the pleased blush that rose in her cheeks. Liked better the idea of her curled up in his arms, in his bed, in the house that was now his.

"I'm really sorry you had to go through all this," Hayley said. "Especially here at home."

Tate smiled then. "It was worth it," he said quietly, then turned to look at Lacy. "Because I found out what home really means."

Her color deepened, but that didn't stop her from leaning in and giving him a sweet, long kiss. When at last she pulled back, he was wishing them anywhere but here. And only when the daze she always seemed to put him in lifted did he notice both Hayley and Quinn were looking at him, smiling broadly.

"Don't mind us," Quinn said with a laugh.

"We're used to it by now," Hayley added, gesturing with a thumb toward where a contented Cutter lounged before the fireplace, looking immensely satisfied. "Thanks to him."

"You were serious about that matchmaker thing," Lacy said.

Hayley grinned. "Besides us, you're couple number six."

Tate was getting used to it, being openly referred to as half a couple. He liked it. He looked over at Cutter.

"Thanks, dog."

Cutter woofed an answer, and gave him what could only be described as a doggy grin. Tate laughed.

And realized he was getting used to that, too. Laughing again.

Chapter 36

He'd gotten so used to sleeping at Lacy's that it seemed odd to be back in his own place. During the first few days there had been a second of reorientation as he was waking up, because the bed—the new, solid four-poster that he'd finally bought, that Lacy had picked out—was placed in a different direction, but the instant he felt her soft warmth beside him the world righted itself. And now, after three weeks, they'd settled into a pleasant routine he savored every moment of.

He simply held her as the morning light grew brighter. He had no desire to move. Ever.

The damage at her place had been extensive, but while she'd obviously been upset, she had been surprisingly composed about it. The only things irreplaceable had been photos she had digital copies of. Her work files had all been in another part of the house and important documents had been in a fireproof box. His Lacy was ever practical and prepared.

She had even found a bright side in the destruction of her closet; she'd just done laundry and hadn't put it away yet, so she had some clothes still.

"What about that sexy little black dress?" he'd asked, not liking the thought that he'd never see her in it again. His tone made her smile.

"At the dry cleaner's," she'd answered.

"Whew."

"See? It could be worse."

That it could have been much worse, that either or both of them could have been killed, was something they had acknowledged once and then put aside.

"Let it be a lesson in not taking anything for granted," she'd said. He couldn't have agreed more. And that exchange had landed them back in bed, before she'd had to get ready for her next tutoring session.

She was set up for work in the guest room, but there had never been any question of where she would sleep. He hadn't yet broached the subject of her moving in permanently. He was already trying to figure out what to do about her extensive garden. Maybe her landlady—who had been remarkably calm about the damage to her property, saying she was just glad Lacy was all right, a feeling he vehemently shared—would rent her just the land it was on, although that might make getting a new tenant tricky.

Then again, who wouldn't want to look out at all that carefully tended beauty knowing they didn't have to do the tending?

But the repairs on the house would be lengthy, so there was time enough to figure all that out. Just as he would figure out the unexpected offer from Sloan Burke, to join her in working for Accountability Counts. He liked the idea, and she said they'd gotten so big she honestly needed the help and that his service record and experience were something invaluable to their mission.

Later, while Lacy was working, he settled in to go through some of his grandfather's papers, a task he'd postponed amid the chaos and his work—hard to keep a secret with Lacy here now—on that crazy idea he'd had. But after a trip back to that restaurant and seeing her once more admire the artwork, he'd settled to it with renewed enthusiasm. He had one more thing to do and it would be finished.

So now he sat down at the big rolltop desk that he knew had been Gramps's favored place for paperwork. It was locked. He looked at it for a moment, at the brass plate that surrounded the small keyhole. It hit him then, what that small gold-colored key on Gramps's key ring was for. He went and got the keys from the hook by the back door and came back. The key slid in and the lock turned easily.

The top rolled back smoothly.

Of course it did, he thought with a smile.

But the smile was wiped away by surprise as he stared down at an envelope lying dead center on the desk pad neatly squared away on the desktop. His name was on it, written in a familiar and much-loved hand. Probably with one of his preferred old fountain pens, a rack of which was tucked in below the row of cubbies that ran across the top of the desk.

For a moment he just looked at it. Clearly Gramps had meant for him to find and read it, and he probably would have weeks ago if it had not been for all that had happened. He picked up the envelope, running a finger across his name, an odd feeling going through him as he touched his grandfather's writing. Had he known, when he'd put this here, that he would not be returning home this time? Or had it merely been one of Gramps's "just in case" things?

He pulled out the single sheet. Unfolded it. It was dated back on Gramps's ninetieth birthday. Which had been Tate's thirtieth. He felt the need to take in a deep breath before he started to read.

Tate,

Since life is complicated and often unpredictable, on this our shared birthday, I wanted to set down in writing some things I wish I could say to you in person. I have complete faith that you will return home safely to read this, for any other thought is unbearable.

Firstly, and most importantly, you must know how incredibly proud I am of you. You are everything any man could wish for in a grandson, and so much more. Not simply because you have served with courage and honor, but because of the kind of man you have become. If I have had some small part in that, my time has been well spent.

I hope that you will want to make this your home, for I have always envisioned you here, when your time in uniform is through. There should be enough money for you to be able to take your time in deciding what you want to do from here. But Tate, you must do something. You are like me—a fact your mother despairs of, I'm afraid—and you would never be happy without productive work.

I hope that you will find something you can be as passionate about as serving your country. (Again you are like me, and again your mother despairs.)

But most of all I hope you find what I found with your grandmother. For that is what makes all the rest worthwhile. It is worth waiting for, and when you find it, hang on to it whatever the cost. Don't settle for less, Tate. You deserve to know that kind of love, the kind that lasts a lifetime.

I love you, my boy.

Gramps

PS: On that last one, you could do considerably worse than starting next door. Lacy Steele is a keeper, and that's a wedding I'd dance at!

Tate couldn't remember the last time he'd had tears in his eyes and burst out laughing at the same time.

He couldn't wait to share it with Lacy.

He was still holding the letter when Quinn called, asking him to pick him up at the small local airport later this afternoon. Since she would be done with her last lesson of the day by then, Lacy didn't hesitate when he asked her to take the thirty-five-mile drive, although she seemed oddly edgy about it. Given that Foxworth—and Cutter—had done so much, and cleaned up most of the official details afterward so that they could focus on putting their lives in order—and together—it was a small enough favor to ask.

While she was doing her last session, he headed to the workshop for a final once-over on the secret project. When he was done he stepped back and looked at it. It was as good as he could make it.

He barely had time to get it inside and placed on the newly repaired wall in the spot he'd planned before he heard her coming down the hall. He went to her before she could step into the bedroom.

"I have to tell you something."

She looked up at him, the concern furrowing her brow telling him he'd been a bit intense. He tried again.

"You won't ever be able to borrow Gramps's shovel again."

She blinked. "Okay," she said, clearly puzzled.

Then he turned her toward the wall and stepped out of the way.

The now-polished metal of what had been the shovel blade gleamed, the pattern he'd cut into it intricate and delicate against the rough edges and the worn handle. He would put a light behind it, later, to show off the lace pattern, but for now the summer sun was doing a fine job of it. It wasn't art, not like that piece in the restaurant, but he hoped she'd see—

"Oh, Tate."

He'd been afraid to look at her, afraid she wouldn't get it or see everything he was trying to say with this bit of whimsy that was so unlike him.

One look at her face, at the tears already spilling over, told him she got every bit of it.

"It's lacy steel," she whispered. And then she threw her arms around him. "I love you."

It was even more of a kick in the chest than he'd thought it would be, when he'd dared to think of hearing those three words from her. He hastened to return them.

"I lo—"

She cut him off with a finger to his lips. "I know." She gestured with her hand at the shovel that now glimmered on the wall. "You couldn't have made it any clearer."

Her words, her understanding, demolished the last of that already-crumbling wall around his heart. And now the words came easily.

"I love you, Lacy. Stay with me. Here, where my grandparents showed me what love is really about."

"Of course," she said.

He nearly forgot about his promise until, stretched lazily atop him an hour later, Lacy murmured, "Aren't you supposed to go somewhere?"

It was a scramble to dress and get going. Once at the small local airfield Tate followed the directions he'd been given, driving parallel to a runway marked with the dark tracks of countless landings, toward the last hangar in the long row. At a sedate fifteen miles an hour, as ordered.

He hadn't been surprised that Foxworth had an airplane. From what he'd learned of the extent of their work, it seemed almost a necessity. Just as they were nearing the large, metal building, a taxiing plane turned onto the approach road, and he guessed that was it. It was a sleek-looking craft, white with a two-tone blue curved stripe flowing over the body and then sweeping up toward the tail. It had large windows along the side and room for at least half a dozen passengers, he guessed.

"Nice," Lacy said.

"Yeah," he agreed as the plane halted smoothly in front of the hangar where a large, roll-up door was already open.

She still seemed a bit on edge, although better since she'd read his grandfather's letter, which he'd grabbed on the way out and given her once they were in the car. She'd reacted the same way he had, with tears and laughter. And he'd had the uncharacteristically philosophical thought that as long as those were in equal measure, he could handle the tears part.

Unless they were Lacy's tears, and genuinely sad. That would be hard to handle. But handle it he would. As Gramps had written, life was complicated and unpredictable.

And he thought for a moment of the small box he had tucked away, the box that held two rings, his grandparents' wedding rings. The plain gold bands were simple, but he knew Lacy appreciated all they meant; she'd practically cried when he'd found them.

They got out of the buggy. He caught Lacy watching him and again got that sense of edginess. But before he could ask about it, the clamshell hatch of the airplane opened, drawing his gaze. The lower part of the hatch was steps on the inside, and he grinned when Cutter leaped out, forgoing the bottom step. Tate expected the clearly excited dog to notice and maybe run toward them, but instead he looked back toward the plane and gave a soft yip.

And then a second dog followed.

Tate stared in utter shock. Not so the sunny yellow animal whose head suddenly came up. The retriever let out a joyous howl and headed for him at a dead run. Tate dropped to his knees, not sure he could have kept standing, anyway.

"Sunny," he breathed as the dog bent herself nearly double in the wriggling effort to smother him with kisses. He threw his arms around her, burying his face in the soft fur, feeling the same comfort she had always given him. She whined, twisting once more to lick his face, her tail wagging so furiously her hind end was practically dancing. She knocked him on his backside, but he didn't care.

For the second time in a day his eyes pooled with moisture. He wiped at them before he looked up at Hayley and Quinn, who had now also deplaned.

"How…?"

"Don't ask us," Hayley said, wiping at her own eyes. "We're just the delivery service. This was all Lacy's doing."

Belatedly he understood and looked up at Lacy. All trace of that edginess was gone, and the joy he was feeling at this reunion seemed to echo in her face.

"Lace?"

"It wasn't all me," she said. "I made some calls, wrote some emails, then called in some Foxworth help—and Sloan—and we got it done."

He hugged the dog again, then stood up. He pulled Lacy into an embrace even more fervent than he'd given the joyful Sunny.

"They were about to retire her anyway," Quinn said. "She hadn't been the same since you left."

"I can understand that," Lacy said, hugging him tightly.

He pulled back slightly to look at her. With her in his arms and Sunny dancing at his feet, he felt richer than any man in the world. All because of three females. This dog had saved his life, Lori Collins had kept him alive and Lacy had given him the reason for it all.

It wasn't how he'd thought about doing it, but he couldn't stop himself.

"What do you say, Lacy? Shall we have that wedding Gramps wanted to dance at?"

He heard her breath catch. And then she smiled and lit the last, dark corner of his life with her answer.

"Only if we wear their rings, so their love will always stay with us."

The kind that lasts a lifetime, Gramps, he thought.

And kissed her.

* * * * *